'I can't get the list,' said Taylor. 'I'm sorry.'

'What's the problem?'

Taylor was hesitant. 'There's a block on it. Restricted information.'

'A block against Special Branch? That's impossible.'

'A block against you, Laurie. They knew I didn't need it and they know we are friends. Who have you upset? I'm sorry, I did my best. This is about your brother, isn't it?'

'Yes. I'm not happy about the way he died.'

'They won't be either. But you'll have to leave it to them . . . You left the force because of him, Laurie. You felt that strongly. Don't do a somersault, mate. He'll drag you down into his own grave.'

Remote Control

Kenneth Royce

CORONET BOOKS
Hodder and Stoughton

First published in Great Britain in 1994
by Hodder and Stoughton
a division of Hodder Headline PLC

Coronet paperback edition 1994

10 9 8 7 6 5 4 3 2 1

British Library Cataloguing in Publication Data

Royce, Kenneth
Remote Control.
I. Title
823.914 [F]

ISBN 0 340 61734 9

Printed and bound in Great Britain by
Cox & Wyman Ltd, Reading, Berkshire

Hodder and Stoughton Ltd
A division of Hodder Headline PLC
338 Euston Road
London NW1 3BH

To Stella

1

Terry was dead. The reckless renegade committed suicide in prison at the age of thirty-five which some say is the best age of all. But not for him. Laurie Shaw drove steadily north thinking how little he had known his brother. It was over two years since they had met and that had not been a happy occasion. Their rare meetings never had been.

Terry had been wild since a teenager and had served time in Borstal. Oddly enough he had never been convicted as an adult until six months ago when he had been found guilty of armed robbery. It was this more than anything that had decided Laurie Shaw to quit Special Branch. His superiors tried to stop him resigning; he was not his brother's keeper. The pleas for him to stay were genuine but he felt uneasy about the situation. And there were those in the force who resented his quick promotion to Detective Chief Inspector at the age of thirty-nine and would know how to use his brother's reputation against him. It might not actually have harmed him, he was too good a copper, but it could make life difficult and was a pressure he found difficult to handle.

Laurie was conscience-ridden for a brother he had never really understood. They were opposites, and, as is often the case, the bad egg got the parental favours and sympathy especially from their mother. Throughout her life she made excuses for her younger son. Shaw wondered how she was feeling now, for he had yet to see her about the death and wanted to leave it until he had found out more. Terry had been a bad lot but had possessed an irrepressible personality that women seemed to admire; he had never been short of their company.

As Laurie Shaw drove in the early morning spring sunshine

his mind ranged back to their schooldays and the scrapes he had saved Terry from even then. Terry had always been wild but was no coward. Suicide? What could possibly have happened for him to do that? Terry had never been a whinger. He had been a fighter all the way and that was part of his problem. Suicide? It just did not gel, yet it had happened.

Shaw stopped at a motorway service station to freshen up and have an early lunch. He was not really sure why he was going all the way north in order to pick up a few of Terry's personal items when they could be sent to him. An enquiry into the death had already been instigated but he wanted to hear what the prison governor had to say. He reached the prison about mid-afternoon, the weather still holding fine.

He parked the car opposite the prison and walked across the wide stretch of road. He did not immediately go to the gates but veered to the small cemetery alongside a twenty-foot wall which marked the boundary on one side. He wondered if Terry would be buried here. There was no family grave, the family was too scattered, some as far as Australia. He gazed round the small cemetery, and to the tops of the prison buildings above the huge wall. He walked round to the prison gates and produced his visitor's pass.

During the course of his police duties he had visited many prisons and invariably wondered why prison governors seldom looked the part. He was not sure what they were supposed to look like but Greville Saunders appeared to be an academic, long thin body and hands, and sharp blue eyes staring from a gaunt, hungry face. Shaw knew the governor had only held the post for a short time following the retirement of his predecessor. "It seems unfair that this should happen so soon after your appointment," Shaw observed as the two men shook hands. He sat down and felt the gloom of the room without looking round but perhaps all prisons affected him this way.

"That's a magnanimous way of putting it, Mr Shaw, the tragedy is yours."

"Well, my brother's actually. Let me say straight away that we were never close. But I would certainly not have wanted

8

anything like this to happen to him." Shaw refrained from making the obvious protests about how could it happen. He knew how. No prisoner, even in top security prisons, could be supervised all the time. It was impossible. "What are the details?"

The blue eyes stared across the tidy desk. "Would you like tea, coffee?"

Shaw shook his head. "No, thank you. I want to get back to London by tonight." He did not know why he said that. He had nothing on at the moment, nothing to go back to but an empty flat.

"They were banged up at the usual time. He was found dead the next morning after one of the warders saw blood seeping from under his cell door. The alarm was sounded and he was found still on his bed with slashed wrists. He had been dead for some hours and the doctor considered he must have done it shortly after entering his cell."

"What was the weapon?"

"A plastic knife honed down to a rough but sharp edge. He must have hacked himself."

Again Shaw expressed no indignant surprise at a weapon being smuggled into a cell. It was not too difficult to do.

"We have spot searches, as you know, but things had been quiet for a while and there was no whisper of any kind."

"I understand. I'm not trying to blame anyone. But it's just not like him. He was too awkward a bugger to give in like that. Had he been depressed? Sick at all?"

"No. There were no warning signs that anyone had noticed. He had friends inside. Even one of the warders. But none of us knows what goes on inside someone else's mind. This is by no means the first prison suicide and we both know that it won't be the last. I'm really very sorry."

"Would it be possible to speak to these friends?"

The blue eyes gazed steadily at Shaw. "For what purpose?"

"To see if anyone can throw any light on why it happened."

There was a slight hardening of attitude from across the desk. "Mr Shaw, we cannot allow a private enquiry. Even if you were still in the force, which I understand you no longer are, I could not permit that. We have set up our own prison enquiry which will have to be thorough enough to satisfy the Home Office, and, of course, there will be a Coroner's Inquest. To add to that would not be helpful."

"It would be to me." Shaw watched the long fingers intertwine and the lips tighten. "I'm not trying to be difficult but you are all acting on the assumption that my brother committed suicide. I've yet to be convinced."

"As nobody was in the cell with him it could have been nothing else."

"Really? All I want to do is to talk to some of the people who knew him to see if I can arrive at what drove him to it. As his brother, and a trained interrogator, I'm more likely to be able to do that than most. I simply want to satisfy myself. I would have thought that a very reasonable thing to ask."

The blue eyes flickered. "I understand your point of view. But it could complicate matters. The present procedure is more than adequate. Indeed, we have a lot of people to satisfy over this disastrous business. Life won't be made easy for us."

Shaw relaxed in his chair. He always felt easier when knowing what he was up against. He said quietly, "Mr Saunders, I could put up a convincing argument for seeing these people, but I've driven a long way, I'm tired, so I would rather cut through official bull by saying now, that if I don't see them I'll go public through the yellow press who will scream cover-up. The public will love it and the do-gooders will swamp you."

"That's blatant blackmail, Mr Shaw. It smudges your police reputation."

Shaw smiled. "Just now you were quick to point out that I am no longer in the police. But I would say it is more of a threat than blackmail. Perhaps something of both. It should not take long to ask a few questions. Or are you worried about what I might discover?"

"That's offensive. We have nothing to hide."

"Then what are we arguing about?"

*　　*　　*

10

There were the usual plain chairs facing across the bare-topped table. The small room was stark and Shaw arranged his chair to face the door which was built like a cell door. The warder was the first to enter. He did so alone, closing the door behind him. He took off his cap, stood awkwardly in front of the table and said, "I'm sorry about your brother, Chief Inspector. He wasn't all that bad a bloke."

Shaw rose and shook hands. "I'm out of the force now, Mr Healy, I'm plain mister. Or Laurie, if you prefer." They sat down before he added, "You probably find it strange that a villain has a copper for a brother. It's not unique. I just want a little more information than they are willing to give me upstairs. Terry was invariably in trouble but he was spirited and I just find it difficult to equate him with suicide."

"So do I," said Bert Healy solidly. "We all do. But he had a kind of pride, and freedom was a strong part of his nature. Perhaps he could not take the idea of being banged up for ten years." And then, with a slight grin, "I hope you don't mind my saying so, Mr Shaw, but you look like him, do you know that? Same unruly black mop, same sort of keep-fit features, and the same solid build. You're as tall as him, but above all you have the same grey eyes. Uncanny. I always thought he looked far too honest to be a villain but sometimes they come like that. Were you twins, sir?"

"I'm four years older. He must have put on weight from what you say. Now, the opinion so far seems to favour him slashing his wrists shortly after being locked up for the night. If that were the case, wouldn't the blood be seen some time during the night?"

"Well, we do have a look through the spyholes but unless there is something obviously wrong or we have reason to expect problems from a particular prisoner, it becomes much of a routine. We're only human. Our main aim is to make sure they are where they should be, in bed. It would be difficult to detect blood without light. And very little came through under the door. It was just enough to check upon and then to raise the alarm."

Shaw gazed at the friendly face and reflected that screws

11

came in all shapes and sizes and that this one would be kinder to most prisoners than some; it was a thankless job. "Was he acting normally up to then?"

Healy considered the question carefully. "Over the last few weeks he had lost some of his cheerfulness. Maybe that's too strong a word for someone with a long sentence. But he always had a strong sense of humour, but more recently, it faded and he became quieter."

"Morose? Depressed?"

"I'd say bitter. Something seemed to have riled him. But there was nothing to suggest he would top himself. He was a strong character."

"So you don't think he committed suicide?"

"Ah, now, Mr Shaw, you're putting words in my mouth." Healy changed position uneasily. "I'm not a doctor. I don't know how his mind was really working."

"Okay. That was unfair. But as you seemed to get on, con and screw, did anything change in that relationship?"

Healy was slow to reply, aware that his opinion was taking on more importance than he wanted. "Maybe he became polite rather than friendly."

"And you know of no reason for the change?"

"No obvious reason. But I don't want to make too much of it. No-one can be cheerful all the time."

"Thanks, Mr Healy. You've been a great help. Now can I check with you those cons my brother seemed to have befriended?"

Carlos Mandova certainly looked like a Spaniard, dark skin and hair, black olive eyes, and could play a guitar passably. The walls of the small North London room were covered in press cuttings and photographs of bullfights and bullrings and of one matador in particular whom he quickly claimed to be his father.

When Carlos Mandova spoke he killed the illusion in an instant: he had a marked Cockney accent and had been born in the East End of London within the sound of Bow Bells. His crimes usually centred round travellers' cheques and currency frauds. He was reckoned to have contacts with the villains who had left Britain in a hurry to enjoy the sunshine of the Costa del Sol on the Andalusian coast of Spain. He had a quick smile and a sense of fun, his jokes mainly directed at his own inability to keep out of prison.

"It's good of you to see me," said Shaw as he found somewhere to sit in the overcrowded room. "Particularly since you've only been out a few days."

Mandova grinned sadly. "I'll be back there. It's the first time a copper's been in here unless he's come to nick me. You're bloody privileged, mate. Fancy Terry having a copper for a brother. Could have been useful for tip-offs."

"Which is one of the reasons I left the force. Tell me about him."

"Tell you about your own brother? You've got to be kidding."

"While he was in prison. You must have formed an opinion."

Mandova scratched around some piled-up crockery in a cupboard and produced a half-opened bottle of Spanish red wine. He pulled some glasses from an overladen sink. "I was bloody sorry to hear he was gone," he said with visible emotion. "I liked old Terry. He understood me." He suddenly stared hard at Shaw and then gazed round for a place to put the glasses. "He thought the world of you, you know."

To cover his surprise Shaw said quickly, "No wine for me, Carlos, if I may call you that."

"You can call me what you bloody well like, mate. Why did he always call you Artie?"

"Didn't he tell you?" Shaw smiled with recollection. "I'm surprised he remembered, it's so long ago. I used to play jazz on clarinet. Still do when I get the time."

"We should get together sometime." Mandova searched around for his guitar. As he did so he said, "Terry was sold down the river." He poured a glass of wine and it smelled vinegary from where Shaw was sitting; no doubt it had been uncorked for some time.

"What do you mean?"

"Well, I reckon he was stitched up. Should never have been inside."

13

"He stood trial for armed robbery, for chrissake. Your loyalty is laudable but what makes you say that?"

"Maybe I understood him better than you."

"I never understood him. You'd better explain."

Mandova decided to keep the charged glass in his hand and drank half of it in one gulp; he seemed to enjoy it. "I suppose they'll want me for the enquiry. Well, it's nothing I could tell *them*. It's all impressions, knowing something about the man. Terry had only been inside for six months. I'd already been in for four years. At first he seemed all right. Numb like they all are when they first go in. But he knuckled down, made some friends and was tough enough to take care of himself against the rest. He was not troubled by any of the cons."

Mandova raised the bottle and waved it like a sword, then topped up his glass. "He never spoke much about himself and never about the blag that had got him tucked away. I always got the impression that he was searching for someone inside, but that is not always easy as the nick was divided into three self-contained wings to lessen the chance of collusion and riot. And he never mentioned it and I've been around too long to ask. But a couple of weeks before I was due out he changed. He became sort of grim."

"Suicidal?"

"Nah. The opposite. But there was a kind of determination about him. He was the kind of bloke who could show his thoughts, not that he couldn't hide them when he wanted to. He never told me what had happened. But there was a change in him."

"Did he have any visitors?"

"A girl used to see him at odd times. A bloody cracker. I only saw her once, when I had a visitor myself. But she called more than that. The screws couldn't take their eyes off her. He said it was his girlfriend."

"I don't suppose you know where I can find her?"

"I haven't a clue. That's about all I know." He rubbed the spare glass with his sleeve. "You sure you won't have one?"

"Some other time. I must get back." Shaw rose, feeling

14

the mustiness of the room rise with him. "Do you think he committed suicide?"

Mandova rose unsteadily. "Who would want to top himself with a bird like that waiting?" Then more seriously, "You realise what you're saying? If he didn't, what's the alternative?"

"Is it possible?"

"Topping him? It's been done before. But as far as I know he had no enemies there. So why would anyone want to do that?"

"If you don't know I've got to find who does. It looks like being a long search."

"Then you'd better make sure it's not a bloody dangerous one, mate. There are a lot of nasties out there. Get some wing mirrors stitched to your arms."

2

The press made little use of the prison death. It was reported in every newssheet but with little emphasis and in every case tucked away so that the item was barely noticeable. This struck Shaw as unusual. Prisons had come under a lot of criticism in recent years and there were always those who would seize on something like this to make a point. Yet the reports of the death were uniform in their brevity.

He sat in the lounge of his flat in North London and stared at the freshly painted walls. He had felt lonely since leaving the force. He missed the activity and his friends. His life had changed and he had yet to sort out his future. He had been offered several security jobs but that kind of work did not appeal. He needed to be in the field and wondered whether he had made a terrible mistake in resigning. But it would have been difficult to stay on; it was all a matter of conscience and peace of mind.

Meanwhile, to help the cash flow he had set up a consultancy to help companies against industrial espionage and on general security. It was little more than an advisory service and he was able to point them the right way to obtain the actual necessary hardware. He operated from home and realised it was a half-baked attempt and that if he was to get anywhere he must take it more seriously and expand, and also lecture or hold courses on the subject. He had yet to come to terms with his future. A small legacy after the death of his father, which had been split between himself and Terry, helped meet the financial demands.

After speaking to the warder, Bert Healy, he had been allowed to see a couple of the cons who had claimed to be friendly with Terry but he had really got nowhere. They were either too thick or had decided which side their bread was buttered and told an almost identical story of Terry becoming depressed a few days before he died. Neither was convincing and he wondered, if Carlos Mandova had still been in prison would his account have been similar to theirs? Had they been under pressure to make life easy for the prison authorities then it was to Bert Healy's credit that he had been so co-operative.

Shaw was glad he was back in London, a town he liked and understood and as he rose to pour himself a drink he realised he had been so preoccupied that he had forgotten to check his answering machine. There were two calls from old police friends, one from one of the companies he was advising, and one from a woman called Jill Palmer who claimed to have known Terry and could they meet. She had left a number.

They met the next day in a café in Covent Garden. And as it was near lunchtime and early enough, they sat outside in the plaza. It was one more beautiful spring day and looked like becoming something of a record for May.

Shaw had no description of her but it was clear that she had one of him as she approached him as he was about to enter the shadowed interior of the café. She was attractive, his attention drawn more to her hazel eyes than anything else. She was not beautiful in the classic sense, and photographs might not do her justice, but she exuded a personality it would be difficult to ignore. She was tall and held herself well, and her summery dress complemented her coppery hair. Was this the woman Mandova had talked about? Although he would not describe her as a stunner – she did not obviously turn heads – once noticed she would not be ignored.

They chose a table on the perimeter under a sun umbrella and ordered an espresso and a cappuccino. "You don't look comfortable with me," she said perceptively. "What were you expecting?"

"How could I possibly know? I had no description of you but you knew me at once. How so?"

"I've seen a photograph of you. And, of course, you are so like Terry."

Shaw smiled grimly. "It's the other way round. I am the older brother. I didn't know Terry had a photo of me. We seldom saw eye to eye."

"It was in a police magazine. I can't remember the reason but you had obviously done something which pleased the police authority."

Shaw was puzzled. "What were you doing with a police magazine?"

"Terry subscribed to it. They are easy enough to get. Don't look so suspicious."

He suddenly saw that the banter was a cover to hide her feelings. For just a moment he thought she was about to burst into tears. Her lips trembled, her eyes filled and then she seemed to sweep away the emotion and was smiling again.

"Was it you who visited Terry in prison?"

"Yes." The coffee arrived and she waited until they were alone again. "How did you know?"

"I went up there two days ago. I'd never seen Terry as the suicidal type so I leant on the governor in order to speak to a few people." As he spoke he felt that she knew this while continuing to give the impression that she did not.

"And did you learn anything?"

"Not really. I have an open mind. I'm still not convinced."

Jill put down her cup. "Not convinced about what?"

He suddenly realised he expected everyone to be on the same wavelength as he was. And now he found it difficult to be as open as he had been with the others. Jill had been Terry's girlfriend; he must be careful. "I find it difficult to believe he committed suicide. He was made of tougher stuff."

"It would be natural for you to feel like that. For me too. But what is the alternative?"

It was the second time he had faced the question and it was much more difficult to answer the girl opposite who had become visibly uneasy.

Shaw tried to think of another answer, to avoid using the

18

word he must, for there was only one alternative, an accident of that nature was impossible; the wrists had been hacked. "Murder," he said at last. It sounded crazy and he almost retracted.

Jill stiffened. "Murder? In prison? Do you realise what you are saying?"

"I should do. I was on more than one murder squad at the Yard before . . . well anyway, it sounds stupid but I simply can't come to terms with suicide."

"I can't believe he committed suicide either. Nor can I accept murder." Her distress was now obvious.

"Did you see any deterioration in him during your visits?"

"Yes, I did, but not of the kind that might induce suicide. He was dejected because he was the sort of man who could not stand being restrained. But he would have attempted escape rather than give up like that."

"When was the last time you saw him?"

"About eight weeks before he died. Just before the new governor took over. He seemed reasonably all right then."

"A lot can happen in eight weeks. He might have gone downhill. Did you usually leave it so long?"

"That sounded like a reprimand. I did the best I could. I used to see him every few weeks but eventually my application for a visitor's pass was refused. I was still trying to find out why when he died. Tell me, how many times did you see him?"

Shaw winced. "I never saw him inside. Not because I was a policeman but because we never agreed on his lifestyle and we drifted apart years ago. What do you imagine he did for my mother?"

"Yet you went to check on the way he died. Why should you care?"

"He wasn't the type to kill himself and it struck me as odd. Perhaps it was a policeman's enquiring mind."

"But you went there just the same. Maybe you had a spark of feeling for him, after all?"

"A spark of concern. He caused a lot of family problems along the line and perhaps I thought I owed it to our mother to find out what I could because she will never believe he killed himself. He was her favourite son."

"Did that upset you?"

"In the early days it rankled. I later understood her attitude. She loved him and could not believe what he had become."

"Did you feel you owed it to him to enquire into his death?"

He gazed at her squarely, disconcerted by the beauty of her eyes. "I owed him nothing. There is a case for arguing the other way round. I just wished he had been different."

"I'm sorry if I've upset you. He thought so much of you, you see."

"Someone else said that. It seems he told everyone but me. Had he done so I might have made the extra effort to help him." And then to change the painful subject, "So you don't know why you were refused a visitor's pass?"

"No. Maybe they thought I had a disturbing influence on him."

"I should have thought your visits would give him something to live for. They don't have to give a reason for refusing a pass. They are a privilege. Do you find it strange that they stopped you visiting?"

"In view of what followed, yes."

"Do you think he was murdered?" It was becoming easier to say.

She stared at her cup, pale and nervous. "Is it possible to do in prison? In the way Terry died?"

"Oh, yes. I won't go into too much detail but it would have needed at least two men to kill him like that. He would have had to be held until weak enough to let go. They would have had to avoid the blood, so if it happened that way it was almost certainly premeditated. They knew what they were doing."

She covered her face and it was a little while before she removed her hands. "This sounds ghastly. It's easier to believe he did it himself."

"Yes, it is. Would you prefer to leave it like that?"

20

When she did not answer he said, "How did you become involved with Terry? I can't see the two of you together."

"Why?"

He stumbled over his words. "There's no answer to that. I just see you as somebody, I have to say it, with more sense. Terry went through life from one crisis to another. The only surprise to me was that he was not tucked away before."

"Perhaps he was cleverer than you thought."

"I never said he was not clever." And then in exasperation, "We could go on like this all day. I've had long experience of him and some suffering. To the family he was trouble. And he's carrying it beyond death. Perhaps he behaved better with strangers. You must have seen something in him."

"Would you like another coffee?"

"If it's a peace offering, yes."

She smiled. "I didn't know we were at war." She ordered the coffees and gazed around. The place was almost full and summer clothes brightened the plaza.

"How did you get on to me?" asked Shaw after the coffees arrived. "And what made you ring me?"

"Terry had your number on his phone pad. I felt I should contact someone in his family. It seemed the right thing to do."

He gazed at her with faint suspicion. "It wasn't because you weren't satisfied about the way he died and that you knew I was an ex-copper?"

"Perhaps that, too. But we haven't got anywhere, have we? What happens next?"

"I'd already decided to start digging around."

"Wouldn't it be better to wait for the results of the Home Office enquiry and the inquest?"

"I've a feeling it will be a waste of time. Not necessarily for sinister reasons but because cover-ups can be second-nature to authority and preferable to scandal. I don't think the Coroner's Inquest will help much either. Do you have Terry's last address?"

"Of course. Do you want me to take you there?"

* * *

21

The apartment was in one of the high rise blocks in south-west London. The area was respectable and reasonably quiet. They took the lift to the fourth floor and Jill produced keys to open the front door. The air was quite fresh and Shaw wondered whether Jill had been here quite recently. He asked her and she replied that she had not called here for some time.

"Someone has. I would expect it to be musty. Dammit, he was banged up for six months. Is there a cleaner?"

"Not that I know of."

He glanced at her sharply and then they went along the narrow hall and entered the living-room. The furniture was fairly new and of good quality, the taste haphazard as he would expect, but there was no shortage of comfort. Terry had always liked his comfort, usually at someone else's expense. There was a small bathroom with shower attachment and a kitchen-diner. There was one bedroom with a king-sized bed which made the room appear smaller than it was.

Shaw went round the place, touching nothing, aware that Jill was watching him closely. "Did you clean up when you last came, Jill?"

"Not that I recall. I might have tidied the odd thing but no general tidying."

"And you haven't been here for some weeks?"

"Don't you believe me?"

He looked across at her. "I'm sounding like a copper. I'm sorry. But if you haven't been here somebody has. Terry was an untidy so-and-so, you must know that. So why is the place looking so perfect? Unless he had changed considerably."

"Well, I would have the odd onslaught on tidying up. I never thought about it. Perhaps I did more than I realised."

Shaw did not answer but went back into the bedroom and started to open drawers. Clothes were neatly folded and the wardrobe had five suits hanging tidily from a rail with shoes neatly stacked on a rack below them. "Was this how it was when you left?"

"I don't think I looked in the cupboards or wardrobe. In

fact I'm not sure why I called at all except perhaps to get a sense of him."

"You did not live here with him?"

"No. I have my own place."

They returned to the living-room and Shaw sank on to the arm of a lounge chair. He gazed up at her. "You didn't live together?"

"I've just said so."

"Then what the hell was your relationship with him?"

"I visited frequently. But I would not give up my own place. What sort of relationship we had is none of your business. Perhaps I'm just an old-fashioned girl who listened to Mother." She sat down opposite smiling at his disbelief.

While he was still trying to work it out she said, "Are you married?"

"I've nothing to hide. My girlfriend was killed in a train crash. And, yes, we did live together. Are you having me on? I mean, you must know what he was like. Is this how you would have expected to find the place?"

"No. I hadn't thought about it. But it is rather tidy for Terry. So what does it mean?"

"It means that an overpaid bunch of so-called pros have been over the place and have tidied as they went to give the impression that nothing has been touched. They've overdone it. It's difficult to leave a place untidy in the same way as an untidy person does. Little things show. That bunch of newspapers there, neatly stacked; Terry wouldn't have left them like that, some would be askew. They should have taken better stock of how they were in the first place; but it's difficult to remember. So what were they looking for, or were they just making sure that there was nothing to look for? I must say I'm surprised you did not notice how un-Terry-like this all is."

"It didn't cross my mind. I wasn't thinking along those lines. Besides, his bad habits are obviously ingrained more in your mind than mine. Is there any point in staying? It brings back too many memories."

"Yes. I've got to do just as thorough a search. If the power is still on what about a cup of tea while I get on with it?"

It was some time later, having got nowhere and not leaving the place anywhere near as tidy, that he remembered the personal effects he had brought back from the prison. He had dumped the bundle in a cupboard in his kitchen, not wanting to be reminded of its association.

"That's as far as we can go here," he said. "I want to go through his prison effects. They're at my place. You want to come?"

She collected the cups and he heard her washing them up in the kitchen and when she returned she stood in the middle of the living-room and slowly pivoted, her expression gradually changing to one of distress until the shield came down and there was no expression at all. He had no idea what was going through her mind but felt, by searching so callously, he had somehow desecrated her memory of Terry. He just stood watching her, not wanting to invade her thoughts. And, after gazing once more round the room at the obvious signs of his search, she observed quietly, "You had at least one thing in common with him, then. Now it does look how he might have left it."

He could find no reply.

They had travelled by underground and taxi from Covent Garden to Terry's apartment. Shaw had an old Ford garaged in a lock-up a block from his home in North London but had not used it owing to the parking problems. So it took them a little time to find a cab and he decided it could take them all the way.

This made it difficult for the man waiting at the corner of the high-rise who formed one of a team who had been following Shaw since he first left his home that morning. He had to follow very carefully until Shaw found a cab and then he whistled up a waiting car and climbed in to follow the cab although he was fairly sure of where Shaw would be going next.

With the distraction of Jill and the preoccupation of his brother's death, and the fact that he had no reason to expect it, Shaw had no idea they were being followed. When they entered his own apartment his main thought, as he saw Jill

24

gaze round at everything, was the disconcerting notion that she was again comparing him with his dead brother.

While she sat down in the lounge he went to the kitchen to produce Terry's personal effects and, as he rejoined her, said, "You mentioned you got my number from Terry's phone pad. Where is it?"

"He kept it on the telephone table in the hall."

He dropped the parcel on to the floor. "It wasn't there. There was no pad. I picked up the phone to make sure it had been cut off; there was definitely no pad."

"Then I don't know where it is."

"It must have been nicked." He studied her quietly and chose his words carefully. "You must be tired and pretty distressed. Maybe it was not a good idea bringing you back here. I'll drive you home."

"I've come this far, so seeing what he wore before going to prison can't make it any worse. Get on with it, Laurie, and stop trying to spare my feelings."

In spite of her bravado she was clearly affected by what he unravelled. It was not just the heavy winter sweater and the thick cords, the shirt, undergarments, the MCC tie to which he had no claim, the blue blazer, but the personal items Shaw spread on the floor.

There was a leather wallet with five ten-pound notes in it. Some loose change. A bunch of keys. Two very early and faded snaps of the two brothers with their mother which shook in Shaw's hand until he fumbled it back into the wallet. There were two letters from their mother which Terry had kept. Six unused stamps were now stuck together. And there was a small field book on birds which was well thumbed and brought back boyhood memories of picnics in woods and trying to identify the birds. It was perhaps the one interest they had shared. Shaw was surprised that his brother had continued with the hobby.

Shaw's mind ranged back over the years as he went through the pathetically few items. For a while he was lost in reminiscence and it was not wholly bad.

"Perhaps you wanted me to leave to hide your own feelings?"

He had almost forgotten she was there as he slipped deeply into his memory. At least Terry had been vibrant and he could feel some of that charge running through him as he handled his dead brother's things. What he found surprising was that there was nothing about Jill; no letters, no snaps. Perhaps he had found it too painful to be reminded of her. "What are the keys?" he asked suddenly. He handed them over.

"Well, that's obviously the apartment key. This one is for my place. That looks like a car key, and could that be a garage key?"

"And the other two?"

"I've no idea. They're very small."

Shaw took the bunch of keys back and balanced them in his hand. "Too big for suitcase keys. One could be an alarm key, the other is more difficult to place. I'll have to see a locksmith."

He sank into the chair and viewed Terry's effects laid out at his feet. This was all there was to show of a man of thirty-five who was supposed to have committed suicide but had more probably been murdered. For whatever reason.

"I'll need a list of names of all your mutual friends. Anyone you knew that he knew. I'm not going to get anywhere through official sources, I've got to work backwards at it. Make sure you don't leave anyone out."

Jill stared at him uncertainly. She seemed suddenly unsure of herself. "I'm sorry, but I'm not sure that I can help you. I didn't know any of his friends."

3

"You don't know any of his friends?" he snapped incredulously. "What do you mean?"

"He kept part of his life away from me. My relationship was with him, not anyone else he knew." Jill was struggling, knowing Shaw did not believe her.

"Just how often were you seeing him, for chrissake? With any normal relationship you must have known of at least a few of his friends, if only through him talking about them."

"He never did. We were just happy in ourselves."

"So happy that you did not live together? What are you not telling me, Jill? Because I can't accept that you didn't know some of his friends. And if there was a side to him he never revealed to you, weren't you just a teeny bit curious?"

"Of course. But there was nothing I could do about it. I either accepted it or we split. I knew there were no other women involved."

"How could you possibly know that?"

"I just knew. He could be very up-front at times."

"That's obvious by the way he confided in you about the company he was keeping."

"Don't be sarcastic. You can't take the truth."

"I haven't heard the bloody truth." He rose angrily. "Just what was the point of you contacting me?"

"You know why. I was not happy about the way he died. I thought I could help."

"The only thing you've done is to take me to his apartment which turned out to be a very negative exercise. I could have found his address anyway and obtained access. The one area where you might have helped you've frozen up because I

27

don't accept what you say. This isn't going to work between us. You'd better leave." He started to pick up Terry's effects and pile them on to the chair he had vacated.

Jill rose slowly. She appeared to want to say something but in the end said nothing. She opened her handbag and scribbled on a small pad, tore off the sheet and placed it on a side table.

"What's that?" he asked.

"My telephone number. Just in case you need it."

"I won't need it. There is nothing more to talk about." He straightened up and felt some remorse. "You must know that any enquiry into this matter must involve the people he knew. It's the essence of an enquiry like this. How else can I start? If you can't help in that direction I don't see how you can help at all. I'm sorry. The offer to take you home still stands."

She hung the bag on her shoulder. "No, thanks. I can manage. If I do think of anything helpful I'll let you know."

"Sure." He escorted her to the door, sorry that it had ended like this but furious too that he had wasted time. He opened the door for her and for a moment they gazed at each other frostily.

"I'm not a liar," she said as she went past him.

"I didn't call you one. But only you can know whether or not you've just uttered one. I'm sorry it did not turn out better."

She shot him a murderous glance as she walked away.

When Jill had gone Shaw finished packing his brother's things and then picked up the note from the side table. It was a central London telephone number, the prefix covering much of the Soho district. He rang the number on the off-chance of someone else being there. There was no answer and no answering machine. He realised he knew very little about her and was annoyed, for his police instincts should have at least enquired into what she did for a living.

He checked the telephone directory and found that there was no entry under that name. He then rang an old colleague at Scotland Yard who ran down the address through the telephone number. It was just off Dean Street. Almost certainly an apartment. He then rang directory enquiries, asked for the number to go with the name and address and was told it was ex-directory. An ex-directory number and she had given it to him. Jill Palmer was full of surprises.

Although it was only late afternoon he poured himself a stiff whisky and sat down in the chair she had used as if by so doing he could sort out some of her contradictions. Terry's apartment had shown no sign that he even knew her. There were no photographs, letters, not even in his wallet. Yet she had a key to his apartment and apparently he had one to hers. If one of the keys on Terry's key ring did belong to her place he felt the strong urge to use it.

He was now even more annoyed with himself that he had let her go so easily, but it was an emotional time and his policeman's mind was too clogged with personal feelings. If he had still been in the force he would not have been allowed to make an investigation in which he was so emotionally tied.

He went through Terry's things once again. Checked through the bird book to make sure nothing was hidden among the pages, but if there had been anything to hide it was too obvious a place. It was difficult to know where to start. He doubted that he would be allowed in the prison again, but he could run down Bert Healy and press him for further details and also Carlos Mandova. But it was old ground and he doubted that he would get any further. He badly needed Terry's old contacts and the only one he had had clammed up.

He put Terry's things back in the kitchen cupboard and left the apartment. He went to the lock-up, got out his old Ford and drove into Soho. Central London was congested and he had difficulty in parking leaving him with a long walk back to Dean Street. He still kept his old distinctive Police Car Club badge on the grid, which had occasionally helped illegal parking. He strolled down Dean Street in the direction of Jill Palmer's home.

There were two apartments over a restaurant. The names were on brass-framed cards on the door beside the restaurant.

The door was open and stairs could be seen at the far end of the hall. He continued walking towards Shaftesbury Avenue until he found a call-box. He called Jill's number and there was no reply. Had she gone straight home she would be there by now.

He crossed the street and went back towards the restaurant. Soho was always busy but it was now into the rush-hour and the streets were crammed with people and traffic. The confusion made it easier for him. He managed to find a recessed doorway flanked by protective railings and he slid into the cavity, having to move aside only now and then as people came out of the building.

Half an hour later there was still no sign of Jill Palmer. He was tempted to go in but held back and was rewarded a little later. She made up part of the crowd coming from the Old Compton Street end and once he focused on her he kept her in his vision.

She was walking quite fast, as erect as he remembered, and she skipped in and out and around people on the narrow pavement. He was fascinated by her approach and the nearer she got the more outstanding she was among the others. He knew this was illusion of course, it meant only that he had recovered some of his concentration and that those around her were sidelined by his single-mindedness. When she turned into the doorway and disappeared he had a vague sense of let-down. Nothing else would happen for some time. He went back to his Ford and began the tortuous journey back home, wondering just what he thought he had achieved.

He spent a lonely evening of indecision and suffered a restless night, but he was away by 7.30 the next morning, found a garage in Brewer Street which was willing to take his car at a price, by which time it was after eight and he was already wondering if he had left it too late.

He took up position in the doorway he had used before, closed his mind to time and waited. He had been there almost an hour, constantly moving to let people enter the doorway, before Jill appeared. She was smartly dressed as if for work and she walked hurriedly south without turning her head.

He was half inclined to follow but held position, and when she was well out of sight crossed the road and entered the doorway beside the restaurant.

He went straight up the stairs to the second floor and was confronted with a steel covered door. The key he had was a Chubb and he turned it, relieved when the tumblers sprang. He went in and closed the door behind him. At right angles to the entrance was a long passage off which were doors to the left. There was also one opposite. Before moving off he examined the front door, to find there were heavy bolts and two heavy duty chains.

All the doors were closed, and using a handkerchief, he entered the nearest room. He glanced round a bedroom, not moving from the open doorway and then went to the next room and did the same. Each time, he left the door wide open which created more light and confirmed which room he had visited. There were two bedrooms, a lounge, small study, a narrow dining-room, a large kitchen and a bathroom. The building was deep and most rooms surprisingly large for so cramped an entrance.

He returned to the chintzy lounge, comfortable and nicely furnished, drapes arched back from the large, old-fashioned windows. It was easy to associate the room with her but he could not really think why. There was a central low marble table on which were two piles of magazines and newspapers, and separating them was a shallow, possibly Dresden, comport with exquisite porcelain flowers running right round the rim. She did no work in here. He went to the study.

It was a room well used. The small desk was covered with piles of letters and books. One wall in the narrow room was taken up with shelves of books, mainly reference books covering a wide range of subjects, most dealing with natural history and geography. There was a small section on bird books. So Jill had shared at least one interest with Terry.

The desk drawers were locked and it took him a little time to open them with a pick-lock the police had taught him to use. He sat down at the desk and systematically went through the contents. As he studied various papers

31

he wondered why she had troubled to lock them away; at least half the drawers contained stationery. He picked up no clue as to what she did for a living and began to believe that what he examined was so much camouflage. As time passed he was no wiser but he did discover an answering machine behind a pile of books at the back of the desk and it was not switched on.

And then he found a typewritten sheet under some blank copy paper in the central drawer. It was not addressed, nor was it signed:

"It is difficult for me to take much more of this. For the first time in my life I don't know what to do. My options are limited so it should not be difficult to choose. But because I'm being driven in one direction I find it is almost impossible to grasp. What has happened? Sooner or later something will break. Oh God, this doesn't sound like me at all. Whatever you do don't contact my brother. This is my own problem."

The sheet wavered in front of him and he put it down on the desk top. He felt cold, suddenly. Apart from the content, on which he accepted he had put his own interpretation, there was nothing to indicate that this was from Terry. But where was the original? This had been copied. He searched again but found nothing else and realised that it was too risky to stay longer. He set about returning everything as he had found it and it was something that could not be hurried. By the time he got round to closing the doors it was after mid-day, much later than he had wanted.

As he went down the stairs he wondered why Jill had not told him about the note. It was undated. But he refused to believe it did not originate from Terry. The content was a massive coincidence if it did not. He stepped out into blinding sunshine, hesitated in the doorway while he looked up and down the street for any sign of Jill. The restaurant was now busy, but Shaw was too preoccupied to glance inside its doors as he strode briskly away. From the gloom of the restaurant interior a man emerged and watched him go, giving a faint nod to someone further up the street.

By the time he picked up his car Shaw was bemused. He did not know what to do next. The inquest was the following day and he decided to drive north straight away and spend a night in a hotel instead of driving through the night. He returned to his apartment, picked up a travelling bag which he always kept ready, a habit from his police days, and started the long journey. He had plenty to think about on the way.

Over and over again he asked himself why he had not been told of the note. And because of that, why Jill had decided to get in touch with him, particularly as the request was that he should not be contacted. About fifty miles from London on the M1 he glimpsed a police patrol car in a lay-by and realised he was speeding and not concentrating as he should. He slowed down and kept his mind on the business of driving.

He arrived late and picked a hotel at random, going straight to his room as the bar was already closed. He slept little that night and cursed himself for being unable to take a detached view, unable to isolate himself from the strange emotions he was suffering. Had he and his brother been close he might understand his deep concern, but they had not and he was puzzled. Perhaps his conscience was pricking him but, on reflection, in the early days anyway, he could not have set out to help his brother more. But in some way or other he felt that Terry had been short-changed and that rankled.

He had no real wish to go to the inquest because he expected nothing from it. But he knew he must go and arrived on time the next day. The Coroner's Court was quite small and was already busy by the time he arrived. There were several reporters but only one he recognised. Shaw stood at the back of the court so that he could see all who entered and noticed a face near the door he thought he recognised but the next time he looked the man had gone. And then he saw Jill in a dark two-piece and she gave him a nod of acknowledgement, no more. He had no idea she intended to come all this way for an official hearing and felt guilty that he had not offered her a lift. Then he noticed that she was with a tall, supercilious looking man, although the relationship seemed quite formal.

The inquest began and the evidence of two prisoners was read out from sworn testimony. The Coroner was at liberty to ask for personal appearances of witnesses if he felt it necessary but that would mean extra warders and handcuffs and a security risk. Their written evidence was little different from that they had given to Shaw direct. He had expected nothing more.

The surprise came when Bert Healy, the warder who had been friendly towards Terry, gave his evidence. It was now slanted towards the official line of suicide. Yes, there had been attacks of depression and Healy managed to indicate that, after a good deal of thought and heart-searching, it had come as little surprise to him when the prisoner had committed suicide, a point on which the court had yet to decide.

Shaw was somewhat numbed by this volte-face; he had considered Healy to be fairly solid. He tried to catch Healy's attention as he went past him to leave the court after giving evidence, but the warder either did not see him or chose not to. Jill Palmer was seated about mid-court and did not turn round after Healy had finished speaking, although Shaw had told her about him and his viewpoint.

Shaw felt the proceedings were fast becoming an official fix. He was tempted to stand up and protest but, although he was Terry's brother, he had no evidence of his own to offer. Carlos Mandova was not called at all and was certainly not in court.

The proceedings ground on, the prison doctor came and went, and the evidence given was all pointing one way. The prison governor contrived to ignore Shaw completely and Shaw began to feel increasingly like an interloper at his own brother's funeral. He left the court before the verdict and waited outside the door. It was almost another hour before they streamed out and he did not even bother to ask anyone the verdict.

The reporter Shaw had recognised came up to offer his condolences and shook Shaw by the hand before saying, "It must be rotten for you. Mind you, if I was banged up I might feel like ending it, too. Poor sod. He must have been in utter despair. I'm so sorry."

"I know your face but can't recall your name. I might need you some time."

"Peter Givens, Chief Inspector." The cynicism of years of reporting, of so often seeing the wrong side of life, showed in guarded brown eyes. Givens swept his straw-coloured hair away from his eyes. He was tall and lanky with nicotine-stained fingers, not often seen these days. "I'm with the *News*."

"Yes, I know. Hadn't you heard I'd left the force?"

"A rumour. But I wasn't sure. Any particular reason?"

Shaw smiled. "Too long a story."

"Well, if you do need me, I'll be happy to help. Anything to do with that cover-up in there?"

"Is that what you think it was?"

"Prisons have had a bad press over the last few years. The problems go much deeper than the staff and the governors. They have a difficult time. So they don't want waves. Keep it nice and simple. Suicide while of unsound mind. The man was in for armed robbery, why make life difficult? It's over."

"There's a prison enquiry. In fact the Deputy Inspector of Prisons is over there, chatting to the governor."

"I had noticed." Givens turned his gaze back to Shaw. "You expect a different result?"

Shaw smiled bitterly. "No. It will be the same. They'll try to avoid any embarrassment. You can't blame them; they have to go by what they are told."

Givens frowned. "Are you saying that someone has lied to the coroner?"

"How can I do that? I was not there at the time of death, the witnesses were. But if I ever had cause to change my mind I could use someone like you."

"That sounds promising. Sure, I'll help."

"This is off the record. Strictly. I still have friends who could persecute you something rotten."

"It's off the record even without the threat. We're used to waiting."

35

"So am I, Peter. I'll be in touch." They shook hands and Shaw looked around for Jill Palmer.

She was standing talking to the tall man who was with her in court. Her back was turned to him and the man seemed not to notice him. Most of the others were moving away to their cars and the pavement was suddenly a lonely place. The tall man was backing away from Jill, saying his goodbyes in an elaborate manner. Shaw moved towards Jill but before he reached her she turned and said, "Sorry to keep you waiting."

"You must have eyes in the back of your head. What did you think of the verdict?"

They were alone now and started to walk towards the car park. "It was no more than I expected."

"Healy gave me quite a different story to the one he gave the coroner. He must have been primed."

"Perhaps he's just afraid of losing his job, and the whole issue is not important enough for him to go out on a limb and annoy the prison authorities."

Shaw nodded. She was probably right. But there was something strange. "You're taking this very calmly. Not showing too much grief."

She looked up at him, trying to match his pace. She said coldly, "What would you know about my grief? You want me to burst into tears? And for that matter I've seen damn all grief from you. You're not too concerned that he's dead, but just puzzled in a policeman's way, whether or not it happened as they said it did."

It was like a huge slap in the face. "I'm sorry," he said. "I did have feeling for him, you know. I wanted nothing more than for him to lead a straight life. The fact that we did not get on has no bearing; that arose from the way he chose to live. Did you drive here?"

"Yes. I'm going back after lunch." She was trying to get ahead of him now as if in a sudden fit of anger.

He caught up easily. "Will you have lunch with me?"

She stopped immediately and turned to face him. "What would be the point?"

He managed a half-grin. "To eat. I'm hungry."

36

"You certainly know how to make a woman feel wanted."

"Do you need false flattery?" And then quickly, "I didn't mean it like that. Honest flattery of you would present no problem. But we don't exactly see eye to eye, do we?"

"Then why ask me to lunch? We have nothing further to say to each other."

He made no attempt to stop her as she strode off. He decided to stay one more night before driving back to London. From his hotel room he telephoned Sandy Taylor, a good friend and a detective inspector in Special Branch, to ask if he could get a complete list of prisoners in C Block of the prison at the time Terry died. He would ring again the next day and call at Scotland Yard to pick up the fax whenever it came through.

He had a lonely dinner in the hotel and started out early next morning for London. He decided to leave his phone call to Sandy Taylor until the following day, realising he had given very little time for a private favour, but Taylor rang him late evening, uneasy and apologetic.

"I can't get the list," said Taylor hurriedly. "I'm sorry."

"What's the problem?"

Taylor was hesitant. "There's a block on it. Restricted information."

"What the hell are you talking about, Sandy? I could get it through the Home Office only they would take far too long. I could get the press boys to dig it out. I came to a friend who could do it more quickly than anyone else, that's all. How can a block be put on it?"

"I don't know, Laurie." Taylor was clearly uncomfortable. "But there is. It's classified."

"A block against Special Branch? That's impossible."

"A block against you, Laurie. They knew I didn't need it and they know we are friends. Who have you upset?"

"*They*? Who are we talking about now?"

"Come on. You know how many they's there are. I'm only a detective inspector, I'm not going to be told that. And if you try to get a list from any other source I'll gamble that it will be bogged down in administrative blunders, delays followed by wrong lists and you'll be generally pissed around and will

37

get nowhere. It's a ploy we use often enough ourselves when we want to sit on information, so you should know the form. I'm sorry, Laurie, I did my best. This is about your brother, isn't it?"

"Yes. I'm not happy about the way he died."

"They won't be either. But you'll have to leave it to them. It might be difficult for you but you can't get anywhere on your own anyway. If they don't want you interfering they'll make sure you don't. You left the force because of him, Laurie. You felt that strongly. Don't do a somersault, mate. He'll drag you down into his own grave."

If there had been any doubts there were none now. Shaw put the phone down, his mind clouded, but one thought came out clear. There was much more to this than a prison cover-up.

4

It was only then, cloistered in his own rooms, that Shaw felt the kind of intrusion he had been involved with against so many others. It was more than intrusion, there was a distinct feeling of threat and he belatedly wondered if his movements had been monitored and if so by whom? There were few choices and yet he was certain that it was far from being that simple.

He checked the obvious places for bugs, including the telephone and bedroom extension but he really needed de-bugging apparatus. He had thought from the beginning that there was obstruction, believing at first that authority did not want outsiders meddling, even the suicide's brother. But it was more than that now. It was becoming sinister, the hidden hands against him effective and doing just enough at a time to close him down.

He waited until it was dark before leaving the building. He was now alert to surveillance, a part of him still not wanting to accept the possibility, but very quickly he learned that he was being followed, not by a full team, as far as he could judge after half an hour of walking, but by professionals nevertheless.

It was difficult for him. He did not want anyone to know where he was going on this particular trip, at the same time he did not want to show that he knew he was being followed. If he wandered aimlessly for too long they would know. He caught a cab to Soho and walked up Dean Street to Jill Palmer's place. The street door was now closed and he found the buzzer tucked away to the side of the recessed door. He rang and almost immediately Jill answered and he asked if he could come up. She released the door and he mounted the stairs. She was waiting in the open doorway to her flat by the time he reached the landing.

She just stood there leaning against the doorjamb, arms folded. In white slacks and beige shirt, hair framing a face which carried a vague expression of disdain, she might have been posing for a fashion shot. She made no greeting but waited for an explanation of his call.

"You certainly know how to make a guy feel wanted," he said as he crossed the landing. As she smiled at that he added, "Can I come in?"

She stood aside and, as she closed the door behind them, asked, "Do you want a drink?"

He sank down on a chair. "I need one but I'd better not. I need my wits more at the moment."

She poured herself a scotch and ginger and sat on the arm of a chair opposite him. She raised her glass. "Cheers. What calls you to stay sober?"

He gazed up at her not sure of her or of what she was thinking. She had put up a barrier between them and he supposed that he had too.

"I'm being followed. Probably have been from the time I visited the prison. I need your help."

"Who would follow you? And why?"

"I haven't a clue. It's all tied up with the way Terry died and they would rather I went away and stopped making waves."

She expressed no surprise at what he said but she was being very guarded. "You want my help? You've already spurned it."

He held up his arms in surrender. "Let's not start again. I wanted to get a list of the prisoners in the block Terry was in. I still have friends at the Yard. Someone has put a stop on it. Somehow I've got to get one but first I want to see Mandova again. You recall my mentioning him. Is there a back way out of here? A way I can return by?"

"So that it looks as if you stayed the night?"

"Not that long. They wouldn't swallow that anyway – usurping my dead brother's mistress a few days after his death. What would that make me look like?"

40

"Girlfriend sounds better. And just what do you think it would make me look like?" She barely controlled her fury.

They were on the fringe again. Shaw realised he had handled it badly and not for the first time. "I never seem to say the right thing. I'm sorry."

"That's because you don't think the right thing. How long do you want?" She glanced at her watch. "It's now nine o'clock."

"I'd make sure I was back by midnight. But sooner if possible. You'll help?"

"I'll tell you where the fire escape is. The rest is up to you. It comes down in the yard of the restaurant next door. There are a lot of dustbins to avoid and a wall to get over at the back which you should be able to climb. The alley you land in leads either way so you have a choice. What's wrong with your own fire escape?"

"I'm not sure I even know where it is. But it's too exposed at the back anyway." He rose. "I really am grateful to you."

She put her drink down. "Don't be. I'll probably shop you as soon as you've gone."

He glanced at her sharply but her expression was well veiled. She was getting her own back. He had to believe so.

"Come on. I'll show you," she said. As she walked past him towards the kitchen door, she said over her shoulder, "Do I get to know the result?"

"If I get one." He wondered why he was being so cagey when she was helping him like this.

To add to his misery she said, as she opened the kitchen door, "I do realise that you have been forced to come to me because you can no longer be certain of your old friends at the Yard."

It was a parting dig from her and what made it worse was that she was right.

He felt a wreck by the time he got over the wall. The yard was more cluttered with bins full of meal left-overs and rotting vegetables than he had expected. Without a flashlight it

41

became an obstacle course. But once in the alley he felt relatively safe and picked his way round a couple of derelicts housed in old newspapers and cardboard boxes. When he reached Shaftesbury Avenue he hired a cab quite easily as it was too early for the theatre and cinema crowds.

By the time he reached Carlos Mandova's place he was satisfied that he had not been followed, but he had been edgy during the ride and the cab driver had kept an eye on him through his mirror.

Mandova was in and well on the way to being drunk. The reek of cheap wine competed with that of stale air as if the windows had never been opened. The atmosphere was foul. The living-room was as untidy as before but there was one noticeable addition. A space had been cleared for what was obviously a brand new guitar.

Seeing Shaw's attention was attracted to it, Mandova said with difficulty in his Cockney accent, "You want to 'ear me play?"

It was no use trying to protest. Mandova picked up his new acquisition lovingly and began to strum and then to play more seriously. Shaw was quite moved by the beauty of the music and guessed that Mandova played better drunk than sober. But time was limited.

"Beautiful," Shaw said. "I'll have to listen another time. I want a few more words about my brother."

Mandova made an effort to sober up but was too far gone, though not enough to be careless with the guitar which he put down with great care. His bleary, bloodshot eyes tried to focus on Shaw. "I told you a lot of crap about your brother. Don't believe any of it."

"Oh!" Shaw's hopes fell. With Mandova so drunk it was going to be heavy going. "I only want to know a few names of other cons in the same block. Any you can remember but especially those who knew Terry. Not necessarily friends but those he spoke to or might even have argued with."

Mandova almost fell off his overladen chair. He steadied himself and looked around for a bottle. There were three, all opened, and placed in strategic positions to be easily reached. But for some reason the system had broken down and he was unable to reach any without standing up and that put him in danger of taking a fall. "I'm too pissed to answer," he said with a high degree of truth. "Right now I can't even remember my own bloody name."

Shaw noticed an unopened crate pushed under the table and partially hidden by scattered papers and magazines. "Have you come into money, Carlos?"

Mandova became guarded, suddenly taking the risk of standing to clutch at a bottle and to hold it close to him like a baby. He stared at Shaw resentfully. "I've just been paid for a little job. But it's none of your bloody business, copper." He fell back on to his chair.

What had happened to the previous friendship? "With all that booze why don't you throw a party?"

Mandova bemusedly searched for all the traps in that question. "I like being alone. I've always been a loner. The rest can buy their own bloody booze." And then with a brief lapse into his natural friendliness, "You can have some, though." But he made no effort to release the bottle clutched to his chest and Shaw had the distinct feeling that he was unable to let go, as if some sort of paralysis was setting in.

"Just a few names," Shaw coaxed. "You can remember." He pulled out pen and pad. "I'll just jot them down as you say them."

Mandova was trying to get his mouth to the bottle but his lips were turning blue and his arms would not move. Shaw realised that Mandova was in a worse state than he had supposed. He stood up to reach forward to take the bottle from the folded arms to place it somewhere safe, for although still held tightly it was now at an acute angle and was beginning to drip.

When he tried to take the bottle it seemed that Mandova held on more tightly and it would not budge. Then he noticed the eyes were beyond being bloodshot and had started to bulge, the veins swelled from pressure. Mandova was having some kind of fit and Shaw looked around for a telephone.

There was no phone, not one that could be found in the general rubble of the room, at any rate. And then Mandova toppled forward and slid sideways from the chair, reaching the floor at an angle to rest with his head against the chair arm as Shaw struggled to stop him.

When Shaw bent over him he saw the eyes again and they were focused on space, the veins slowly receding. In spite of the stuffiness of the room he felt suddenly chilled. He managed to reach out a hand, his fingers groping for the carotid artery. Mandova was dead, still clutching the bottle as though he wanted to be buried with it.

Shaw kicked a couple of cheap, torn cushions out of the way and tried to get nearer. There was barely a clear patch of floor. Sheet music, too, was strewn about the place. He bent over to smell the open bottle which had straightened with the Cockney's fall, the aroma now right under the dead man's nose. It was difficult and inconclusive. He had no intention of forcing the bottle from its cradle, and instead produced a handkerchief and wiped clean all exposed parts of the bottle where he had touched it. Lack of prints would raise questions but it was better than advertising his visit.

As he straightened he reflected that he was acting as if this was not a natural death. Yet it would be very easy to assume that Mandova had died from alcohol poisoning and it certainly looked like it.

Shaw stood gazing round wondering what else he might have touched. It occurred to him that he might search the place but quick assessment convinced him that Mandova had not been a man to hide things surreptitiously, even if there was anything to hide. It was all on open view, the complete wreck of his life scattered about the room, the one highlight of sane living reflected in the recent acquisition of the guitar which stood out like a homing beacon. The whole lesson of Mandova's life was still inside his head, dead like the rest of him.

Shaw stepped back carefully, aware that he had given plenty of thought to getting here but perhaps not enough to leaving. He reached the door and wiped the knob. He did not think he had touched anything else. He accepted that his attitude was ridiculous, that he had nothing to hide. And yet he continued with extreme caution.

He stood outside the building for a while experiencing the confusion and fear some of the men he had arrested over the years must have felt. But he had done nothing wrong and it was crazy to feel like this, yet the bitter taste of persecution persisted. He collected his wits and moved off. He walked for a long time before searching for a cab to take him back to Shaftesbury Avenue and by the time he reached there the pavements were full of the theatre crowds.

To mix with them gave him a feeling of comfort, even of protection, letting them shield him as Mandova had the bottle. Twenty minutes later he was back in Jill's apartment and she was pouring him a drink without his asking.

"What went wrong?" she said, handing him a strong whisky.

He lay back in a chair, legs splayed, holding the glass tightly. He took a swig. "Mandova died on me." It was still difficult to believe.

Jill stared at him, realised that he meant it and went to pour herself a drink. "What happened?"

He told her, trying to correlate events sensibly. A good deal of his bewilderment had arisen since he left Mandova as all sorts of implications began to creep in.

"You think the drink killed him?"

"One way or the other."

"I don't like the way you said that. What are you suggesting?"

"How the hell do I know?" He struggled upright in the chair. "One more source of information has been cut off and it happened right in front of my eyes."

"You think the wine was doctored?"

He shook his head slowly. "I don't know. I could smell nothing but cheap booze from his mouth. He said he'd been paid for a job but that would not suddenly make him uncooperative. My guess is that he was paid off. Maybe he did just die of booze, he'd had enough."

"If an alcoholic is deliberately fed drink from which he dies, how does that stand in the eyes of the law?"

"I'm not a judge or a lawyer. I guess a case for murder could be made out but it would be difficult to prove intent."

She left him to his thoughts for a while and then asked quietly, "Did you try resuscitation?"

He gazed at her thinking how smart she looked and what a wreck he must appear. "No. I should have. But it would have needed a strong nerve and a stronger stomach, neither of which I had at the time. It did cross my mind, but in all honesty I don't think it would have made a scrap of difference. My main thought was to get away. And, before you ask, I did not phone the police either. There was no phone in the place and no call-box immediately near."

Her tone softened as she asked, "You don't want to be involved in his death?"

"I am involved. But I don't want to be officially involved. A bloody strong instinct tells me to stay out of it. I'd better phone anonymously."

"You can do it from here." She brought the mobile phone across. "You want a directory?"

He shook his head, dialled 999 and asked for the ambulance service. He told them where they could find Mandova's dead body and hung up. He said to Jill, "They might think it a hoax and call the local police. The last thing I wanted to do was to call the Yard."

"I'll make some coffee." Before he could reply she went to the kitchen, leaving the door open. She called through, "And how do you feel about investigating Terry's death now?"

He did not reply until she returned with the mugs. She placed one on his side table and returned to her seat. "Inadequate," he said eventually. He gave her an inquisitive glance. "You seem to be taking all this very coolly. Had things petered out between you and Terry?"

"I'm simply good at hiding my feelings. You must blame my mother who considered it a disgrace to give way emotionally in front of others. It does not mean that I do not feel very deeply. I do." She toyed with her mug. "On the other hand you seem to wear your heart on your sleeve."

Shaw noticed that she had neatly passed the ball back to him without actually answering the question. But he was willing to believe that she did feel deeply. "You've never seen me in an interrogation room," he replied.

"And now you are beginning to feel like one of your suspects."

He looked across sharply. "What makes you say that?"

"Oh, come, look at you. You arrived in a dreadful tizzy. Not at all like a policeman. You gave a good imitation of being on the run. Are you going to give up?"

"How can I? But I am beginning to get an inkling of what I'm up against. You've been very helpful this evening and I'm really grateful, but I'd better get back."

"I told you I could help. Has it occurred to you that I too, might be being watched? For whatever reason. Hadn't you better go by the fire escape?"

He grinned. "They followed me here; they'll expect me to leave some time."

"You should have told me you were followed here."

It was going to end on the usual sour note, he could feel it coming. "I'm sorry. I thought I had made it quite clear. Otherwise I wouldn't have had to go to Mandova's the back way." She must have known, surely?

"You're right. I couldn't have been thinking too clearly." She smiled a little too brightly. "Now you can take them all back with you again."

What had triggered her sudden change of attitude? What had happened to the new rapport? Fleetingly, he was looking at a stranger and their parting was quite formal, the earlier friendliness not gone but definitely suspended, and it worried him.

"Are you all right?"

"Take no notice. I got caught up with the idea of helping you. I should have thought it through."

The copy of what was probably Terry's letter flashed into his mind and he began to see the contradictions in her again. She still hadn't mentioned it and he was back to wondering why, and whether she was part of the forces that seemed to be building up around him.

5

Veida Ash was a senior section leader in MI6. A striking woman, she looked younger than her thirty-eight years and had kept her figure. She dressed plainly, usually skirts and blouses but could still look good in slacks. Her main concession to outward femininity was high-heeled shoes; she had good legs and was not beyond exploiting them. Her hair was naturally fair as was her complexion and she had sky blue eyes that verged on hardness.

Veida had reached her position in the face of persistently hostile, and conniving, male opposition, because she was extremely good at her job and could be just as devious as those who opposed her. There was no disputing her loyalty or her efficiency and she had served in the field for some years before becoming comparatively desk-bound.

She had just returned from a prolonged lunch-break shopping spree at Harrods to find an agitated Gerald Ratcliffe impatiently waiting for her outside her office. She handed him her carrier-bags then unlocked her office door and said, "You look as if you're having a baby, Gerald. What's the matter?"

He followed her in, his stoop natural and nothing to do with the weight of the bags which he placed on the floor beside her desk. She gave herself a brief check in the small wall mirror beside the desk, touched her hair, and sat down, slightly amused by him. Gerald Ratcliffe was a good man but had a reputation for being a bit of a panicker.

"What is it, Gerald? You're acting as if you're beyond it."

He sat down the other side of the desk and brushed back greying hair that was constantly falling over his eyes. "It's no joke, Veida. Phil Sims is beefing like mad about the use of his men. He can't keep it up. He needs them himself, and I must say I can see his point of view."

"We've done five plenty of favours. Does he want us to encroach on his territory and do the job ourselves?"

"Yes. Or get Special Branch to do it. They can't keep it up. Besides they feel they are monitoring a man for whom they have a great respect. They see no reason."

"I respect him too. Very much. That has nothing to do with it. As for seeing no reason, who on earth are we dealing with here? When have they needed a reason for general surveillance? Phil Sims is acting naive and he's hardly that. They just resent helping out, Gerald. Tell him we'll stop passing information about the Julien brothers if he goes on like this." But she knew it was not that simple and sooner or later she would either have to come up with a sound reason for calling on the help of a sister service or supply her own workforce on their patch.

"It would be better if you told him."

"Yes, well, I might have to do that, Gerald."

She reached down to the side of the desk and moved her shopping against the wall behind her as if unaware that Ratcliffe was still there.

"What's it all about, Veida?"

"Nothing much." She gave him an understanding smile; she could be quite warm at times. "It's not that I mind Laurie Shaw poking around about his brother's death so much, he was bound to do that, but that he might unearth a scam it had taken me a long time to set up. That's why we blocked off access to prison lists and further interviews with prisoners. His brother was working on something for us. I want it to die with him. Cut our losses. We can't win them all. I just want to steer Laurie Shaw away for as long as it takes for him to realise he will get nowhere. It should not take very long. He's got to get on with trying to make a living."

"If we're forced to use SB a good many of them will know him and there might be resentment. His early promotion may have made him enemies there but he had a lot of friends, too. They might tip him off."

"If they did, they should be kicked out. They're professionals, Gerald, just like the rest of us. They'll do the job if they have to." Veida hesitated before adding, "I know I sound like a cold-blooded bitch. I hate doing this to him. Let's hope it won't last long."

"Why don't you level with him?"

"That's impossible. The issue is dead. We had bad luck. He'd still look into the death, and who can blame him, but he would find it very difficult to believe his brother was in any way involved with us. I can't tell him some without telling him all, and that is out of the question. He's been a bloody good policeman, for God's sake, he would not accept a part explanation. Drop it, Gerald, and I'll give Phil Sims a ring and tell him it should not take much longer."

As Ratcliffe rose, stooped over her desk as if trying to read what was on it, Veida said, "If the worst comes to the worst we'll have to employ outside help. We've done it before."

"God help us," muttered Ratcliffe as he walked to the door. He reached it then turned. "Almost forgot. That ex-con Shaw went to see; he's dead."

Veida was already studying something on her desk and apparently did not hear. Realising he was still standing there she said irritably, "What was that?"

"Carlos Mandova, the Cockney with the guitar and bottle, he's dead."

"When was this?" Veida became attentive.

"Last night, I believe. Liver flapping against the knee. Too much booze. He was a chronic alcoholic."

"Who told you?"

"It filtered down from the police." What the hell did it matter who told him? "That's one joker you won't have to steer Shaw away from."

Veida offered a smile. "It makes no difference. Mandova knew nothing about anything, except maybe a little music. He was a recidivist by all accounts. Was completely lost out of jail. Still, I wouldn't wish that on him. Or anyone. Poor fellow." Which dismissed both Carlos Mandova and Gerald Ratcliffe.

Veida raised her head again once Ratcliffe had closed the

door behind him. She sat quietly for some minutes before picking up the scrambler to ask for a connection with Phil Sims at MI5 in Curzon Street.

Veida was right in one respect. Shaw had to work to live and had been neglecting the few tenuous outlets he had. The next few days were taken up by dealing with enquiries he should have dealt with earlier and, by working long hours, he regained some of the ground he had lost. But during that time he could not take his mind off Terry, the strange death of Mandova, or the fluctuating attitude of Jill Palmer from whom he had heard nothing.

Shaw had no other leads to follow. It was convenient for those who wanted to thwart him that the people he most wanted to talk to were all in prison. He felt trapped by a silence surrounded by prison walls and could see no way through. Several times he was tempted to ring Jill to find out if she had made any sort of progress but he knew it would be futile and that, anyway, she would almost certainly have contacted him had she any news.

By the end of the week he was feeling frustrated. He buried himself further into the promotional side of his own work, but the deep suspicion and bitterness, and the way he was being blocked, gnawed at him and he became edgy and bad-tempered. The thought of Terry was always there, because he simply wanted the truth to lay the ghost once and for all. But it would stay there until he got some answers.

The telephone rang on the Saturday evening. Life had become lonely after working hours and he was becoming something of the recluse Mandova had become. He was even drinking more. The ringing startled him and he was surprised to hear a familiar voice, but one that did not give a name nor could he give one to it.

"Is your phone bugged?"

"Not the last time I checked but the Indians have the wagon surrounded. Who's that?"

"Operation Terry. Go to the Red Lion. Be there in half an hour. That should give you time to slip through the Indians

51

and reach the cavalry." The phone cut off and Shaw was left wondering if it was a sick joke.

It was dusk when he left home. He made no attempt to shake off his tail and walked slowly to his local, the Crown, just a few streets away. He had not been there for some time but was greeted by many friendly faces. Most of his friends would have heard what had happened and he knew they would steer clear of the subject.

The place was crowded, and because of the heat, the doors were wide open. He saw a face near the main door he thought he recognised, not a friend but someone he had once worked with some time ago. The man now wore a moustache which did nothing for him. If he saw Shaw at all he gave no sign.

Shaw turned back to his ale, joined in a conversation with a couple next to him, talked a bit, laughed a bit. He was doing what the others were doing, having an enjoyable night out. He asked the man next to him to keep an eye on his half-finished drink and squeezed his way towards the sign for the toilets. The men's toilet was outside in the yard where there were a few tables and chairs for those who preferred the open air. Merlin, an amiable Irish wolfhound belonging to the landlord, roamed the yard looking for affection and scraps. He found plenty of both.

Shaw skipped past the tables, jumped on one of the empty kegs along the wall and rolled over to drop into the rear street. Once outside the pub he had the advantage of being a local with a keen knowledge of the district. He ran as fast as he could.

The Red Lion was not far away and whoever had telephoned must also have had a knowledge of the area. He went in. It was just as crowded and as lively as the Crown, the pubs separated merely by a little distance and customer preference for the type of drinks served. He knew the landlord here too, and ordered another pint.

It was too crowded to stay at the bar and he managed to find a space; the few tables and benches had been taken long since. He knew fewer people here but some gave him a nod. He took his time gazing round trying to puzzle out who might have phoned him.

"Do you remember me, guv?" The voice was gravel, the body granite, the features carved from the same uncompromising block. The clothes were so tight they might have been glued on. He was barely above medium height, but that would not have mattered in an argument. And yet there was a basic friendliness about the face, eyes that wanted constantly to smile. A pint mug was held in a hand that had once pounded brick walls to toughen them up for the next fight. But the problem was the weight went sideways instead of up, and he had been too heavy for his height at boxing. So he turned to all-in wrestling.

"Max Fuller," said Shaw warmly, holding out a hand. "When did you get out?"

Fuller grinned. "Yesterday. I'm on parole. Lucky, really." His grin widened and there was no malice as he said, "You certainly got me bang-to-rights that time. No hard feelings, guv. Although I had them at the time. You ever marry that dish you were shacked up with?"

Shaw stopped smiling. "She died." And then quickly. "It must be eight years since I nicked you. Just before I left 'B' Division."

"You should have left earlier. I might have got away with it. You remember I got a stiff sentence because of other charges taken into consideration. Sorry about your girl. It was me who phoned but it was Bert Healy's idea. He's not a bad bloke as screws go."

"Bert Healy? He's certainly got something to answer for. But if you've got something to tell me we'd better move away from here." Shaw's gaze was roaming the room again.

"We can sit in my car. A bit hot but so is this."

They finished their drinks and left separately, Fuller having told Shaw where to meet him. The car was a Mercedes parked a block away, well clear of the main road.

Shaw climbed into the passenger seat. "And they say crime doesn't pay," he remarked dryly. "Is this new?"

"Naw." Fuller sat with his hands on the steering wheel as if he wanted to drive off. He lowered all the windows to get some air in. "It's a couple of years old. As if you didn't notice by the number plate. Guv, you're either losing the knack or are getting cagier. The car is legit, paid for in cash, receipt available."

"That takes care of the car, what about Terry?"

"Bert Healy knew I lived this way and asked me to contact you. You want a cigar?" He produced a box from under the dashboard.

"I gave up smoking some years ago and so should you."

"You're right." Fuller put the box away while Shaw wondered when he would get to the point.

Fuller made a quick check of his mirrors and said, "Bert Healy asked me to apologise for him about the evidence he gave at the Coroner's Court. He said there had been pressure on him to stick to the medical report and not to complicate things. He was told that whatever he thought was merely opinion and the coroner needed facts and they spoke for themselves."

"I knew he had been told to toe the line. That was obvious. Is that it?" Shaw turned to watch the craggy, shadowed face beside him; the profile was surprisingly impressive, strength in every line.

Fuller rubbed his broken nose. "What exactly do you want to know?"

"What I've always wanted to know. I find it impossible to believe that Terry committed suicide."

"I'll go along with that. I'm pretty bloody sure he was topped."

Shaw was not certain how he felt then. It was what he believed but it was the first time somebody had come straight out with it. Murdered. It had now been said, by a villain. Shaw calmed down, wary now, wondering why Fuller should stick his neck out. He said carefully, "Every time I've tried to find something out I've been blocked one way or the other. How did you escape the net, Max?"

Fuller smiled. "Because I'm an old hand. I did not come forward as a friend of Terry's. But I did get to know him because I wanted to meet the brother of the guy who nicked me. At first it was a sort of twisted satisfaction. I told him

54

you nicked me and he laughed his head off, thought it was bloody funny that you, as he put it, should be as straight as he was bent. But as I got to know him – we used to talk football together, both Spurs supporters – I began to think he wasn't as bent as he made out. But when he was found dead, I kept right out of it. There's no future in getting involved in that sort of thing. Hear nothing, see nothing, say nothing. It helps get you through prison life. I didn't want to be involved in any way at all. I wasn't the only one."

"So what are you doing here now, Max?"

"Well," Max tapped the steering wheel, "I thought there might be some kudos in it for me. Bert Healy's one of the decent screws and asked me to help. I might land back there some day. It's useful to have a screw on your side."

"Don't give me that, Max. I've got no money. I couldn't afford the wing mirrors of a car like this. Now what's your angle?"

Max sat staring straight ahead. "I knew you wouldn't fall for it if I said I did it from the kindness of my heart. After all, you put me away for a good long spell. So as sure as hell I'm not doing it for you. All I agreed to with Bert Healy was to offer his apologies and I've done that."

Shaw was turned in his seat watching Fuller closely. "You've dragged me out for that? Bert Healy can sort out his own conscience."

"I liked your brother and I didn't like what happened to him."

"And now you're out you'll put yourself out on a limb? You must have liked him a hell of a lot."

"Don't sound so bloody cynical. Terry got some satisfaction from the fact that you nailed me. He was proud of you and you're like peas in a pod to look at. So we talked maybe more openly than most. I told him how you finally got me on that roof." He turned suddenly. "I could have thrown you off like a sack. No trouble at all."

"I know you could. If you hadn't been afraid of heights and couldn't move another inch."

Fuller burst out laughing. "You bastard," he said with a tinge of affection.

"Did Terry ever talk about the job he pulled?"

"Never. Not once. It was queer. Most of us would have a laugh about this job or that, but he never mentioned it. I don't think there was a job to talk about, I don't think he ever pulled it."

Shaw felt chill. "He wasn't the type to confess to something he didn't do. And anyway, he pleaded not guilty."

"It was just an impression. He wouldn't be banged up for nothing."

"No." Shaw was uneasy. He was still not convinced of Fuller's motive. "It would need more than one man to do that kind of topping. He wasn't a weakling. They'd have to hold him down, stop him yelling, and hack his wrists. Is that what you are saying happened?"

"You think he was topped, don't you? Isn't that what this is all about? You've answered your own question."

"Shit." Shaw shivered. "Who the hell could do that?"

"Two strong men just before closing time."

"Do you know who?"

"If I knew I would have to have been there. And I wasn't. I've an idea who."

"Don't piss me about, Max, give me names."

"It wouldn't help you. You're up against a code of silence, only this time there's a lot of fear as well. It could happen again and they're running scared. It needs a lot of bottle to pull a caper like that."

"And maybe some inside help. A blind eye. Who were the screws on duty that night?"

"That's not something I'm likely to remember. I didn't know it was going to happen. You'd have to get hold of a duty roster and you'd be bloody lucky to get that."

"And that's what you came to tell me?"

"Yeah. I'm beginning to wonder why I bothered. You don't believe a word I've said."

"Oh yes I do. But there's something you're not telling me. What I find difficult to stomach is that you'd stick your neck out like this simply because you got on with my brother. From what I hear he seemed to get on with almost everybody. It's your angle that's missing."

"Once a copper always a copper. You're a suspicious bugger. I didn't care for the bastards who I reckon did it. One had killer written all over him but was in for car theft. They were not afraid of the barons and nobody tried to buck them. Nasty bits of work. Even the screws were scared of them."

"That shouldn't have worried you, Max. Couldn't you have taken care of them?"

"We're not talking of face-to-face stuff here. We're talking about a knife in the back. Or slashed wrists."

"So you want revenge? How can you get it? You've given no names and with the prison authorities putting their heads deep in the sand, what could be done anyway? You yourself have no proof. You may be motivated by sheer hatred. You want it to be them. Which is why you won't give names in case you are wrong."

"Johnnie West and Hugo Klatt."

It was like an explosion in the confines of the car. Shaw sat still for a while and then pulled out a notebook to jot down the names.

Fuller shifted nervously at the sight of the notebook but it was probably the reaction of a villain who always thinks the worst when one comes into view.

"I've never heard of either of them, but then I don't know every villain in the country. Hugo Klatt sounds German."

"He is. Speaks passable English. Lived here for some years as far as I can make out. Naturalised British. He's killed before, guv, I'm telling you. Johnnie West is a blag man and always goes armed. Works up north mainly where there's less serious competition. I don't rate him without Klatt. He has the muscle but he needs Klatt's cold-blooded guts to hold him together."

Shaw stared through the windscreen at the row of pale street lights converging in the distance. "Thanks, Max. Thank you very much." He put his hand on the door catch. "I still don't know what your real motives are, but I believe what you have told me. Don't let anyone else know and keep your head down. Let's go and get a drink."

They climbed out and Max tested the doors to make sure

they were locked. "So you still think I have an angle," said Max as they turned away from the car.

"Everyone has an angle, if it's only to be on the side of the angels but I know you wouldn't expect me to go that far. When you feel like telling me I hope you will."

A drunk came lurching out of the darkness and almost fell off the pavement. Shaw made a grab to steady him and for a moment it seemed that both would fall, and then Fuller pulled the drunk away and hit him a savage blow in the guts, caught him as he fell and dumped him against the factory wall they were passing.

"Why did you do that, for chrissake?" Shaw demanded. "He was cloud high."

"Not enough not to pick your pocket. Here's your wallet and your notebook back." Fuller handed them over to Shaw, adding, "You really are rusty, guv. So soon."

Shaw felt foolish as he put away his wallet and notebook. He leaned over the drunk and lifted his head by his hair. The man was gasping with pain, arms folded across his stomach. Even in the poor light Shaw now recognised him, it was the man he had seen in the Crown. As Shaw went through his pockets the man tried to struggle but Fuller clamped a huge hand round his jaw and squeezed until Shaw thought the jaw would crack. The only identity was a credit-card case in the name of R. L. Andrews. He made a note of the name and card numbers.

As Fuller watched him he said dryly, "This is a turn-up, ain't it? You're doing my job. I should make a citizen's arrest." He pushed Andrews aside as Shaw finished. "Do you know who he is?"

"Vaguely."

"Not a copper? I haven't busted a copper?"

"Worse," said Shaw. "The last time I knew him he was in the Security Service."

58

6

Restaurants, mostly cramped these days, made security conversation difficult, and clubs were largely anti-feminist so Veida Ash and Phil Sims found the convenient excuse to meet in the Victoria and Albert Museum at mid-day. Both had a genuine interest in the ceramics department and could easily lose themselves among the Lowestoft, Pinxton, Crown Derby and the rest. To them it was therapy to wander round the display cabinets never tiring of the magnificent contents. Both had porcelain collections. Their mutual interest also served as a salve.

It did so now with Sims as he stood before some rare Swansea. He sounded quite reasonable as he said, "I'm sorry, Veida, but I can't spare the people. And one of my men has got himself almost battered to death by an old lag who was with Shaw last night. It simply can't go on."

"An old lag? With Shaw? Do you know who?"

"What the hell does it matter? I believe it was a safe-breaker, a peterman as they say, called Max Fuller. Out on parole. My man saw them together in a car – a Mercedes, I ask you, and noticed Shaw making notes. Our brief was surveillance, not to pick bloody pockets. It actually served the stupid bastard right. He was trying to be too clever and paid the price. But it's still not good enough. You'll have to get the Home Secretary to sanction further help but I will fight it all the way."

"Even if I make out a good case for carrying on?"

"You've already tried to do that. You may well have convinced your own people but you've not done enough to convince me. It simply isn't important enough."

"Come on, Phil, since the Soviet empire collapsed twenty

per cent of our people have been looking around for new enemies. I'm saving you from redundancies, probably including your own."

"It won't do, Veida. It's no joking matter."

Veida wondered if Sims would recognise it if it were; he was not noted for a sense of humour. She knew that at MI5 he was called the curate, although his language often belied the description. "Okay. I'll ask the chief to have a word with the Home Secretary. I'll be as quick as I can."

It was the last thing Sims actually wanted. He could do without an inter-services war. "Well, what is it you really want? You must come absolutely clean about this."

They moved on to the foreign section. "I could quite easily have used some of our own people, many of whom are at present trying to unwind various networks and others are twiddling their thumbs, not yet used to the new situation. Terry Shaw was working for us and was trying to make contact with another prisoner, someone who had information about funny business in Yugoslavia which the eternal peace-makers needed to know.

"This man had already shown he was not going to volunteer to tell us. We had to get someone close to him. We had used Terry Shaw a few times and he had a reputation as a wild boy which suited us fine."

Sims reluctantly took his gaze from some Meissen. "Did his brother know this?"

"Don't be silly. They didn't get on. Which is one of the reasons I'm so surprised that the elder brother is making such a nuisance of himself."

"It's obvious he's not satisfied with the way his brother died."

"Nor am I, for goodness sake. It's bloody strange. I don't think for a moment Terry committed suicide."

Sims turned his back on the showcase, finding it a sudden distraction. "Then why on earth haven't you done something about it? If you had done, you might have got Laurie Shaw off your back."

"What can I do? I can't prove a damned thing. I have to find out in my own way and if that's not possible then it will

60

remain a suicide as found. Terry might have been careless in making contact. He might have shown his hand. In which case I have a good idea who did it. But none of this would stand up in a court of law and I don't want it known why Terry was there, or how he got there. If the press got hold of that lot we'd have the brakes put on to satisfy the public and to tone down a few red faces. And we wouldn't be able to pull that sort of stunt again for years. I mean that kind of thing doesn't happen in England, does it? I don't want Laurie, or anybody for that matter, finding out why Terry was really there. I don't want the man who is still inside to get any edgier than he is. He must feel that he has dealt with the problem. My motive is quite simple: I want the information I wanted in the first place, not justice for Terry Shaw. He accepted the risks. If Laurie continues as he is he might even put himself in danger. And those he contacts. My eyes won't be the only ones watching his antics with interest. He must be discouraged."

Sims shoved his hands in his pockets and stared languidly down at Veida, quite liking what he saw. "You'll go to all this trouble over Yugoslavia?"

"Don't trivialise it, Phil. In any case that's an over-simplification. There's more to it than that."

"You've really told me little more than you did before."

"That's all I've got, Phil. The con Terry was trying to befriend has got to speak to someone sometime. Maybe when he finally does it will all be too late. In which case it will have been a waste of time. It happens."

"There are times when you can be a really cold bitch, Veida. No word of remorse about Terry Shaw. I hope his brother doesn't get to know why he was there. For your sake."

"Now you're being melodramatic. Laurie was with SB, he's no shrinking violet. Besides, he should be pleased that his brother did odd jobs for us. We didn't know it would turn out like this. But it does show we are on to something."

Veida turned away and noticed the disdain shown by Sims. She smiled up at him. "I'm not as hard as you think, Phil. If I let myself go now, I'd burst into tears. I liked Terry. I liked him a lot. He had charm and a lot of guts. I know he had a bad reputation and I'm sure he earned it, but maybe he was late to come round. Perhaps Laurie set too good an example for him. And perhaps the hate Laurie had for him was not hate at all but love and despair. I don't know. I don't want anything to happen to the surviving brother. While your men are there it's not likely to happen."

Sims had not seen this side of her before and was almost moved. But at last he said, "Until the end of the week, Veida. With the best will in the world, I can't do more. I hope you don't go to the Home Secretary but if you do I'll simply have to make my stand."

Shaw and Peter Givens were not so reticent about where they met although they did have a mutual interest in a tankard of good ale. They met at the Cheshire Cheese in Fleet Street where Dickens used to sup, and sat in one of the cubicles to have lunch at Givens' invitation when Shaw had telephoned him. They decided against the famous pie but did have roast beef in spite of the continuing hot weather.

"So what's new?" asked Givens, sensing he was nearer to a story.

"I need your help." Shaw added uncomfortably, "But still off the record."

"I'm a newspaperman, Laurie. I obliged you before, but there has to be a limit unless there's a bloody good reason."

Givens' straw-coloured hair fell about in waves, which he would occasionally sweep from his eyes. He was tall and gangly. His eyes were brown, forever searching and basically cynical; the man had seen the sleaze of life and it had left its mark.

"You offered to help at the inquest. Off the record or not at all. I think you'll find it worth waiting for the green light. I'm not kidding."

"Exclusive," said Givens who had heard it all before.

"Would I lie to you?"

Givens chuckled. "That's a neat gauntlet you've thrown. You'll have to trust me. You'd better eat your beef before it gets cold."

They ate in silence for a while, but Shaw was eager to get on and ate too quickly. He said, "I want the prison list of C Block where Terry died."

"You mean you can't get it? I should have thought your old contacts could have coughed that up."

"They've been gagged. So far as I'm concerned, anyway."

Givens chewed thoughtfully. "Really? That's interesting."

"And it's true. I can't get it. And I'm being followed."

Givens appeared slightly alarmed at that but Shaw added, "Don't worry. Now I'm wise to it I just get rid of them. Unless you're being watched too, which is unlikely at this stage, they don't know we're here."

"How can you be so sure? And who's doing it?"

"The one face I recognised belonged to a guy I worked with in Northern Ireland. Well, I didn't actually work with him but we were doing the same job from different angles. If he's still with MI5, then it's them. Unless he's doing freelance; times are tough after all."

Givens smiled wryly. "But you don't believe it? Well, this is getting even more interesting. Do you know why?"

"They're trying to stop me digging over my brother's grave. He was murdered, Peter. My bet is that they know it too."

Givens let the waiter take his plate. "Just coffee," he said. "Black." He glanced at Shaw before adding, "And the same for my friend." He sat back, expression blank. "Go on."

"Go on what? That's it. That's what I'm trying to find out. What the hell is going on and why an invasion of my privacy?"

"So you really do think Terry was murdered?"

"I've thought so all along. Now I'm sure. If you can get a list there are two names I would like you to look into if you possibly can. Johnnie West and Hugo Klatt."

"Klatt? That rings a faint bell." He tried to remember, then shook his head in frustration. "Too faint," he said at last. "Might take a little time. And I might be blocked too."

"That's possible. But you're able to make much more noise if you are, than ever I can. Besides, you can enquire

63

through different channels; you wouldn't approach SB as I did. A bribe or two might do the trick."

"You must have been a bent copper to suggest that." Givens was trying to be light about a serious subject. "Okay. I'll see what I can do. Do you think they know it's murder and are trying to cover it up? If so why?"

"I don't know. They must believe he was murdered to take so many pains. But I think there's something else. Don't ask what because I haven't a bloody clue."

Givens was letting his coffee cool. "Do you think your brother was ever involved with the Security Services? Did he buck them at any time?"

Shaw did not like the question and realised it was one he had been running away from. "Most of his life was spent in bucking almost everyone."

"Could he have worked for them at any time?"

Why had he not considered that himself? Was he willing only to believe bad about his brother? Although working for the Security Service did not necessarily mean he was doing something virtuous. "I shall never know the answer to that. All they have to do is to deny it. They would never admit it anyway." He felt his hands shaking under the table. "An old lag I put away some years ago suggested Terry was in for a crime he did not commit. But that means nothing. There are plenty of cons who protest they never did it, and Terry could be very plausible."

Givens said coldly, "That's a bit severe on your own brother, isn't it?"

"It must sound like it, I suppose," Shaw faltered. "But all I've heard since he died is what a bloody good bloke he was and how he admired me." He shrugged in despair. "That's not my recollection of him. He was always denying things, sometimes with the blame placed on me. It wasn't funny. If he changed, it can only be over the last couple of years or so."

"Perhaps he showed his worst side to you more than anyone else. Perhaps he was envious and knew he couldn't match you, so you were his target."

"Match me? Peter, what the hell are you talking about? I

was a detective chief inspector not the chief bloody constable. What was there to match?"

Givens tossed his napkin on the table. "It's a matter of degree. He probably realised that he could not match your general attitude to life."

Shaw managed a wry smile. "Well, let me tell you something about my general attitude to life. With the way things are going now, with the way I'm being bitched around, the lack of co-operation from people who owe me one way or the other, my attitude is becoming more like my dead brother's. Maybe there's more of him in me than either of us realised. I'm going to get the truth and if it means doing things the way my brother did, then that's what I'll do. There's much more to this than a killing."

Givens could see that Shaw was emotionally charged. He waited for him to cool down and said quietly, "I'll help you as much as I can."

There was a message on his answering machine from Jill Palmer. She wanted him to go round to her place as soon as he could after 5 pm. There was no need to ring first, she would be there.

It was now nearly 4 pm and Shaw had only just returned from meeting Peter Givens and was still mulling over what they had discussed. He was not too keen on trusting a newspaperman, the temptation to print was so strong. He hardly knew Givens, yet felt he had to take the chance of trusting him. His old friends in the service were now out of reach. He waited impatiently for 4.30 and then left, losing his tail long before reaching Soho.

When he arrived at the alley he made sure it was empty, then used the fire escape. He tapped on the kitchen window and Jill raised it almost immediately.

"I thought you might come this way," she said as she helped him through. She closed the window behind him and led the way into the lounge.

He sat down and she produced a drink so quickly that it must have already been poured. "A bit early," she said. "But you might need it."

"That sounds ominous." He raised his glass. "Cheers."

She sat down in her usual chair and he considered what about her was different. She'd had her hair done, a bob which suited her.

"I thought we wouldn't be seeing each other again," he said. "But I'm glad I'm wrong. I hate bad feeling."

"I was unaware that so far we had any between us." She made herself comfortable, tucking her legs under her.

He thought it best not to answer that; they too easily got off on the wrong foot. "So what's new?"

To his surprise she produced the sheet he had read after breaking into the apartment. She stretched out to hand it to him. "You'd better read that."

He hoped he gave nothing away as he tried to cover his guilt. He took the sheet and read it as if having never seen it before. He was aware that she was watching him very carefully.

After reading it he expressed his surprise and concern, trying not to overdo it. "Is this supposed to be from Terry?" he said as he placed the sheet on a side table. "It's not signed."

"It *was* from Terry," she replied emphatically. She was still waiting for a real reaction and he found the steadiness of her eyes disconcerting.

"But how? He hadn't a typewriter inside. And I still think he would have signed it. Don't you?"

"Never mind that. What do you make of it?"

"Well, I haven't had a lot of time to make up my mind. If it is from him it reads like a suicide note, or at least a preliminary to one. How on earth did you get it? That would never get past the prison censor. Unless they wanted it to."

Jill raised an eyebrow and then her glass in a mocking way. "You've had plenty of time to read it," she said. "It is not the first time you've seen it."

"What are you talking about?" He tried to cover his feelings. She knew, but it was how that worried him more. He felt like a guilty child caught in the act.

"You read it the day you broke in here. You didn't

66

put it back properly. You used Terry's key to get in and decided to check on me." She spoke quite calmly but her tone was cold.

Shaw tried to be indignant, but before he could protest he saw the futility of it. "I wasn't sure about you."

"And now?"

"I'm still not sure. You have made a very strange claim and you have kept it from me. If that is something akin to a suicide note you have a lot of explaining to do."

"You bastard. You break into my home and you say I have a lot of explaining to do. Just what the hell did you think you were doing?"

"You didn't add up. I found it strange you did not know any of his friends."

"Really! And that gives you the right to burgle my flat?"

"I had no right at all. But it had to be done. And I was right, wasn't I? You did have something to hide." He pointed to the typewritten sheet. "You wouldn't be raising it now if you thought I had not already seen it."

She was breathing deeply, trying to control herself. "Let's talk about the reason I did not know his friends. The last few months of our association he started to act strangely and to shut me out. During that time I never met anyone he knew, although he was always something of a loner. When I raised the matter of the change in him he would laugh it off. He could be very convincing, as you very well know. But there was something wrong and then he pushed off for a week with some futile excuse about a job and the next I knew he was awaiting trial for armed robbery. It was a bolt from the blue, for whatever I thought he might be up to it certainly was not that."

"Why didn't you tell me this?"

"I thought about it. But I hardly knew you and you were very anti-Terry. Apart from him our only common denominator was that we both believed he was too strong a character to commit suicide. And, anyway, what have I told you? It's nothing conclusive. It takes us no further forward because I know of no way we can find out who

67

he was seeing during that time. It's a dead end. I wasn't sure of you and was being cagey. And so were you."

"What about the letter? Why didn't you tell me about that?"

"I was in two minds. If you hadn't broken in I might never have told you, that's true. But only because, if I did produce it, it might look as if I was trying to show that he did indeed kill himself. I didn't want you to think that. And it's misleading; I don't think he meant to give the impression he would take his own life. I think it was despair at something that was happening. I said to you at the outset that he was much more likely to try a breakout and I think that was what he intended."

Shaw picked up the letter again and read it once more. Terry had written: "For the first time in my life I don't know what to do . . . Sooner or later something will break." He said after a while, "You could be right. It would still have been better had you come clean in the first place."

"I don't think so. Had anyone known of its existence I would have had to present it to court and that would have clinched the findings. Your enquiries would never have stood a chance."

"They don't stand a chance now, for God's sake."

"We didn't know that then. And don't be so negative."

"How did you get the letter? Was it smuggled out?"

"Not really. He dictated it to a visitor who simply took her notes home and typed them. That's why it isn't signed."

"A visitor? You?"

"No. A prison visitor. Terry asked her to see that I got it. It was at that time he refused to see me any more."

Shaw thought it through. It would be easy to dictate a letter; the simplest tricks were always the best. He was still uneasy about the whole affair but he began to see why Terry stopped Jill visiting. "He might have seen an attack on him coming and did not want you involved. Someone might think he passed something on to you and that could have put you in danger."

"That occurred to me."

He suddenly realised he had not touched his drink. "Am

68

I really so intimidating that you were afraid to pass on information to me?"

"You were full of anger. I'd had much more time to think about it. I wanted to help, but I had to be sure of you. You made it quite clear from the start that the two of you were hardly buddies. I was on his side."

"I had to be sure of you too." Shaw drained his drink and shuddered.

"And are you now?"

He gazed at her evenly. He did not like the sensation of doubt building up in him. "No. I was going to apologise for breaking in but I don't think I should." He put his glass down carefully. "You see, I think you knew I would break in. I think you wanted me to find that unsigned letter and I think you knew I would find nothing else. Not even a hint of what you do for a living. You knew I had Terry's keys which included the key to your door, yet you did not ask for it back. I think that so far you've outsmarted me."

"And just why would I want you to find that letter?"

"To put doubt in my mind. Finding it gives authenticity to it because you had not foisted it on me. Had you shown me I might not believe it to be genuine. Now I don't know what to think." Shaw rose unhurriedly. "I don't know what your game is, Jill, but you're quite good at it and you're an accomplished liar. Were you playing a game with Terry as well? Is that why the poor sod is dead?"

Jill paled, her tension reflected in every line. She stood up, eyes full of anger. She struck him so hard across the face that he went reeling against the chair, falling back into it. And then she looked round for a weapon.

7

Max Fuller mixed uneasily with some old friends in the Red Lion. His discomfort was caused by the fact that he was preoccupied by his talk with Shaw, and the company he was with at present were largely villains, most of them old lags. The two were incompatible.

It was difficult, too, because a small party was being thrown in the pub to celebrate his parole and his return to the land of the quick buck. He had already been offered two jobs of the 'we can't lose' variety. They had to believe that luck would shine on them and that they would make their fortunes. But if Fuller violated his parole he knew it would be a very long time before he saw this kind of freedom again.

So his good humour was muted, a fact which puzzled his friends, two of whom had seen him with Shaw the previous night. Neither had cause to recognise Shaw, particularly as a policeman, but the presence of a copper was something they sensed.

They did not have to be told, and nor did Fuller, of their suspicion. So he said to all at large, "The copper who nicked me was in here last night. Bloody funny. I had a drink with him. He's been kicked out of the Bill. He's now one of us." He laughed and most laughed with him.

"Here's to bent coppers," said one and raised his glass high. "May they rot in the can."

Fuller wasn't sure how he felt. He was at home with these people, they were mates of long standing. And yet he had enjoyed Shaw's company in a way he had not expected. He felt sorry for Shaw because he had liked his dead brother. It was difficult for him to see the difference between them.

The evening continued noisily and Fuller began to relax

with the flow of beer and soon they were singing old numbers their fathers had sung before them. At closing time they dispersed without trouble because the landlord was always good to them and they did not want the bar to be closed by the law.

Fuller had only a mile to walk to his bed-sit. They stood talking in small groups outside the pub until they finally dispersed and for the final half-mile Fuller was on his own.

He had been born into crime, but a peterman was a specialist, a craftsman respected by other villains; a true professional, or as one wag had put it, "A consultant surgeon among the GPs." He had never been involved in violent crime and had too good a reputation to be mocked by those who did. Up to the time he had gone to jail he was still doing the odd bout of all-in wrestling just to keep his hand in. He was generally liked but a new, rising breed of callous villain despised him, though they would never dare say so to his face.

Fuller was basically a lonely man. His wife had left him years ago, tired of travelling the country to this prison or that and finally acknowledging that he would never reform. She had taken her two daughters with her and none of them communicated with him. The divorce came through while he was in prison this last time.

Fuller was not sure whether it was the unaccustomed liquor that had got to him or realisation of his true present position. But he was morose and that was a new experience. He staggered a little as he headed towards his one-roomed home. He was not short of cash, had salted much away, and he could easily have afforded a larger place to live, but where he lived was adjacent to where he and his parents were born, a link he did not want to sever.

It felt good to be free though, lonely or not. He swayed against somebody's gate and gave a little chuckle and as he steadied himself he heard something move. There was movement and movement and this sound was the wrong kind. He tried to clear his head. A quantity of beer would not normally have affected him too much, but he was years out of practice and his thoughts were muzzy. Until danger threatened and then, by an enormous effort of will, he partially cleared his mind.

He stood by the gate to steady himself and strained to listen for the movement again. He heard it. Stealthy. Not an animal. Someone creeping along. More than one. Behind him and across the road, and now in front. Fuller slipped off his jacket and hung his coat over the gate, and waited. There was silence again as whoever was following realised he had heard them.

There was a painful silence and then a sudden rush of footsteps and three men came at him from three different angles. As they converged towards him he stood his ground, and then, at the right moment, jumped forward, to kick one in the crutch and to reach out his long arms to those on either side. Before they knew what had happened he had them in headlocks and was squeezing the very breath out of them.

They tried to pummel him but could have been striking a concrete block. Fuller was really enjoying himself for the first time that evening. He lifted the heads from under his arms and cracked them together with an awesome sound, and then did it again. He dropped the bodies like carcasses and went forward to see how the man with the groin injury was faring.

The man was doubled up and groaning in the gutter. Knowing he had nothing more to fear from the two unconscious bodies he had left by the low garden wall, Fuller moved forward and it was then that the amount of drink let him down. His reflexes were slow as the man suddenly lashed out with a knife cutting into his forearm. He felt the pain and let out an almighty roar as he seized the knife hand, crushing it in his, and then pulled, twisted and flung the man over his shoulder, breaking his arm in the process. The knife fell at his feet and he kicked it away.

Fuller gazed round at the damage. The knifeman was now lying face down in the middle of the road, his broken arm spread out, his face bleeding on to the street. All three were unconscious. Fuller retrieved his jacket and wrapped it round his injured arm and then strode on as if little had happened. It did not occur to him to ring for the police; he had never done that in his life. And he knew that some of what had happened would have been seen behind twitching curtains and that someone would raise the alarm.

He went past his house to a short row of lock-ups in a mews street behind. Drunk or not, he unlocked one of the doors and drove the Mercedes out, locking the door again afterwards. He drove off, considerably sobered but not enough to fool a breathalyser. He feared that that could affect his parole if he was stopped, so he drove carefully.

Shaw was bathing a swollen eye when the doorbell rang. He saw Fuller through the spyhole and opened up to let him in. He noticed the blood on the sliced shirt sleeve at once and led the way to the kitchen before anything was said.

"How did you do it?" he asked as he cut off the sleeve. Fuller did not reply. Shaw bathed the long gash, recognising it as a knife wound, and that Fuller had drunk a few. "You might get away without stitches, it's a clean wound. Go to a doctor tomorrow to check." He was sure that Fuller would do nothing of the kind. He put prolonged pressure on the arm to stop the bleeding and then sanitised and dressed the wound before leading the way back to the living-room.

"Now you can tell me," he said.

Fuller sat down, for the first time seeming a little shaky. "Feel dizzy. Must be all that blood I've lost," he explained.

"More likely the booze," Shaw rejoined dryly. "Do I get to know what happened or not? And why come to me?"

When Fuller faced that question he was not sure. He had plenty of friends, why come here, he had never been here in his life. "I dunno," he said. "Maybe I don't want any of the boys to know and you'd have more influence on my parole officer. I was mugged. Three of them."

"Which hospital are they in?"

"I dunno. I left them lying there. I thought I should tell you."

"Why? Because you think that the mugging was a result of our chat in the car?"

73

"Sure. They didn't ask for my wallet. In fact they didn't speak at all. They wanted to duff me or even kill me. This is a knife wound."

"I know that." Shaw was finding the connection difficult to believe. If it were true, someone had not done their homework on Fuller. "What do you want me to do?"

"You've already done it, guv. Patched me up. I couldn't go to a doc and my mates would think I'm losing my touch. You could give me a drink."

"You've had enough, Max. You've got to drive home. Why would they want to do that to you?"

"To stop me talking to you. Word gets round; it would stop anybody else too."

Shaw did not want to accept it. And then he thought of Carlos Mandova. He had seen nothing in the newssheets about him, he supposed he did not rate, but he would have liked to obtain the post-mortem report. It might be worth trying his friends at SB again. "You want to stay here tonight?"

"Would you mind? It might be kind of busy round my way when the police and ambulance arrive."

"Were you recognised?"

"There was no-one on the streets at the time but anybody could have been looking through windows. But it was pretty dark so nobody could be sure. I can't afford to report it on parole. Nobody would believe I took out three muggers without going for them first."

Shaw sat reflecting. Death. Violence. Intimidation. He really must find out about Mandova. He wanted to reject the whole idea. Fuller had come to no real harm and he himself had not been attacked or threatened in any way. But Fuller was a one-off; someone should have found out his background before sending thugs to deal with him. It seemed that it was those around himself, those who might be in a position to help him, who were being affected most.

"If you're staying the night, Max, you might as well have that drink."

Shaw got up without thinking. So far he had managed to keep his face averted or, while sitting, keep a hand up to shield his eye. In the kitchen Fuller had been too engrossed with his own problems but now, as Shaw rose, he saw the ugly bruising and the cut under the eye.

"What the hell happened to you?" Fuller demanded.

"It's too long a story. And too sore a subject. Someone clobbered me. We've both been mugged."

Fuller started to laugh. "Was she worth it? I mean a man wouldn't scratch you like that. I reckon it's you who needs the drink."

But Jill Palmer's attack on him, justified or not, had convinced him that she had something very much to hide. It would appear that, in spite of her offers to help, she was not being intimidated. This made him even more wary of her. He did not know where he stood. Or where she stood either, and that was worrying.

He handed Fuller a drink and hoped he was sober enough to answer some questions. "Do you know who they were?"

"They weren't in a state to tell me. Cheers, guv."

"You mean to say you didn't go through their pockets?"

Fuller looked surprised. "That would have been dishonest. And, anyway, I wasn't going to hang about." With safety and relaxation, the drink was taking over again.

Shaw sprawled in his chair. He was tired and his eye felt as if it had been ripped out. Fuller was a blur through a screen of fatigue and he was already sorry he had invited him to stay; the spare bed had to be made up. But the other, inquisitive side of him was pushing for answers.

"Did Johnnie West and Hugo Klatt have any visitors?"

Fuller tried to focus but was near to falling asleep, his glass tilting in his hand. He jerked. "Who? Oh, yeah. I think so. I'm not sure."

"Don't go to sleep on me or I'll kick you out. Think."

"Unless I'm actually in the visitors' room at the same time as they are how can I know? They're not the type to tell everybody if they're expecting anyone." It was an effort for Fuller but it pulled him round a little.

"That helps a lot. How long were you inside, Max?"

"Okay. A carrot-top. Hair bunched out like a bird's nest. Heavily made up but not a bad looker just the same."

75

"Whom did she see?"

"Klatt."

Fuller had not hesitated, so the redhead must have made quite an impression on him. "What about West?"

Fuller scratched his head. His eyes were glazing over again. "I can't think. Can't we leave this till morning? I mean, I've been mugged."

"No," said Shaw mercilessly. "The other guys were mugged. I've been mugged. All that's happened to you is that you've drunk too much. What was the redhead's name?"

"I never got to ask her." He chuckled with recollection. "Wouldn't have minded though."

Shaw could see that he would get no further that night. And the way he felt then he wondered if he ever would. "Let's get you to bed," he said.

When Shaw woke next morning Fuller had gone. The blankets were folded neatly at the foot of the bed in the spare room with a note taken from his own stationery held down by a ballpoint from his desk:

"Thanks, guv. I didn't want to disturb you. Haven't yet broken prison habit of rising early drunk or sober. Always was a quiet mover. Years of practice in places I shouldn't have been. Carrot-top's name was Molly Winters, I think. But definitely Molly. Johnnie must have had visitors but none that left an impression. I'll let you know if I come up with anything more. I've used your bread, toaster, and tea. Left as found. Tidy. Be lucky. Max."

Shaw made himself coffee. He must have been flat out not to have heard Fuller leave no matter how quietly he moved. His eye was still painful and, when he looked in a mirror, red and swollen. Jill had certainly caught him. Every time he met her he thought it would be the last but this must surely be true now. And he was beginning to wonder if she had not typed the letter, supposedly from Terry, herself.

He had no idea what to do next. He had no leads to follow and had to be patient to wait for Givens' research. Later

76

that morning, from frustration, he rang Sandy Taylor, his old friend at Special Branch, and asked if they could meet for lunch. He was surprised when his friend agreed, having already refused the prison list, and they arranged to meet at a restaurant in Victoria Street.

Shaw booked a table and was there by 12.30. He went inside to claim the table and wait. To Shaw's surprise Detective Inspector Sandy Taylor arrived on time. Shaw was relieved as the two men shook hands. "I wondered if you would come," he said.

"Why? I said I would." It was difficult to see how Taylor had obtained his nickname. He was almost bald but threads of sandy hair had been trained across his head. His Celtic origin showed in a freckled skin. Thin and tall, his features verged on the gaunt.

They chatted about old times, had some drinks, ordered a meal before Shaw came to the point. "What's going on, Sandy? It didn't stop at blocking the prison list. I'm being shadowed all over the place."

"You mean they are here?" Taylor showed alarm.

"No. Once I knew I started to shake them off. They haven't a full team, otherwise it wouldn't be so easy. I ran into one of them; belonged to Five. Know anything about it?"

Taylor was worried. "I wouldn't be here if I did."

"Would you have been here had you known I had a tail?"

"That's a low one, Laurie. Maybe not. Well, not without making some enquiries first."

"Do you think you could still make those enquiries? Because I would like to know what the hell is happening."

"I can try. I'll probably meet the same stone wall I did before. Is this all about Terry's suicide?"

"No. It's about his murder."

"Jesus. Are you sure?"

"I can't prove it. If I could do that the whole world would know by now. But he was murdered, all right. I have my source of information."

"Narks can be highly unreliable."

"He's not a nark, Sandy. They don't want me to prove

77

that Terry was murdered. They're trying to sideline me and are interfering with some of my informants. I believe they got at one; he's dead."

Taylor had expected nothing like this and was disturbed. "It's nothing to do with us," he said lamely. "I'd have picked up a vibe."

"It's the Security Service but exactly who and why, I haven't a clue."

"But why would they want to kill Terry?"

"I didn't say they did it. But I'm sure they know he was killed if not by whom, and don't want me to find out."

"Maybe they're tackling it themselves and don't want your clods to get in the way."

"Maybe. If they did and found out they wouldn't go public and that's exactly what I want to do."

"You won't get past them. You haven't the strength of the force around you since you resigned. You won't get anywhere on your own, Laurie. You don't stand a dog's chance."

Shaw shrugged. "You're probably right. But I can't sit on my backside doing damn all. It's a pity they won't let me work with them instead of shutting me out. They're arrogant buggers."

"That's a fact. They're even worse since Five were nominated to head the anti-terrorist squads. They're not answerable to anyone."

"Can you get me a list of prison visitors over the last six months? They must be on record."

"That's a tall order, Laurie!"

"Can you try? You don't have to spread it around."

"Sure." Taylor did not look too hopeful. "But if I'm stopped I won't battle too hard to go on. It's not my fight. Your brother has already been the cause of your resignation; I don't want him to be the cause of mine." Taylor hesitated then looked his friend in the eye and Shaw braced himself for something unpleasant. "I never really understood your resignation," said Taylor evenly. "It didn't make sense. I know a bloke high in one of the security firms whose brother is on the creep; one of the best cat-burglars in the country. Why should he resign because his brother is a villain? The funny thing is they have a huge respect for one another, but one's dead honest and the other dead bent. They go their own ways. You could have done the same. Did you really resign on a moral issue or did you want to show the world what a crass bastard your brother was? Your way of getting back at him?"

"Or maybe even to stop him," Shaw replied too quickly. He was shaken. "You've obviously thought about it. If that was my reason I can only say it escaped me at the time."

He wondered how many more of his friends thought like that.

He drove north again the next day. It seemed to him that he was being forced round in tight little circles; seeing people he had already seen and who probably had little else to offer. He had been corralled and the restriction was demoralising. By the time he arrived it was early evening and he went straight to Bert Healy's terraced house in a neat, modern street on the outskirts of town.

Healy's wife answered the door, a pretty woman with fluffy hair and kind eyes who told him Bert was still at the prison and would not be home for another hour or so.

Shaw had balked at telephoning first because Healy might have made excuses not to see him. He said he would return but Daphne Healy invited him in to wait.

"After that long journey you just relax. I'll get you a drink." She turned as she left the room: "You should bathe that eye."

He took the glass of ale and sat down in a cosy sitting-room and she left him to watch television while she went back to finish the ironing. He felt he was deceiving her and that Healy would not thank her for letting him in. It was a long way to come for an extreme long shot but showed a stubborn relentlessness which partly explained his early promotions.

When Healy eventually came into the room he was more angry than Shaw expected.

"I can't help you any more," Healy said before Shaw could say a word. "And I bloody well resent you conning your way past my wife."

"You'd better keep your voice down or she'll hear you. I haven't conned her; I simply did not give her the full details of why I'm here and I'm sure she would not have wanted to hear them. Steady down, Bert. After all, you did put Max Fuller on to me. It's just a follow-up."

"I did that because I reckoned I owed you one. But not now."

Healy was still standing and Shaw felt at a disadvantage so left the chair. The television was intrusive and he turned it off, hoping Healy would not start another outburst.

Healy glared. "Taken over the bloody home as well, have you? You'd better get out."

Shaw could see that Healy was not only angry but afraid of something. "Has someone threatened your job?"

"Don't be daft."

Shaw sensed he was near. "Look, Bert, I'm in no position to intimidate you. And I wouldn't, anyway. I just want to know if you can tell me anything about the visitors Johnnie West and Hugo Klatt had."

Healy appeared to be transfixed by the question. He slowly recovered, the steam gradually leaving him. He was still angry but more with himself it seemed than with Shaw. He was torn between a desire to help and the possible result of doing so. He was confused and wanted to get back to the life he understood. Mention of West and Klatt had definitely unnerved him.

Healy impatiently indicated the chair Shaw had left and Shaw sat down again. Healy lowered his bulk on to a settee. "Those bastards are poison, particularly Klatt. Nasty piece of work." He waved his arms. "Look, I'm sorry, but I don't want to get mixed up in this. It's my bloody job and I'm not willing to risk it. Anyway, how can you expect me to remember visitors like that? There are hundreds of them."

"Max remembers a redhead who visited Klatt. And Max reckons Klatt and West topped my brother."

"Max is talking through the top of his head. And Max wants to keep his bloody mouth shut."

"Then why send him to me? What was the point?" Shaw reached for the glass of beer he had put down.

It was clear that Healy was still torn between a natural honesty and what might happen to him if he followed an open line. "I felt bad about going back on what I said to you. We weren't told what to say in court but it was made clear that loyalty lay with the official line. I just wanted Max to tell you that but he obviously opened his big mouth further. He told you what he thought you wanted to hear. You know Max. You can't rely on anything he said beyond what I told him to say."

"So you don't remember a redhead?"

"Oh, yes. Nobody could forget her. An over-made-up flashy scrubber."

"Do you remember her name?"

"No. And if I did it probably wouldn't be the right one." He watched Shaw's grim expression and felt some of his original compassion. "Look, you're flogging a dead horse. I can't help you any more because there is nothing else to tell. Honestly. You could have saved yourself a bloody long journey and now you've got a bloody long one back, and no further forward. Give it up."

"Do me one favour. Give me the prison number of Hugo Klatt."

"It won't help you."

"Will you get it for me?"

"I'll phone through now." Healy went into the hall and made a call to one of his friends at the prison and came back with the number scribbled on a scrap of paper. "Where will that take you?"

Shaw tucked the number away. "The only way I'll get to see Klatt is to drop him a line and ask for a visitor's pass."

Healy stared in disbelief. "There's no way he'll see you. You're off your trolley."

"I think he will," said Shaw, "and if he does it means I've broken out of this tight little prison they've put me in."

"Why the hell would he see you? He'll know by now that you're stirring it up for him."

"And that's exactly why he'll see me. He'll know where

I will be at a precise time. And so will others."

"Don't do it," Healy pleaded. "You're mad. You're setting yourself up to join Terry. You don't know what you're up against."

8

The envelope was not even addressed to him. It was buff and plain but well sealed. Instinct made him feel along the edges for anything other than paper. He took it into the living-room.

It was very early morning and Shaw was exhausted, having driven back through the night. His injured eye was sore, approaching headlights still pounding the optic nerve. In spite of his tiredness he went to his desk and scribbled a note to Hugo Klatt requesting a visitor's pass, and sealed and addressed the envelope. He wanted to catch the first post.

He drew the curtains back, the grey light creeping in as he sat down in the nearest chair. He was asleep as soon as he relaxed and did not wake for over two hours. He felt wretched then and was annoyed he had not managed to stay awake. He made coffee and while he waited for it to cool retrieved the buff envelope he had picked up in the hall.

He felt over it again and then slit it open. There were three sheets stapled together with roughly fifty names on each sheet. A prison number was beside each name and Johnnie West and Hugo Klatt were included. It was a list of the prisoners in Block C and it still included Terry's and Max Fuller's names so was not completely up-to-date.

Shaw sat down and went through the list carefully, fighting off sleep with difficulty. It was what he had wanted in the first place. But who had brought it by hand? He had asked Peter Givens only for details of Klatt and West. Sandy Taylor had not been able to get the list. He reached for the phone and rang Jill Palmer.

"Sorry to wake you so early but did you deliver a prison list?"

"The one you spoke about?" She was so sharp that Shaw thought she must have been up for a while.

"Yes. Someone delivered it here. I thought it might be you."

"Why? If it was from me it would have been fictitious."

He swallowed on that. He should not have phoned her. "It was just a thought. I'm sorry . . ."

"Well, it wasn't me."

The line went dead and Shaw regretted phoning. Then who had delivered it? Because the phone was there in front of him he did another check for bugs and went into the bedroom to check the extension. He went round the usual places where a bug might be hidden, as a matter of routine after being away. In spite of the external surveillance he was again surprised that as far as he could see there was nothing inside the house. It seemed that it was his movements which interested them most and their results of late must be poor, the way he had been evading them.

He prepared breakfast and went through the list again. He recognised a few villains he had dealt with himself. And two terrorists. The list now was really of little use since Max Fuller had given him the names of Klatt and West.

After breakfast he went for a walk to post the letter to Klatt and to clear his head. There was no need to take evasive action and he did not check to see if he was being followed, although the sensation was still there. It was still early, the weather still fine and the trees were twitching with fluttering birds. With less on his mind it was a morning he would have enjoyed.

He waited until after ten before phoning MI5, asking for Phillip Sims. It was just the same as phoning any business except calls were monitored. Sims came on, expressed delighted surprise, and then regret about Shaw's brother, and agreed to an appointment at mid-day. As Shaw was retired, so-to-speak, it was better that the meeting took place away from the building in Curzon Street.

They met outside a pub off Trafalgar Square. They did not go in as Sims decided to take on a cloak-and-dagger stance, much to Shaw's amusement. They walked towards the Square and faced the white façade of South Africa House, tourists and early lunchers feeding the endless pigeons around them. Nelson reared on his column casting a shortening shadow. "What happened to your eye?" Sims asked politely.

"A pigeon flew into it while waiting for you."

They discussed Shaw's resignation. Sims had been devastated at part of the service losing such a good man and it seemed to Shaw that Sims was trying to talk enough to put Shaw off whatever it was he wanted to raise.

Eventually Shaw turned to face Sims and thereby Nelson as well. "Why are your men following me?"

"What! What on earth gave you that idea?"

"I recognised one of them. He probably went sick after Max Fuller gave him a thump or two while he was trying to pick my pockets. His name is Andrews."

"My dear fellow, you must surely have been mistaken. If any of our people were doing that I would almost certainly know about it."

"Exactly. So I wondered why they were doing it. Any idea?"

"It can't be us. It's impossible. Why would we do such a thing?" Sims gazed round the square. "And where are they now, I ask you? You're not up to any hanky-panky, are you?"

"Someone seems to think so. As for where they are now, they're not likely to show themselves while I'm with you. You'd sack them. By the way, did you know my brother was murdered?"

Sims had recovered and was far from the fool he portrayed. "That's news to me." He gave Shaw a searching look. "Murdered? That's a pretty monstrous thing to say in view of the coroner's findings."

"You know about them, then?"

"I do read the newssheets. Including the yellow variety. Surely they would have cottoned on had there been anything in what you say. You must be mistaken."

"No, I'm not mistaken. What about this guy of yours Max clobbered? You evaded the point."

Sims shrugged, stooping over the grounded pigeons as if counting them. "When things are slack, and they've been fairly so since the Eastern bloc collapsed, some do spare-time work. They are not supposed to and we stamp on it heavily, and if it conflicts with what we do they're out. The claim is always that they're underpaid, and compared with industry, and the importance of what they do, I suppose they are."

"So you know nothing about any of your boys following me?"

"Certainly not. You must be dreaming it, old boy."

"Well, the next time I dream one, I'll trap him, clobber him, and get Max Fuller to finish the job. All in the interests of invasion of privacy."

"And quite right too. Do let me know at once." Sims gave a rare smile. "Was there anything else?"

"No. I'm relieved to hear what you've told me."

"Yes, well, you do realise that I have extended to you a special privilege for old time's sake. I really shouldn't be talking to you at all. You are no longer one of the family."

Shaw smiled. "I've always quite liked you. And I love listening to your bullshit. You came to find out just what sort of cock-up your people made. Cheers, nice to see you haven't lost your touch." He strode away chuckling but only to annoy Sims. Once out of sight he wondered just what he might have achieved by the meeting.

He returned home to find a call from Peter Givens on his answering machine and called straight back. He decided it was best to meet away from his home so grabbed a couple of sandwiches from a delicatessen on the way to the *News* offices.

He travelled by underground as far as he could, it was no time to find a cab, and walked the rest. It was half-past two by the time he entered the spacious lobby of the newspaper building and a few minutes later when he arrived in Givens' office.

They shook hands, Givens sweeping the hair from his eyes, and sat down either side of the desk. Even with the door closed the bustle and constant ringing of telephones intruded.

Shaw produced his sandwiches and by the crumbs already on the desk he could see that journalists sometimes did the same as he. "A busy morning," Shaw explained. "And I had to shake off the men who MI5 say aren't there. So I'm late."

"What happened to your eye?" Givens seemed amused.

Shaw regretted he had not worn dark glasses. "Ran into a door."

"What else? You need a new technique." Givens' desk was covered in papers. He buzzed the intercom and ordered coffee. He shuffled the papers around as if he had no idea what they were, but suddenly from the apparent chaos came order and several neat piles appeared from one of which he extracted two typewritten sheets.

"John Arthur West," Givens said. "Born Liverpool, July 1954. Married twice, both wives left him for the same reason; wife beating. Odd that; beaten wives often have a strange habit of staying with their husbands until almost too late. So there were probably other reasons. Quite a bit of form, mostly for GBH. Recidivist. Several sentences ranging from three months to twelve years. Graduated to blag man and has been on smash and grab for some time now. As far as is known always goes armed. Mindless slob, will never reform, and a waste of taxpayers' money." Givens glanced across the desk. "He's never actually shot anyone so far as records show, and most of the GBH has been inflicted with boots and knuckle-dusters. No case of actual killing. Okay?"

Givens shuffled the sheets again. "Now Hugo Klatt is a bit of a mystery. Wasn't easy to trace and I cannot vouch for the accuracy of what I've got. I've checked as far as I can though, and it seems to stand up. Date of birth, 12 March 1944 in Dresden. That makes him forty-nine. His father was killed on the Eastern Front shortly after his birth. Mother and he were trapped in what became East Germany and after his mother died in 1966 he was one of the few to escape over the Wall. He stayed in West Germany until 1975 when he came to Britain. As soon as he met the statutory requirements he applied for naturalisation. Up to that time there was absolutely nothing against him. Clean as a whistle. Owned a printing works which I am told is still going. We can check. Couldn't have been entirely satisfied with printing because he went into car theft. But no record of violence."

"Why do you find that a mystery?"

"You were in Special Branch so you know better than me. It's often difficult to check on these political escapes. For all sorts of reasons. Was he allowed to go? That sort of thing. What was he doing in West Germany while he was there? So far I haven't been able to raise anything on that. Although it's all down on paper it's nowhere near as clear-cut as Johnnie-the-moron-West. We can check with the German police and Interpol, that sort of thing, but journalists are a bloody nuisance, if you haven't already noticed. The police would not try too hard, particularly if there is a possibility of us finding them wanting."

"Then I need to go out there. Do my own checking."

"Is it that important?"

"If he killed my brother it is. The one thing in this is the complete lack of motive. You say neither has a reputation as a killer, yet my information is that they did the job, in prison, under extremely tight conditions. Either there was something very much to hide, or they were paid an enormous sum. Otherwise it would be too risky, which really leads back to the first premise."

Givens was leaning back in his chair looking at the papers without actually seeing them. "There's another reason why I think Klatt is a bit of a mystery." He tossed the papers on to the desk. "That could be a load of crap."

"You mean his background might be rigged?"

"As you know, where Germany is concerned there's a lot of it about. They were infiltrated something rotten."

"I have run across it," Shaw responded mildly. "But Klatt's occupation as printer and car thief hardly puts him in a position of espionage. And if he was he must have made a cock of it or he wouldn't be in prison."

"Just the same, there's something wrong."

Shaw respected Givens' gut feeling; he had experienced

many himself although some had been wrong. "Any mug shots?"

Givens opened a large envelope and drew some photographs out. "That's West. Police shot, looking straight into the camera with the sincerity of a con man."

Shaw held the glossy print. The arc lights shone straight into the eyes, giving them circles of light which really destroyed their true expression. Dark, greasy hair, pulled back and almost reaching the shoulders. Because of the crudity of his features he missed being good-looking but it was easy to see how some women might be attracted to an animal magnetism. Shaw handed the print back. "And Klatt?"

Shaw expressed surprise as he took the print. "Is this it?"

Givens nodded, a slight, satisfied smile on his lips. He did not say anything, content to let Shaw form his own opinion.

"It could be anybody." Shaw studied the picture of a young man scrambling to his feet at the foot of the Berlin Wall, partly obscured by three men rushing towards him to help. The top of the wall could not be seen, but the graffiti on the wall itself were clear. The young man, in jeans and loose jacket, was crouched forward as he tried to rise, hair hanging down over his face. Underneath was the press caption: Hugo Klatt escaping from East Germany on 8 November 1966.

Shaw could not put the print down. He was fascinated but had no idea why. After a while he looked up to say, "What happened to all the press shots that must have followed? He was one of the few escapees for God's sake. A hero."

"A hero serving time for car theft in one of HM prisons and who you think killed your brother. It's a long jump from the Berlin Wall, if you'll excuse the pun." Givens took back the print and said, "There are no other shots. None that we can trace. Of course there were others taken at the time." He pointed to the print which he had placed on the desk. "That particular shot was in all the nationals over here and abroad at the time. America too. One of the most published shots of the day. A victory shot. Helping hands from the West running to assist him. Great stuff. But hardly a studio shot. So what happened to the others, Laurie?"

"Shouldn't we be asking what happened to Hugo Klatt?"

"Phew!" Givens inclined his head in acknowledgement. "You think he's a ringer?"

"The only publicity shot is so indeterminate of the individual that it could be almost anyone. You say later shots are missing. What about the police mug shot?"

"Oh, that's a beaut." Givens handed it across.

Shaw looked at it and a pudding-faced bald-headed man of forty-nine stared back at him. As far as a head-and-shoulders can show, Klatt appeared to be powerful. His lips were full, and the eyes, even allowing for indifferent lighting, were arrogant and threatening. Prison had not dented Klatt's opinion of himself. He had faced the camera and managed to intimidate the photographer at the same time.

"Is there a passport photograph?"

"It's little different from that one. Just a few years older. I saw it at Petty France but did not ask the passport people for a copy. Interesting, ain't it? A press photograph of a young man in his early twenties jumping the Wall, face obscured by his own hair, and the next shot is of a middle-aged baldy on police files." Givens offered a faint smile. "You have to admit that people can change physically an awful lot during that time. Lose weight, put it on, go to seed. It's possible."

"Sure." Shaw got up. "Look at you."

Givens held out an envelope. "Take this. It contains copies of the mug shots and the personal details. Meanwhile I'll contact some journalist friends in Germany to see what happened to the other photos. Maybe they were simply lost or thrown out after so long."

Shaw offered an old-fashioned look. "I've applied for a visitor's pass to see Klatt."

Givens said nothing but his hand reaching out to tidy the papers suddenly stopped moving. He withdrew it. "That means applying to Klatt direct and for him to ask the prison authorities. In the very unlikely event of him agreeing the authorities won't. They already know you're trying to stir it up."

"That's what makes it so interesting. We might see a show of outside influence in which case my bet is that the pass will be sanctioned."

Givens was still seated and he gave Shaw a long look. "Are you suggesting that Klatt might be instructed to see you and someone is powerful enough to pacify the prison staff?"

"I'm saying it might be suggested to him and that the prison authorities might be placated thereby."

"I sometimes forget that you were with the SB. Crafty devil. But you could be wrong."

"Of course. It's all pie in the sky. But in any event it might give Klatt an opportunity to find out what I know. He might want to do that."

Givens leaned back with fingers intertwined across his stomach. He said seriously, "I admit that I see a really good story in this and have already spent some time on it, but I wouldn't want it at the expense of finding your head rolling in the gutter. It seems to me that you are not only looking for the killer head-on but are also summoning the devil you seem to think controls him. That is a very dangerous thing to do, Laurie. And you could be wrong about everything."

"It's one way of finding out. Thanks for all you've done, Peter. I really appreciate it."

Givens rose to shake hands. "I just hope to God you know what you're doing."

9

On the second floor of Century House, Veida Ash accepted that this time Phil Sims really meant it, and had taken some preliminary precautions. "So you let Shaw frighten you off," she accused.

"Don't be silly." Sims sipped his coffee and grimaced. "We make better coffee than this at our place and that's bad enough. He's known almost from the beginning that we've been watching him. That did not matter so much except to show how standards have slipped, but the reason is what it's always been: lack of manpower. And he knows that his brother was murdered."

Veida sighed. "We knew that. We're as sorry as he is about it; more, actually, because Terry might have had something to tell us before he died. That's not the issue. I still don't want him bumbling around with the possibility of picking up on his brother's task. It could put him in the same danger as his brother."

"Are you saying that you knew Terry Shaw was sticking his neck out when he went in?"

Veida gave the sort of sigh that irritated Sims as if he was a backward schoolboy unable to grasp the obvious. "Not in that way," she said. "Do you think we would have put him in had we considered that might happen? It was a disaster that he was killed. Look at the repercussions now."

"Why don't you simply have a straight talk with Laurie Shaw? Just explain everything. He'll understand."

"I'm sure he will. But our aims are different. He wants whoever murdered his brother. That to us is a side issue and we're pretty sure anyway, although we don't want it known. He would not tolerate that attitude and would make life more difficult than now. I understand his position only too well but I very much doubt that he would ever accept ours."

Veida curled up in her chair and then stretched, arms reaching high. She yawned, then gave Sims a warm smile and said, "Don't think I'm ungrateful, because I really do appreciate your help. But don't complain if you find us crawling over your patch."

Sims put his cup down on her desk. "I'll bring a jar of something decent next time I see you. I hope you sort out the problem."

When Sims had gone Veida's affability vanished and her expression changed to one of deep concern. She would have to handle matters herself.

Shaw was not certain at which stage he felt free from observation. He had become so used to intrusion that he accepted it as normal and dealt with it accordingly. He had not expected to be picked up at the *News* offices as he had taken precautions on his way there, but from the moment he neared his apartment block he became alert, expecting his tail to pick up the threads.

It was such a strange feeling that he walked round the block in an effort to locate a tail. He was suddenly alone and it took some getting used to. He went back to his apartment still not completely sure, and picked up a letter on the way in. He peered through the curtains but his regular watcher across the street had gone.

He was not certain he liked the sensation of being left alone; there was an ominous feel to it; he preferred the enemy he could see. So they had changed their tactics. His talk with Phil Sims might have had an effect but he did not think so. Sims had already known that his men had made an obvious job of it. It would not have swayed him except to make him more careful. Inexplicably, Shaw felt more threatened than before.

He opened the letter. It was from a solicitor stating that if he would make contact he would learn something to his advantage. There was still time; he rang and introduced himself. He had been left £45,000 by his brother and if he would like to call at the solicitor's office with solid identification he could collect a cheque. Settlement of the estate seemed to be extraordinarily quick.

Shaw sat down heavily. He was bemused. People he had only met during the last few days had been unanimous in saying that Terry thought the world of him. He had believed that at least some of it was lip-service to console him. According to the solicitor he was the sole beneficiary. Why wasn't Jill included? He must find out when the will was made.

The actual sum was £45,000.87. He didn't know what to think. Was it bent money? He had no intention of trying to find out because he was tired of looking in corners in an effort to discover just how bad his brother had been. Another side was being forced on to him whether or not he liked it.

He telephoned Jill. There was no reply so he left a message on her answering machine, now working. He was surprised when she rang back an hour later by which time he had drunk a few whiskies. He tried to steady his voice. "Did Terry owe you any money?"

"If you mean by that did I lend him any, then no. I suppose you've heard about the will."

Shaw felt cheated. How the hell did she know? When he stumbled over his reply she continued.

"I was one of the witnesses. I did not want any of it. I have some of my own."

Shaw ferreted for words. "Do you know how he got it? No, forget that, it really doesn't matter."

"After all you've said against him it's made you feel humble, hasn't it?"

"Well, yes. It was totally unexpected."

"The booze has made you maudlin. Go to bed early and put a compact on that eye."

"Don't go." He thought she was about to hang up. "When did he make the will?"

"Just before he wandered off and got himself a prison sentence. I witnessed it with the solicitor's clerk at that time."

"Did you know its contents?"

"Not at the time. And I had no intention of asking. I don't

94

know how much either. It was later, during a prison visit, that he told me he had left his money to you."

"It's forty-five thousand quid and I'm sending it to our mother."

"He didn't want you to do that. He wanted you to use it to find out who killed him."

Shaw went numb. The immense cold was immediate. His voice was shaking as he said, "Are you saying he knew he was going to be murdered?"

"The last time I saw him he told me he had left his money to you and that if anything happened to him he hoped you would use it to find out who did it. He asked me to put pressure on the solicitor to expedite. From then on all my applications for a visitor's pass were rejected. He would not let me see him."

"And you didn't bloody well tell me this? If I hadn't phoned you I would never have known."

"Yes, you would. When you go to collect the money his solicitor will ask you to make contact with me. I would have told you then."

Shaw glared at the phone as if what was happening was its fault. "But why the hell didn't you tell me before?"

"There was no need. I didn't know so much money was involved and you were already trying to find his murderer. And without the solicitor's back-up you wouldn't have believed me anyway. You don't believe a bloody word I say."

"Look, we'd better meet." The drink was adding to Shaw's confusion.

"Not on your life. We get on better at each end of a telephone. Anyway, I have nothing further to say."

"Oh yes you have. He told you he expected something to happen to him and you did damn all about it. You didn't go to the police or the prison authorities. What sort of person are you?"

"You went to the prison authorities *after* he was murdered. And where did it get you? You know, I sometimes wonder how the hell you ever became a policeman. You are unbelievably naive. I had no evidence of any kind to offer. It was just Terry's notion. Some would say his fantasy. Their answer would have been why did he not complain himself? He had access to the governor if it came down to it. Nobody would have believed me. They would have thought I was up to something, trying to get him moved for some reason. I had absolutely nothing to offer that made any sense at all. And, in truth, I don't think he had either. For whatever reason, he was afraid of something. But as he did not take me into his confidence, and God knows I tried hard enough to get it, I had nothing but his suspicions and they could have been explained away by the depression that many prisoners get which often results in stir fever."

Shaw could hear her anger down the phone and her breathing was irregular. He was about to speak when she added, "It is very easy to be wise after the event. You're very good at it. And your reaction to me reflects what would have been the police reaction had I seen them. Suspicion. Use the money well, Laurie." She hung up.

Shaw felt as if his whole system had been shaken up. He was angry and edgy and confused and no more sure of her than at any time. She always had an answer and never a hesitation.

He sat down in his favourite chair and against his better judgement poured another stiff whisky. He was fast losing control of a situation which was becoming more confusing. He went through the material Givens had handed him, learning nothing more. Whether it was the drink or the shock of being the sole beneficiary of his brother's will, he did not know, but he was fast losing sight of himself. The brother he had so disliked had an obvious faith in him which was becoming difficult to understand, let alone honour.

Adding to the confusion, every time he wrote Jill Palmer off as of no value she showed up again in unexpected ways but still adding nothing to help his problems. He wondered what else she was holding back, for it seemed a mini-crisis was needed each time to prize something from her. It would be unwise to rely on her in any way.

He went out to a nearby restaurant for dinner, feeling lonely now and unsure of what he could do next. An excellent meal helped him feel better but endorsed his loneliness as the other diners all had company. He was being forced away, if not ostracised, by his former colleagues. He was feeling sorry for himself and knew it. He paid his bill and wandered into the cooling night air. His apartment was about a mile away and he walked slowly, leaving the canopied lights of the restaurant behind as he entered the dark zone of indifferent street lamps.

As he was not alone on the street it was a little while before he realised that his tail was back. There was a difference and it took him a while to place it. He stopped to look behind him and someone hived off into a doorway without subtlety, and emerged again when Shaw started to walk. There was more than one man, and he spotted another across the street.

Shaw continued on, using his ears and his experience. These weren't surveillance operators, they were far too clumsy, almost as if they wanted to be seen. These people were intimidators. He continued to walk on and they continued to follow, one of them coughing loudly to make sure he heard. He reached the apartments and they openly stood nearby while he opened the street door.

He slept well because he had drunk a lot but did not wake refreshed. He rose blearily, remembered the men and went to the window. Someone had managed to find parking space during the night and a man was sitting in a car, glancing up quickly as he saw Shaw's curtains move.

He had a shower and, once dressed, checked for mail. There was a follow-up from an estimate for security he had sent off recently. He took his time over breakfast and then went to see the solicitor to collect the amount Terry had left him. He paid it into his account and went back to the apartment. He had to admit that Jill Palmer had told the truth in one respect: the solicitor *had* asked him to contact her once the formalities were over, but as he had already done that he saw no point in doing so again.

The visitor's pass to see Klatt arrived next day. It had taken just two days to clear and that was quite remarkable. Someone had oiled the works but even that would have no effect unless Klatt had agreed to see him. He drove north again that day and gave his tail the slip along the route.

He lost them, in fact, before leaving London. Intimidation required a pinch of expertise and these men stayed at the thug stage. He reached the prison after lunch, produced his pass, and queued up with other prison visitors. In the waiting-room he looked through the protective glass into the reception area where prisoners met the visitors.

It was some time before he saw Klatt come through the far door accompanied by a warder. The mug shot was fairly accurate, although Klatt appeared much tidier in the flesh, blue prison uniform immaculate. Yet even from the safety of the visitors' waiting-room Shaw could see something of the inner menace of the man. Shaw had seen many villains in his time but this one, to him, had more than a touch of evil. Klatt chose a table in the middle of the room and Shaw was called soon after.

Klatt remained seated as Shaw approached. Neither man offered to shake hands and Klatt made matters worse by saying, in his heavily accented voice, "You look as if you've stepped from the grave."

Shaw had difficulty in controlling himself. It was a sick way to say he looked like his brother and he suspected Klatt intended to goad, to threaten too, if he was subtle enough.

"You want a tea?" Shaw asked, still standing.

"Coffee. Black. And digestive biscuits." The bleak, threatening eyes were also mocking.

There was a tea bar in one corner of the room where visitors could buy the prisoners soft drinks and chocolates and biscuits. Shaw bought two coffees and a packet of biscuits. He placed them on the table and sat down opposite Klatt, not sure how he felt but guarded. He had the feeling that Klatt had all the advantages and was playing with him.

"Why did you agree to see me?" Shaw asked.

Klatt almost laughed. "You bloody well asked to see me. But then you're a dumb copper so I must make allowances."

There were phases when Klatt's accent was atrocious and Shaw said, "Your pronunciation isn't very good considering how long you're supposed to have lived here."

It was a good provocative shot and Klatt's eyes glazed over as prudence suddenly superseded arrogance. He was quickly on the defensive. "I agree to see you because it fills in time. Eh? But I don't have to sit here and take insults from a bent copper. What is it you want?"

"You mean you haven't picked it up on the grapevine? Nobody's told you? I want to know why you killed my brother."

Klatt was unwrapping the packet of biscuits as Shaw spoke and the hand holding the packet suddenly contracted and he crushed the biscuits to a mass of crumbs. He stared across the small table, evil eyes screwed up and thick lips pouting, saliva at one corner of his mouth. It needed a massive effort of will to remain where he was but he knew he must hold on to his temper or give something away. What he wanted to do was to throttle Shaw.

It took a little time for Klatt to unwind and during that time Shaw learned quite a lot about him and felt much better about his accusation.

"You're mad. You say something like that in the safety of the prison. You wouldn't say it to me outside. Why would I want to kill your brother?"

"That's why I'm here. To find out." Shaw kept up the pressure, knowing now that this man was capable of snapping but had a basic sense of survival to resist it. There was nothing to stop Klatt leaving the room but Shaw had placed him in a position of needing to know more. And he had a strong, uneasy feeling that Klatt was under instructions.

Klatt won his battle for self-control and sipped his coffee. He wiped his lips with the back of his hand, his gaze never leaving Shaw. "I don't have to put up with this crap. Is your police force full of bums like you?"

"Then why stay?" Shaw leaned across the plastic topped table.

"To see if you're as crazy as your stupid brother." Klatt swivelled his large head, eyes sweeping the room. "You think it's possible to kill anyone in here? Even if I wanted to? *Donnerwetter.*"

"Then humour me, Hugo. There's nothing new about

prison murders. I know you did it." And when it seemed that Klatt might at last lose his control, Shaw added, "I can't prove it. Prisoners have a conspiracy of silence. Nobody is going to take the risk of grassing even if they knew. But I suspect the only other person who really knows is Johnnie West. He's your weak link, Hugo, because you couldn't do it on your own. You'd better watch him; he'll soon forget about the money. And that's when he'll lose his nerve."

Klatt finished his coffee. His control seemed to come in waves. At the moment he was reasonably calm again, perhaps recognising that it would be almost impossible to prove. "Tell me, mister copper, why would I want to kill your brother? To take such a risk in a place like this."

"We've been through that. So I repeat: why? If you can't be caught, can't you at least tell me that?"

The bleak eyes flickered. "You're even dumber than I thought. To give you a reason for something I know nothing about is to give you a confession for something I didn't do. You want me to make up a story? So you can use it against me later? You really are crazy."

"Does Molly Winters know anything about it?"

As Shaw noticed the change come over Klatt he pushed his chair back ready to jump away. Klatt was holding on to the edge of the table as if he was about to toss it. His eyes were shut tight and sweat beads stood out on his forehead. His whole frame rocked as he fought to keep from throttling Shaw.

Shaw glanced quickly at the warders stationed each end of the room and there was another on one side. The warders tried to keep low profile during visiting time but they were good observers just the same. Little missed them and it was only a matter of seconds before one of them would see the agony Klatt was suffering, and the damage that might ensue. That they had not noticed so far was due to the room rapidly filling and the distraction of an increasing number of visitors.

"For chrissake, the screws will be here any moment. Calm down, you murdering bastard." Shaw took an extreme risk but it worked and all the implications got through to Klatt

100

who realised he was on the verge of wrecking the place along with Shaw.

As Klatt slowly unwound, the big arms trembling, the sweat trickling down his face, Shaw again had the strange sensation that his warning was only part of the reason for Klatt's massive endeavour; Klatt was doing it for someone else, someone who pulled his strings from a distance.

By the time Klatt was fit to speak the underlying bragga-docio had disappeared. When he faced Shaw again he was quite different. A seriousness had replaced the arrogance; the eyes, dangerous before, were now quite chilling. His whole manner had toned down and he was much more menacing in a less obvious way. He knew it was too late to deny knowing Molly Winters; he had given himself away. He not only knew her but she was clearly important to him. "So you've been prying," he observed quietly.

"Of course I've been prying, although I'd prefer to call it investigating. I seem to have hit a nerve. Is she your girlfriend? Wife?"

"Leave her out of it. I see you out of curiosity because I heard you are trying to stir things up for me. I did not expect you to make the most stupid accusations about me and your brother. I did not know him so well at all."

"Maybe had you done you might not have killed him."

Klatt blinked. "Perhaps you are not so dumb after all. You are trying to goad me into doing something foolish to try to prove I can be violent so that I get banged up in isolation for some time. And perhaps you came close. But your opportunity has gone."

Shaw nodded in acquiescence. He was well satisfied. He had set out to stir and had succeeded. What he did not know was exactly what he had roused beyond Klatt. He had one last shot.

"If I came so close with you, imagine what I can do with Johnnie West. I already have a visitor's pass to see him. I hope he's still your friend, Hugo. You'd better go and check on him."

Klatt endured another personality change. And in the cold mask that faced him Shaw thought he could see the first hint

101

of fear. And when someone like Klatt was afraid of something he would deal with it in the only way he knew.

Klatt could not resist a final shot before leaving. As he pushed his chair back he said, "Have a safe journey home." He spoke with vicious satisfaction as if he already knew that Shaw would not.

Shaw remained uncomfortably seated until Klatt had passed through the far door to the inner sanctums of the prison.

10

Shaw was happy to be free of the prison. They almost all looked the same to him, many Victorian-built with the same stark double-pillared gates. He stood outside and sniffed at the air. It was moist; rain was on the way at last.

He crossed the street and then walked down towards his parked car, Klatt's oblique parting warning still drumming through his head. Whoever had briefed Klatt would be annoyed at that lapse; it was not the remark of an innocent man. Shaw felt he had learned quite a lot and was easier in his mind. But he knew that to prove anything against Klatt was virtually impossible. No witness would come forward. Suspicions in prison were realities. People like Max Fuller knew for a certainty who killed Terry Shaw. But in court he would stand no chance at all. He had seen nothing. And in truth he knew nothing. But he knew just the same.

Shaw reached the car and felt foolish lying flat to look under the chassis, and to open the door and to release the bonnet catch and examine the engine. It was the effect Klatt could have on people. Someone was working with Klatt and that someone was the right side of prison.

He drove south again wondering how best to use the money Terry had left him and thinking he had somehow missed the apparent esteem Terry had held for him. It made him feel uncomfortable. It seemed that he could hardly have known his brother at all, but that could not be true. He had known Terry all his life and the others like Klatt and Fuller and Mandova and Jill Palmer belonged to a later part of his life and that was the part he had missed. During that time Terry must have changed in some way. Perhaps he would never learn how.

He made little attempt to see if he was being followed. It was difficult on a motorway with all the traffic heading one way. It was at the service stations that he became alert. He stopped twice on the way back. The first time he checked the car before driving off again. The second time Klatt's warning took shape.

As he approached his car he could see the bonnet was up and the driver's door wide open. He stopped but could see nobody near the car. He advanced slowly, tentatively peering down into the engine. A brown paper bag was resting among the plugs. Before touching it Shaw got down to examine underneath, found nothing and rose.

The car interior was untouched, nothing added or removed in spite of the door being wide open, so he returned to the paper bag and gingerly prised it open. It was impossible to hurry in case he tripped a detonator so the strain was increased and the revelation a time-bomb of suspense in itself. The bag contained the remnants of sandwiches.

Shaw's smile was one of sick relief as he lifted the bag out and searched around for a trash bin. After he had dumped the bag and returned to the car he felt shaken. On leaving the restaurant he had not interrupted anything; the leaving open of the car door and bonnet had been deliberate to show him how easy it would be to destroy him.

Shaw felt unsettled for the rest of the journey back to London. A point had been well made and it was difficult to know how to deal with it. He had been placed in a position of having to look over his shoulder all the time now. He was convinced there was more to it than his brother's murder. When he reached his flat, and even that had become an exercise of observation on its own, there were messages on his answering machine from Peter Givens and Jill Palmer, each asking him to ring back.

He rang Givens but he had gone. He decided to leave it until the next morning. He poured a drink, and looked in the kitchen to see what sort of scrap meal he could provide for himself, for it was late to go out.

He took the drink into the sitting-room and switched on the television. The telephone rang in the middle of the ten o'clock news. It was Jill Palmer. Immediately he was wary.

"Did you get my message?" she asked quickly.

"Yes."

"When did you get back?"

"Just over an hour ago. How did you know I was away?"

"Because you weren't in. I phoned about three, left a message, and have phoned several times since without leaving one. Why the hell didn't you phone me back?"

"Because I had nothing to say to you. Why your concern?"

There was a long silence. "I'm not concerned. But you are inclined to do and say silly things. I wondered if you had done something daft. Or perhaps had anything fresh to tell me."

Shaw switched off the television. "No, I've nothing fresh to tell you. Nothing has happened since the last time we crossed words. Have you got anything?"

"No. Nothing. So you're all right?"

"Well, it's me talking down the phone so I suppose I must be." He thought she was trying to ferret information from him. "Why would you think I might not be all right?"

"I didn't really think that. I seem to be saying all the wrong things. I'm sorry, the call was a mistake. Goodnight."

Shaw put down the phone, tired and puzzled. They never seemed to get anywhere even when they were fairly reasonable with each other. But it left him wondering why she had rung at all.

It had been a long, tiring, and threatening day. He decided to go to bed early.

Early the next morning Shaw wrote out an application for a visitor's pass to send to Johnnie West and posted it on his way to meet Peter Givens. They met for coffee in Covent Garden. There had been drizzle overnight but the sun was back and everything had dried out so they sat under a striped terrace awning.

From the beginning they had felt easy with each other so

105

Shaw was not offended when, after the coffee arrived, Givens said, "There's a limit to how long I can spend on this caper without something to show. I'm not trying to squeeze you but upstairs want to know what I'm spending my time on and why I'm being so bloody secretive. I do, after all, work for the paper. So what can I pacify my boss with?"

"Less than before. I'm sorry." Shaw played it shrewdly knowing that his negative answer had been couched in such a way as to suggest there were now deeper issues involved.

Givens was forced to smile. "Crafty bugger. Still the cop at heart. But I meant what I said."

"Okay, I'll tell you what happened yesterday. But if you start leaking titbits we're finished. Perhaps literally. All we've done so far is to turn over a stone but not enough to disturb the mud underneath. What I thought was just a prison killing, and that was all I was trying to prove at first, has far deeper implications. I'm sure of it. I haven't a clue what's going on but I'll bring you up-to-date and you can judge for yourself." He recounted yesterday's events.

Givens let his coffee get cold as he listened and he made no interruption as Shaw spoke of his visit to Klatt and his journey home.

Afterwards, Givens sat thinking, sipped his coffee, pulled a face and called for more, and said, "It's one thing putting on the frighteners, quite another to go the whole hog."

"It's the inconsistency," Shaw replied. "The bums who are parked outside my place have come straight from a school for villains after their first couple of weeks' training. Or third-rate actors from a film set. There is no subtlety about them. Yet whoever messed around with my car must have followed expertly. They might have known I was visiting Klatt but there was no way they could know I would stop at those two service stations. And I wasn't long at the second so they moved fast. They knew exactly what they were doing and I find that scary because I haven't an idea who they are or what they look like or why they did it."

"To stop you chasing Terry's killer."

"That's only part of it and I'm beginning to think a small part. Anyway, now you know as much as I do."

"What about Terry's girlfriend? She seems to keep popping up." He glanced at Shaw's yellowing eye. "All we know about her is that she packs a wallop. If it was her, of course."

Shaw let it pass. "She's an enigma. I'm going to chase it up. But you didn't ring me about any of this. What's your news?"

"I very much doubt that the Klatt you saw yesterday is the real Hugo. A man by that name did escape over the Wall and the shot I showed you is genuine. The reason for lack of photographic material was for security. There was obviously more to Klatt than met the eye at the time. A German version of our D Notice went out once he sought asylum and the press were closed down on further stories. It's possible that some of the agencies might have shots taken around that time but if they have they're reluctant to produce them, probably for the same reason."

"So he must have been important to both the West and the East Germans at the time."

"That's fine, except he disappeared."

"Well, he came here. What do you mean?"

"He disappeared four years before he came here. Nobody seems to know what happened to him. He came over the Wall, stayed a while, vanished. Never to be found again."

"Until he pitched up again here," Shaw insisted.

"Your bloke pitched up here just before East Germany collapsed. I'll bet my house it's not the same man."

"You live in a rented apartment."

"Just the same. I didn't think it was him when I saw the mug shots."

Shaw said slowly, "Somebody here sanctioned his naturalisation papers. Did he fool them or was he deliberately helped?"

They viewed each other in silence, Givens slowly pushing back his hair, Shaw's fingers exploring the tousled mass of his.

"Is it possible to find out who let him in?" Givens' tone was speculative.

"If I was still with SB it would be no problem. It's a Home Office matter. But even my friends in SB offer very little, and are reluctant to help. They've been nobbled. I might be able to find out some other way. I've applied to see Johnnie West, by the way."

Givens burst out laughing. "You're a glutton for punishment. I was surprised that Klatt saw you."

"Klatt was told to see me. I don't expect West to be; I think he was an accessory. But I do expect Klatt to hear of it."

Givens shook his head. "You're still playing a dangerous game, Laurie."

"When most of the evidence is behind prison walls what else can I do? Do you know where Klatt was born? The real one?"

"No. Dresden was the place given but that's no guarantee. If the real one is missing it will be difficult to find out. Masses of documents have been destroyed in East Germany, most of them by the Stasi." They looked at each other again as if a cord had been struck.

Shaw said, "As your phone is nearer than mine, can I use it?"

"Of course. Think your place is bugged?"

"Not as far as I can see but there are plenty of outside mikes that can pick up easily enough. I don't want to chance it."

As they walked back to Fleet Street Shaw said, "Although I didn't bring anyone with me, it might be noticed that we are meeting. Be careful."

"I've got the strength of the *News* behind me."

"That won't help you. Just keep your eyes open. The yobs who are hanging out at my place might be nothing more than a distraction. There's a lot of cunning behind all this."

The two women shook hands politely. The exchange of greetings was just short of frosty. Judith Walker was a tall woman, simply but expensively dressed, and she had done nothing to hide the continuing greying of her hair. She had once been a Group Captain in the Royal Air Force, having spent most of her last years there in Intelligence. She had none of Veida Ash's attractiveness but easily matched her shrewdness and had nice eyes which could ice over in an instant. She was the present Director General of MI5, not the first woman to be appointed to the post to the dismay of most of the males in the organisation.

Veida Ash had similar feelings towards her. She was used to being controlled by men and thereby getting her own way most of the time. Veida was comfortable with a male boss and had never got on too well with other women. She was uncomfortable now with Judith Walker whom she recognised as a formidable woman with a pedigree background, something Veida herself lacked.

They could have sat side by side on the long bench seat at the discreetly lit restaurant, but, perhaps by mutual consent, chose to sit opposite each other where it was easier to test the waters. They took time to order, which did little to improve the atmosphere between them and destroyed any vestige of friendliness. Perhaps that was how Judith Walker dealt with matters, to build up some sort of barrier and to keep things on a purely business level.

Veida slipped into gear to deal with the veiled hostility and could guess what was coming.

"It was good of you to come at such short notice," said Judith with a smile. "I do appreciate it."

It was not lost on Veida that it had been made to sound as if she had obeyed an instruction. But Judith Walker was not her boss and was not even in the same section of the Security Service. "It was just luck I could fit you in," she replied with a matching false smile. But she knew she had to be wary of this woman who had easy access to her superiors. "Is it about my asking Phillip Sims to help me out?" Get in the first shot.

Judith did not answer for some time, eating slowly and clearly relishing her food. She talked trivia for a while and made Veida wait in punishment for her earlier snide remark. She held a far superior post and quietly exercised her authority. Eventually she said, "Might it not have been better had you approached Sir Charles Melville who could have stated the position to me, and thereby, if it was important enough, we could have given you proper backing instead of the shaky support Phillip gave. Of course, we would have had to know what exactly is involved. We would not work in the dark even for our sister establishment."

Veida stirred her coffee, smiling pleasantly at Judith Walker. "It simply wasn't important enough. I could have operated without your help but that would have meant stamping over your territory and would have raised a few eyebrows and perhaps a few hackles."

"Even so. I gather you wanted to discourage ex-Detective Chief Inspector Shaw from looking into the death of his brother?"

"Yes. He thinks he was murdered."

"Do you?"

"Yes, I do. Terry Shaw was planted by us to obtain information which could not be obtained from outside. To me the murder is less important than getting what we first wanted. Shaw could upset a very delicate situation. He might already have done so. I have to hope. And, if this sounds like something you should be doing yourselves it concerns matters in Eastern Europe and our networks abroad." Veida made her first concession. "I'm sorry if I've ruffled feathers. I had only the best intentions."

"Isn't your attitude towards Terry Shaw's death a little cold-blooded?"

"I have had to put it to the back of my mind. I'm not at all certain that his death was connected with what he went in to do. He could be wild at times and might have upset the wrong person. Prison justice can be vicious. It's up to the prison authorities and the police to sort that one out. Of course I'm upset it happened but it's not my priority, which is to gather information."

Judith opened her handbag and checked her credit cards as if she might have forgotten them. "I'm well aware of your reputation and successes in Eastern Europe, Veida. You have a formidable record which cannot be achieved on sentiment. But this is one of those border-line cases where it is difficult to decide who should operate. I applaud your application and if you ever feel like switching channels we'd be delighted to take you on board. But we would appreciate a little more open competition. You have really told me very little." She was aware that she was echoing Phil Sims.

Veida inwardly shuddered at the idea of a female boss. "That's because Terry Shaw was killed before I got to know what I wanted to know. Meanwhile I'm groping and simply following hunches. And I don't want Laurie Shaw making the same mistake as his brother. Something stinks in the state of Denmark and I'm doing my best to find out. You wouldn't expect me to speculate, especially as I haven't got that far with Sir Charles."

Judith Walker smiled quite warmly but her eyes were probing. "At least we now understand each other. We'd be delighted to help any time, but do let me know in future. These inter-service meetings are most helpful, don't you think?"

Veida did not think so but acquiesced. The luncheon finished pleasantly enough on the surface and when the two women parted, this time the handshake appeared to be less formal. But on the way back to her office Veida was far from satisfied. Judith Walker had really added no more to what Phil Sims had said. And she would not normally have taken out a section leader, no matter how important, to register a complaint. Judith would have complained directly to Sir Charles Melville, the head of MI6. So what was she up to? She decided to report the meeting to her chief to cover the possibility that Judith might already have done so. It was important to seem to be doing the right thing. But Veida was unhappy about the meeting, was quietly fuming and not a little concerned. Had Judith Walker seen her then she might have learned a little more. But in one respect Veida was pleased with herself; she had cleared the way to operate as she wanted and had placed a clamp on any interference or complaints from MI5. They could not now complain about her operating in their back yard which was what she had wanted to achieve in the first place. She used a public call-box to issue certain instructions and returned to her office reasonably satisfied.

*　　*　　*

111

Shaw stood outside the revolving sign of New Scotland Yard and waited. It was twenty minutes before Detective Superintendent Bob Reedy joined him. Reedy slapped him on the back and said, "Why didn't you come in and wait? Too many memories?"

They strode north to the nearest pub. Reedy was bulkier and a few years older than Shaw, but they were of similar height. "You still on murders?" asked Shaw as they pushed their way to the bar.

"No. I've seen too many. I'm on fraud now. Fascinating. More complicated than murder. Some of these fraudsters make more than a bank robber will ever make yet get nowhere near the same kind of sentence. A villain may be violent but a fraudster is usually a slimy sod who has done everyone else down behind their backs and often diddles them out of their life savings. Maybe I should be back on the squad."

They ordered pints of beer and edged their way towards the far side of the crowded room.

"Cheers!" Reedy raised his glass in a beefy hand. His smile was broad and honest. He took several gulps and the glass was suddenly half empty. "What is it you want from me?"

"I want to check on who let a bloke called Hugo Klatt into the country. It seems that he might not be the real guy, so someone has been bloody careless or is on the take."

Reedy lifted a shaggy brow. There was a humorous glint in his eye as he said, "Why me? You should be asking your mates in the SB."

"They've closed the door on me. I'm making too many waves because I think Terry was topped. Someone is trying to stop me."

"You really think he was topped?" Reedy's years of working with murder squads showed in a brightening attitude.

"I'm bloody sure he was. I wish to God you had been interviewing the cons up there; you'd have got something out of them."

Reedy's eyes sparkled with memories. He finished his drink and Shaw struggled to the bar to order again. When he returned he could see that Reedy was interested.

Reedy said, "We made a good team. A pity SB nicked you. I'm not sure you did the right thing going to them."

"Nor am I. Will you help?"

"I'll dig around a bit." Reedy raised his glass. "For old times' sake."

"There's one more thing," said Shaw. He pulled out a slip of paper and handed it over. "Her name is Jill Palmer. I wonder if you could get someone to run her down, occupation, any form, you know. Name and address is there."

"Is she the one who gave you the eye?" Reedy was grinning. "That's a bit of savage revenge, isn't it?" Reedy tucked the piece of paper into his pocket.

Shaw was tired of jokes about his eye, particularly as so many of them were accurate. "She's the one," he replied lamely. "And it's not revenge."

By the time Shaw reached his apartment he felt he had done as much as he possibly could for one day. He just had to sit back and wait for information to be fed back to him. It was now late evening and the loneliness crept in. He had felt lonely ever since leaving the force. His life had little pattern before Terry was killed but the long gaps between investigating were as difficult to fill satisfactorily as before.

When he reached the street door he suddenly changed his mind and decided to eat out. He had a meal at his usual restaurant, taking his time, not wanting to go back to the solitude of his rooms and battening on to the light-hearted chatter at the tables around him. He was almost the last to leave.

There were a few people about still and he was alerted late to the constant presence of his tail. They did not dive in doorways any more when he turned to see them. They were either getting lazy or more purposeful. At least they were some sort of crazy company and with a few drinks inside him he almost felt an affection towards them. He called out to the one across the street but he did not reply and it was perhaps this that gave Shaw the first warning. When he had called out before there had usually been an expletive in reply. He noticed, too, that they were nearer and that they had entered what he called the twilight zone, a long, quiet street leading to his own where there was little activity.

When the man across the street started to cross towards him and he could hear the footsteps of the man behind him rapidly closing up, Shaw broke into a run. They followed as quickly and then, from the many shadows, stepped a third man right in front of him.

11

Shaw swerved to avoid the tackle, partially succeeded and was spun round almost to face the others pounding up behind him. Instead of trying to swerve back again he spurted through the gap between the two men. Both made a grab at him but he tore through by sheer speed and kept going as fast as he could.

There were shouts and swearing behind him as the men followed, blaming each other as they went. The shouting stopped when they decided to get on with the business of catching him. Shaw heard one hive off down a small side street and guessed they were trying to block him off at one of the turnings. He kept going fast, knowing he could not keep it up for long. He passed a couple of lovers who turned in amazement and again as the others sprinted past after him. Suddenly Shaw took a right turning. He had the advantage of knowing the district, and almost immediately turned right again which was taking him back the way he had come. He ran up the nearest steps to hide behind a tall pillar of a canopied porch. As the men rounded the corner he was no longer in sight but they knew he could not be far away.

Their footsteps slowed and Shaw heard them separate, one crossing the street away from him. Someone further along left one of the houses and it was clear from the talking and the clack of heels that a man and a woman were taking their dog for a walk. As there was no other sound Shaw guessed that his escort had faded into the shadows as he had. Then he heard another set of footsteps and he guessed that the third man had arrived from his abortive diversion.

Shaw remained absolutely still, more worried about controlling his rasping breath than anything else. He stayed where he was, hoping that the width of the pillar would keep him out of sight. When the couple with the dog turned the corner the other footsteps took immediate form.

Flashlights were now used, shining into basements and up into porches, which must have thrown confusing shadows. The three men were trying to move quietly but the beams gave their positions away. Shaw resisted the temptation to see where they were and stayed exactly where he was.

It had to end one way or the other. Short of going down every basement and up into every porch, which would create its own dangers for them, unless they could spot him they would have to call off the search. Which is what they did when they heard the couple with the dog returning.

When the front door closed the street was suddenly silent. Shaw was having difficulty in maintaining his position and had to clutch the pillar to stay upright. He had no idea whether the men were still out there waiting or had gone. He decided that in their position he would wait. So did he with increasing difficulty.

After a while he gradually slid down the pillar with his back to it, his legs reaching out towards the house. He realised that if a flashlight was shone into the porch his legs could be seen but standing still in darkness provided its own problems and he had to take the risk.

He began to doze, jerking awake every time his head dropped. He was tempted to take a chance and go but in any event he could not return to his apartment; that was one place someone was certain to wait. He dozed on and off for some time, the night cold creeping into him, adding to his discomfort. He glanced at his watch and could just see the luminous dial; it was 1.30 in the morning. He had little idea of when he had first raced up the steps but guessed he must have been there for well over two hours. He simply could not keep awake for any length of time any more and decided he must take the risk of moving. He cautiously tiptoed down the steps and waited for a while at the bottom. The whole place seemed dead.

*   *   *

It was at breakfast that Hugo Klatt caught up with Johnnie West. He took his tray into West's cell and sat down on the side of the bed. West was sitting at the small table and had his back to him. He turned round to see who had entered and swivelled his chair so that he got a better view of Klatt who was not a man to keep his back to.

They had barely spoken since Terry Shaw had died. The prison staff had interviewed everybody in the wing and nothing had come to light regarding the death. It was no surprise to anyone that nobody knew anything about the death other than it had happened. Prison suicides were not uncommon.

West was surprised by Klatt's visit; it was best they kept apart. He continued eating but at an angle so that he could see Klatt. He said nothing but gave a nod of greeting.

"I hear someone has asked for a visitor's pass to see you," said Klatt bluntly.

West turned his head. "You've heard wrong," he said spluttering food across the floor.

"You shouldn't talk with your mouth full," said Klatt. "Is your money through?"

West wondered where this was leading. "I've been told it is. But without actually seeing it I can't be bloody sure, can I?"

"If you've received the message you can take it that it's there. More than you'd make on a dozen blags. Now what about this visitor's pass?"

"I haven't had an application for the last two months. They've all deserted me, the bastards. After all I've done for them."

A burst of laughter came from the next cell and the echoes were eerie in the strange acoustics of prison. When the sound died Klatt said, "Don't bugger me around, Johnnie. You've had an application. What are you trying to pull?"

West started to get annoyed and a little worried. "You're spoiling my breakfast. What's wrong with you? I haven't had an application and that's that. What the bloody hell does it matter anyway?"

"If it's from Laurie Shaw it matters a lot."

117

"Laurie Shaw?" West shoved in the last mouthful and chewed quickly. He was still chewing when he added, "Isn't that the copper brother of Terry? I've heard about him. What would he want to see me for?"

"You've got a short memory and that's dangerous. What the hell do you think?"

West moved his chair right round so that he was now facing Klatt. He wiped his mouth with his hand and stared for some seconds, slow to understand exactly what Klatt was getting at. "Are you off your rocker? He wouldn't write to me for a pass."

"Why not? He wrote to me."

West could not see where this was leading. "But you didn't see him?"

"Of course I saw him. I wanted to know exactly what he knows. And he does know. At least he's satisfied he knows. But it's all in his mind."

West was suddenly scared. "You shouldn't have seen him. He can't know anything."

"He could make things difficult. Don't worry though, it's been dealt with. He told me he applied to you for a pass."

"He's a bloody liar. Even if he did I wouldn't see him. And nor should you have done. It's unnatural, you don't know him."

"I do now. So you haven't had a letter from him?"

"No. How many more bloody times? Leave it off."

"You seem tetchy? Is that the right word?" Klatt ate slowly, gazing upon West, his expression unsettling. "You'd let me know if he applied?"

"I don't see why I should but I would. It's important that we both know what's going on. If you've seen him he won't want to see me."

Klatt finished chewing quite deliberately before saying, "He'll want to see you because he's seen me. He thinks he can get something out of you."

"That's stupid. Stupid."

"He sees you as a weak link, Johnnie."

"What the hell are you trying to do, Hugo? He doesn't even know me."

118

"A man like that does his homework. You'd better not be the weak link, Johnnie. If I thought that, you'd go the same way as Terry Shaw. I'll stick a skewer through your bloody guts. You think about it, eh!"

West sat forward, arms on legs, hands clenched. "Don't threaten me, you German bastard. If I go, you go with me. Just what the hell do you think you're doing? It's you who's running scared. He's got to you."

Klatt rose, tray in hand, breakfast unfinished. "Just remember what I say. You let me down and I'll pig-stick you."

It was later that day, when the mail had been sorted and checked, that West received Shaw's letter. He read it with his back to the cell door afraid that Klatt might come. And when he had finished reading the brief contents he screwed it up and sought for a way to destroy it.

West wondered why he was suddenly afraid to tell Klatt he had received it. The German was mad, unpredictable. Better not to let him know. In the end West ate the letter, tearing it up first into small pieces. There was not much of it but it was a painful process and he had trouble getting it down. When the last unpalatable piece had gone he belatedly realised that he was committed to lie forever to Klatt about receiving it.

West sat on his bed listening to the sounds around him and wondering why he had panicked. It now irked him, particularly as he had shown fear of Klatt. But Klatt was unstable and everybody knew it. Nevertheless Klatt had not believed him when he told the truth about an application for a pass. As he would now be lying when it was raised again it was going to be even more difficult to convince him. West sat uneasily.

Shaw stirred uncomfortably, stiff all over. For a while he was completely disorientated, then realised he was lying on Max Fuller's settee in a most awkward position. He sat upright with a jerk and a pain shot straight up his spine; he felt dreadful. He climbed to his feet and stretched and went looking for Fuller.

There was barely anywhere to look. There was one very large room with a bed one end and a dinner-table at the other. The space in between comprised the sitting quarters, settee and easy chairs and a television set against the wall. There was a kitchen, quite large, and beyond it a shower and toilet. By the layout it was obvious that Max had planned it himself, paying too little attention to hygiene.

Fuller was nowhere about. The bed had been made up prison fashion and Shaw was reminded of Mandova. The windows were open and it was chilly. The time was 8.30 and Shaw was surprised by how little he had slept.

When Shaw had left his hideout at 1.30 he had half expected to be chased again. He knew he could not return home so he went to the only person who might offer him refuge. He had walked a good distance before locating a roving all-night taxi. Fuller did not query his arrival nor protest at the hour.

He was only too happy to return a favour for almost identical reasons. And now he was missing.

Food had been laid out in the kitchen, frying-pan ready, so Shaw, now ravenous from the night's events, cooked himself bacon and eggs and fried bread. It was a very acceptable change from his usual two slices of toast. Afterwards he washed up and pondered on what he should do. Fuller returned a little later. He had been jogging for a few miles, apparently a daily routine to keep himself in shape for any offers of wrestling bouts. He stripped off his track suit and showered.

"Glad to see you helped yourself to breakfast," said Fuller when he returned from the shower. "How do you feel now?"

"Terrible. Thanks for taking me in. I've got to make up my mind what to do. I can't go back to the flat."

Fuller spread himself across a lounge chair. "Bloody funny that an ex-cop has to come to a villain for protection. Now that's a turn-up."

It was the truth. Shaw did not know which of his friends he could rely upon apart from the fact that he did not want to compromise them, particularly his police friends. He went to the window. "I can't stay here."

"You can, but you'd be bloody uncomfortable. I know of a way out so that you can go back, guv."

Shaw turned round. The contents of the room were expensive if not to his personal taste. Fuller was not short of money but clearly had no big ambitions regarding property. "Go on," he said warily.

"You pay me to be your bodyguard. It looks as if you need one."

"I can't afford to pay you . . ." But he could. Wouldn't this be a legitimate claim against Terry's money? "Maybe that's not a bad idea." He did not much like the idea of someone moving in but the alternative was less attractive.

"I don't come cheap," said Fuller with a grin, "but you've already decided you can afford it." He started to laugh, seeing the funny side of it. "I'm not trying to do myself out of a job, guv, but why don't you go to your mates in the police about this?" He found the whole situation so amusing that it was difficult to keep a straight face. It was not something he could tell the boys at the pub.

"That three blokes tried to do me? Happens all the time. They'd tell me to take more water with it. Even if they took it seriously there'd be a layoff until the police got tired of keeping an eye on me. But they wouldn't give protection on anything so flimsy. I accept your offer, Max. Pack a few things and we'll go back."

Shaw found it strange returning, as if the whole area had been desecrated. He expected to find his apartment ravaged but as far as he could see nothing had been touched. It seemed that the threat was against him and not his property, until he found the baby alarm placed on top of some magazines on a bookshelf in his sitting-room. Then he knew someone had been in. And he knew he was lucky to discover it before playing back his answering machine.

He reached for the baby alarm, raising a finger to his lips to warn Fuller. He covered the microphone and said, "Someone is near enough to pick up our conversation. Go down and have a look while I get rid of this."

When Fuller had gone Shaw placed the baby alarm under a cushion and played back the answering machine. Bob Reedy of Scotland Yard wanted to speak to him. He rang back and was lucky to find Reedy in. He arranged to meet him at the same pub that lunchtime.

Ten minutes later Fuller appeared with a pale-looking man whom he held in a painful armlock. "Dragged him out of the car," said Fuller. "Had this to his ear." Fuller pulled a receiver from his pocket.

Shaw took the receiver and now turned off the baby alarm. "Dump him in that chair," he said to Fuller, and then to the man, "Okay, what's your name and what's the game?"

"Tom Jones. I'm a singer." The accent was southern counties.

The next moment Jones crumpled in the chair as Fuller gave him an almighty open-handed swipe. "You be respectful to the guv'nor," he said. But Jones was beyond hearing and they had to wait for him to come round and that required carrying him to the kitchen and putting his head under the tap.

"Don't hit him again," pleaded Shaw. "We want him alive."

"Okay, guv, but I'm not standing for his lip."

His name was Ronald Neames and he lived in Dulwich. He was in his mid-forties, medium height, sallow with a full head of dark hair, and had sorry brown eyes. He worked for anyone who would hire him but the names he mentioned were not people who would give written references. Between them, Shaw and Fuller knew most of the names and they were all villains. There was no point in asking who employed the villain who hired Neames.

Neames had not planted the baby alarm. He had merely been told to sit in a car and listen and make notes. He had picked up nothing worthwhile because Shaw had been quick to spot the alarm. There were no notes on his pad. He had been paid to do the job by a woman called Jody Marsh.

Fuller said, "I didn't know you could pick up people speaking through a baby alarm. Outside the house?"

"Oh, yes," replied Shaw. "But why use one? It was quickly spotted. Why not a more sophisticated bug?" And then, "Let him go."

"What?" It was against Fuller's natural instincts to let Neames go. "I can screw what you need to know out of him first."

"He doesn't know a thing. Take him downstairs and make a note of his car number."

Fuller lifted Neames from the chair with obvious distaste. He propelled him from the room and resisted the temptation to hurl him down the stairs. After they had gone Shaw went round the flat again. The point had been made that his flat was easy to enter and that he had better beware. Was that the object? Just to let him know and, at the same time, pick up something on the baby alarm? They must have known he would see it. He took the alarm and receiver into the kitchen and broke them open. There was nothing sinister inside either of them. He rendered them unusable.

When Fuller came back Shaw told him to get the locks changed while he was out and was not surprised to find that Fuller had a locksmith friend who would do it straight away.

Fuller felt it his duty to go with Shaw wherever he went but Shaw convinced him that daylight was a relatively safe time to move around on his own and convinced him to stay to supervise the locks; deadlocks and double mortice. But Fuller still had something on his mind. "You didn't blink an eyelid when he mentioned Jody Marsh."

"Neither did you. I knew she was bent but when her husband Nat disappeared I thought she must have retired. Apparently not. But listening at keyholes isn't her style, Max. It's a funny business. Maybe I can get something out of her."

Fuller gave a look of warning. "She's a hard case, guv. Much harder than her old man. In fact some say she topped him and he went for pigs' food. She didn't seem too upset when he disappeared. I believe he'd been sleeping around and Jody would never stand for that. You be careful."

Shaw sensed that Reedy was hiding something almost before he spoke. He had that bland look about him Shaw had seen so often when interviewing villains. It was a mask,

123

so lightly cast that only those who really knew him could detect it.

"Hugo Klatt," said Reedy, raising his glass and downing half the beer. "Nobody seems to know who was responsible for letting him in. It's either a political cock-up and they won't admit the mistake – do they ever? – or it's a cover-up."

"I'm not wearing that. It must be a matter of record."

"Of course it is. But nobody is going to tell. I've been politely told to forget about it. Which means the Security Service have a big finger in the pie. Just one thing slipped by although I can't see it as important; the powers-that-be couldn't make up their minds whether Klatt was born in Dresden or a place called Greifswald. I don't suppose it can matter much where he was born."

"Are you saying they brought him in?"

"No bloody fear, I'm not saying anything. But their fingerprints seem to be all over the place. I can't get any further with it. Your mates at SB might do better. That's the best I can do."

"And Jill Palmer?"

Reedy shielded his thoughts behind his raised glass. "Nothing on her. No record. One-time civil servant. Seems to be self-supporting and has an interest in a clothes shop in Chelsea."

"Is that all? Married? Divorced? Kids?"

Reedy lowered his empty glass. "Didn't think that sort of thing mattered these days. Was married to an army officer. Lasted about eighteen months, which seems to be the going period in this day and age. Divorced three years ago. No kids."

"No boyfriends?"

Reedy looked uncomfortable. "Only one. He's dead."

"You mean my brother?"

"You did ask me, Laurie. That's about it. A very average girl."

"You're not holding anything back, Bob?"

"You'd know if I was. You're used to reading me. One of the few who could."

"That's what makes me feel uneasy. Jill Palmer is anything but average."

Reedy glanced at Shaw's eye and smiled. "I can only tell you what I've managed to dig up. Maybe she should be in for GBH."

"Very funny. But I'm grateful. At least you've cast a bloody big question mark over Klatt. He's an evil bastard and whoever let him in should be shot."

"Maybe they were," rejoined Reedy dryly.

When Shaw looked sharply at Reedy he was not convinced that his friend had been entirely joking. But he could see that he would get no more.

Jody Marsh was not as well organised as her husband had been but was infinitely tougher. While Nat had been playing fast and loose, a risky thing to do knowing the nature of his wife, she too was doing the same but with more care and selectivity. The truth was that if she fancied a man, they were mostly afraid not to comply, whether married or not.

Jody, in her forties, was a striking-looking woman. She turned heads and carried the sort of confidence that created its own barrier, keeping the hopeful males at bay and commanding those she wanted.

The police referred to her as Boadicea. She was certainly known to carry blades, usually in the form of sheathed stilettos; a small version in her bag and one strapped to her leg. She had led a life of violence and really was capable of little else outside of bed. And yet she had never been booked, Nat taking most of the raps for her, often out of guilty conscience for his extra-marital affairs. In spite of his infidelity he had loved her right up to the day she killed him for sleeping with her sister. That had been too much for Jody.

The police believed she killed Nat, her friends knew damn well she did. But nobody could break down her story that he had at last gone off with another woman, probably to South America. His form with women bore out the possibility.

So Jody gradually picked up the threads of her dead

husband's enterprises into drugs, protection, and prostitution to which fraternity she had once profitably belonged. But she had lost a lot of friends because Nat, for all his faults, was liked, whereas she held a doubtful esteem by fear. Jody did not understand compromise. When she went out she always had a male companion but everyone knew he was a minder. With some of the ill-feeling towards her she needed one although it would take a very strong character to attempt to harm her. She knew this and held most of her compatriots in contempt.

When her telephone line suddenly went dead she berated British Telecom on a neighbour's phone but even she was surprised at the speed with which they arrived. Two Telecom men came within the hour, they had luckily been in the district and had received a message to call. They went to the top floor of the conversion where she had a maisonette and she showed them where the phones were, her minder at her elbow the whole time. There were two phones; they dealt with them both. She swore at them about the lousy service while they worked but they responded only to each other. She was sure that one was foreign and that disgusted her for Jody, in her strange twisted way, was staunchly British.

When they left they got into their yellow Telecom van and drove off, stopping a few blocks away. The man beside the driver lifted his phone and dialled Jody's number.

When Jody answered she was blown to bits, killed by Semtex and her belief in her own impregnability. Nobody would dare. And somebody had. The explosion blew the top two floors off the base of the house. Debris scattered to cause considerable secondary damage and a gas pipe exploded and burst into flames.

Where Jody's maisonette had been was a ragged square of ruptured brick from the centre of which rose dust and flames and segments of Jody herself together with her minder. Everyone in the street, shaken and scared by the massive explosion, raced from their homes and stood to watch and count the cost of the damage to themselves. Nevertheless, there were many satisfied faces among them even as they murmured, "Poor Jody. What a terrible thing to happen." Jody, who kept most of the detail of her various businesses in her head, had taken her empire with her.

12

Shaw did not reach Jody Marsh's address until the following morning and, had he looked at the newspapers before leaving, he might not have gone. There was still so much confusion around the house that police directed him away from the street and he had to park a couple of blocks away and walk back.

There was still a fire-tender outside, hose pipes trailing through pools of water, a turntable ladder hovering like a vulture over the charred and still smoking gap that had once been Jody's home. A Gas Board van was parked in front of the fire-engine and it seemed that the problem of escaping gas was under control. There were still plenty of spectators and black ash was drifting everywhere.

Shaw did not really need to be told but he asked the nearest person just the same: Jody Marsh had been blown to bits with her latest lover-cum-minder. It was thought to be caused by a gas leak although nobody had reported the smell of gas until after the explosion. Neighbours could now speak more openly without fear of reprisal. Jody was no longer a threat and a whole team of prostitutes, drug-pushers and protection money collectors had to regroup or start their own war.

Shaw had a word with the gas men who were certain that the original explosion was not caused by gas. It was too early to say; the police, fire brigade and gas experts would have to sift through to find the cause. Shaw crossed the street to get a better view. From the gaping open wound of the building charred debris still tumbled with cascading water. The buildings either side were substantially damaged.

Had Jody justified this sort of treatment? Had it been so

important to keep her quiet? This was not gang war. Had it been she would have been shot or knifed or just disappeared. This was an execution and a message to people like himself that they would end up the same way if they did not mend their ways. And yet Shaw felt nowhere near enough to any kind of conclusion to warrant a warning so drastic. Neames had only been picked up the previous evening and it would have been impossible to organise a killing of this impact at such short notice. Jody must already have been earmarked, which meant she knew something and was perhaps getting too big for her boots. She had met more than her match and that was scary, for it was not an easy thing to achieve. Yet in spite of the enormity of the damage, Shaw was left with the impression that Jody, for whatever reason, had merely been brushed aside. It was a formidable demonstration.

Ronald Neames' life would be spared because Jody had lost hers and Neames knew nothing beyond that contact. It was a shrewd move. Few would mourn Jody's passing and the police would secretly be pleased.

Shaw went back to his flat. His tail seemed to have vanished again as if they were deliberately playing cat and mouse to spring when he least expected it. Max Fuller's presence must have acted as a deterrent, though. When he got back he told Max what had happened to Jody and Max did not seem surprised.

Shaw said, "I have to go to Germany. I don't know for how long but meanwhile I'd like you to stay here. Get yourself some food in and I'll pick up the tab when I come back."

"If you come back. You'd better put some cash down in advance."

"Thanks," said Shaw.

"If someone can do that to Jody they can certainly do it to you. Jody could take care of herself and was used to the scene. But someone still got to her. What chance do you stand?"

"I'll make sure you get some cash before I leave."

Fuller sighed heavily. "It's difficult for me to say this. I never thought I'd get to like a copper. I don't need your money. But you're pushing off to unknown parts where you'll be easy to pick off and you don't even have a shooter. I've looked. Do you want me to get you one?"

The suggestion came as a shock to Shaw. To one used to administering the law for so long it was difficult to listen to this kind of talk. It was not the handling of arms that worried him, he had been trained to use small arms in SB, it was the very thought of carrying a gun at all. "No, thanks, Max. I'd never get it on to a plane anyway."

"Then get one over there. It should be easy."

He went to his bank to organise travellers' cheques and returned to find Jill Palmer chatting comfortably to Max. Max looked up and said, "I let her in. She says she's a friend of yours."

"You're supposed to be my bodyguard. How do you know she hasn't come to kill me?"

Before Fuller could reply Jill said, "He told me he is your butler. I haven't come to kill you and I am sure he would have stopped me had I tried. I came to apologise."

Shaw made a slight movement of the head and Fuller remembered he had to make his bed and closed the bedroom door behind him.

"You reckon I asked for it?" asked Shaw, touching his bruised eye. There was something different about her. She always dressed smartly, none of the jeans and jacket touch about her, but it was not her clothes. Her hair style had changed; it had been cut closer and shaped to her head and he thought it suited her well. He almost said so, then remembered that he was virtually at war with this woman.

"You did at the time. But I reacted too strongly. I shouldn't have clobbered you. I know something of the strain you've been through. Both of us. It hasn't been easy."

"No." He sat on the arm of a chair and gazed down, liking what he saw without trusting her. He wished that he could but somehow something always cropped up to put him on the defensive. "Would you like a drink?"

"No, thank you. It's too early for liquor and too late for tea. Are you going away?"

His suspicion was immediately back. "What makes you say that?"

130

She noticed the quick change in him and said disparagingly, "You've just put your passport on the small table over there. They look like travellers' cheques sticking out."

He felt a fool. He was always feeling a fool with her, either that or angry. "Good observation. You should have been in the police."

Jill laughed. "I don't think I'd have been very good at that. You didn't answer my question."

"I'm going to Germany to chase up a possible lead."

"Alone?"

"Of course alone. Why?"

"If you could bear the company I wondered if I could come with you. I've nothing else to do."

He was taken completely by surprise, not for the first time by her. And he did not much like the idea. "It could be very dangerous. They blew up Jody Marsh last night."

"Who the hell is Jody Marsh?"

Why did he think she already knew? "The wife of a gangster. She carried on after he disappeared. Some think she killed him and I wouldn't disagree. She hired someone to tune in to what was being said in here. Someone put a baby alarm in. I ask you. Whoever hired her decided to get rid of her. She probably got over-confident."

"How do you know that she was killed and if so the reason might have been entirely different?"

Shaw slipped into the seat of the chair. "Why do you make life so complicated, Jill? She didn't blow herself up. If she was going to do that Jody would have invited all her enemies in to go with her. Nothing unselfish about Jody. Just take my word for it."

"Okay. So when do we go to Germany?"

"I'd be faster on my own. No offence. I have a slight knowledge of the area."

"It doesn't appear that you're taking Max so you'll need some sort of bodyguard." Jill's expression was bland.

"Max, eh? You worked fast on him. Max would be like a fish out of water and he doesn't like Germans. He'd start World War Three. Apart from which you don't strike me as a bodyguard."

"I pack a helluva wallop."

He burst out laughing. Before he could answer she said, "There's nothing to stop me going independently. I'd just book where you book. We may as well go together."

She was playing it down. Why was she so determined?

"It could be my way of saying I'm sorry," she continued. "Don't make it too difficult for me. A platonic excursion."

At least that was clear. "I planned on leaving the day after tomorrow." He never felt he understood Jill, was not entirely comfortable in her company. Perhaps it was her association with his brother. And yet this might be an opportunity to get to know her better; they could hardly avoid each other on a plane. "Okay," he said reluctantly.

"Are you first going to bring me up-to-date on what you've found out so far?"

It was crunch time. It would be difficult not to tell her if he allowed her to come with him. He was by no means sure he could trust her, yet he would never find out unless he confided something. He told her about Klatt and West but omitted mentioning his friends in Scotland Yard; he did not want them implicated.

Shaw took one suitcase and drove to London Airport by a devious route until both he and Fuller were satisfied that they were not followed. Fuller drove the car back from the airport after giving Shaw fatherly advice on how to handle himself in a crisis.

Jill was already waiting at the airport as if she thought he might try to leave without her. They had adjoining seats on the Lufthansa flight and when they reached height and bumped their way over the English coastline Shaw told her about Greifswald.

"I went out with Sandy Taylor, an SB mate of mine, to collect two IRA suspects being held there. What they were doing in a small Baltic port was a mystery in itself. It seemed they'd been on the run for some time so they might have come in from West Germany and could even be trying to get to Denmark. It was an abortive trip. They escaped before we arrived. Some said remnants of the Stasi helped them. It's

132

possible, for the newly formed Office for State Security had no teeth at that time. So Sandy and I took a couple of days off to look around."

Shaw sat musing as time rolled back and he recalled what it was like in those days not too long ago when East Germany had collapsed as a separate State.

"Don't reflect on it, tell me," Jill urged.

They were too high to see anything but cotton threads representing snowcaps on the North Sea. He told her what he knew.

"It's history now," he said. "And you'll probably find it boring. We missed out on the IRA but picked up on some other news. It started on 4 December 1989. In what was then the East German town of Greifswald, the public became aware that the Staatssicherheit, the Ministry for State Security, was performing an urgent destruction of its most delicate files.

"I can still recall the number of the top secret order that went out, 282/89 which was issued on 27 November, ten days after the Stasi was officially abolished. You probably know that Stasi is a derivative of the full name. They sent out the same instruction to all fifteen regional headquarters and at Greifswald they had sent on the same instruction to the Stasi's 218 local offices. With a population of around only 64,000, the immensity of the full coverage of all regions and their local networks could be judged. The instruction was the more interesting because it proved that the Stasi, now officially defunct was alive and well and still issuing orders.

"It was an impossible order. Greifswald's fifty or so Stasi agents resorted to tearing up documents by hand and stuffing them into black plastic bags. The shredders were unable to cope with incriminating documents covering forty years. The Stasi HQ, in what had been the courthouse, had its attics full by early December, and still had made little impact on the files."

He turned and was surprised to see that she was completely absorbed by what he was telling her.

"On 4 December a citizens' committee of around 300 people demanded to take over the files and were confronted by armed Stasi who backed down only on instructions from East Berlin. The Public Prosecutor sealed every drawer and desk and the citizens' committee kept vigil through the night."

Jill's concentration made Shaw uneasy. "Are you absolutely sure you want to hear this?" he asked.

"Absolutely. Please go on."

"Greifswald represented one tiny fragment of what had ensued over the whole of East Germany. And it particularly stuck in my mind because I became involved with the Office of State Security, and later the equivalent of the West German SB, on trying to block those Stasi who tried to escape to Britain at a time when they were trying to run anywhere.

"The obvious connection is that Hugo Klatt might be a Stasi on the run and had planned his papers and escape. He would have been in the very best position to take on someone else's mantle. He might even have killed for the papers; the real Klatt is apparently still missing. It was also possible that MI6 had found a use for him, or thought he had information they wanted."

As Shaw listened to the muted roar of engines and felt the sudden turbulence as they passed over a storm, he could not convince himself that he had found the answer. Was it worth attacking Fuller, getting rid of Mandova with too much drink, blowing Jody Marsh to bits? It did not make sense. These were all things that someone like Klatt might do to protect himself and, if he was ex-Stasi, he had probably done far worse over the years. But Klatt was in prison and Shaw was convinced that the strings were being pulled from outside. Jody would not have been blown up to protect Klatt. It was too risky. And yet somehow Klatt played a part in addition to being a killer.

"You're ruminating again. Do let me in on it."

"There's nothing more to tell. We'll have to hope we can pick up something at Greifswald." His ears blocked up and he put the whole matter out of his mind while they made their descent.

*　　*　　*

It had been a little time since he had been in Berlin and he still found the new openness strange. He rented a Volkswagen and still expected them to be stopped as they headed north into what had been East Germany. It was still like two separate countries, the differences almost immediately visible.

"It's about 120 miles due north on the Baltic coast," he explained once they were on the road. "Actually founded by Dutch merchants in 1240, it's now the country's smallest university town. Not very interesting country though, is it?" As Shaw drove through the agricultural heartland, his knowledge came back in spurts. But when it came down to it he was merely heading for a small port where he hoped to find information about Klatt. He remembered Max Fuller's warning and suddenly felt vulnerable. He once knew a few people here but had no real friends and might soon have enemies. Many of the Stasi had been caught and imprisoned. And many had not and had their own secret brotherhood.

Shaw hoped he did not convey his disquiet to Jill who had said very little on the latter part of the drive. She might be tired, of course, it had been a long journey although there had been little traffic on the roads, mainly articulated trucks coming from the Baltic ports, loads strapped down under heavy tarpaulins.

It was late evening by the time they reached the outskirts of Greifswald, clustered lights winking ahead of them, the dark sea lost somewhere beyond the town.

As Shaw slowed down he asked, "Ever hear of Peenemunde?"

Jill roused herself, pushing herself up in her seat. "Isn't that where they made the V2 rockets during the war?"

"There's a clever girl. It's just east of where we're going. We'd better find a hotel for the night."

They found one quite central and Jill was obviously impressed by the fluency of Shaw's German. He managed to book them single rooms but only one was en suite so he insisted Jill should have it. They met an hour later in the small lounge, all beams and sea relics. It was almost like being on an old ship. They attracted a good deal of attention, strangers were noticed here and memories of a powerful police state were still strong, suspicion inherited from years of oppression. They had a couple of drinks before going to the half-full dining-room; they were hungry after such a long day.

They had almost finished their meal when a heavily built man detached himself from a small group at another table and approached them. He came hesitantly to their table, gazed at Shaw, yellowed eyes puckered into a smile in his lined face, suit quite smart but unable to hide a thick waistline. He passed a pudgy hand across a balding head and said in good English, "Am I right? Inspector Shaw from London?"

Shaw rose. "You've a good memory. It's a few years since I was here." They shook hands firmly.

"And just how often do you think we get callers from your famous Scotland Yard? We've never forgiven ourselves for losing your men for you. Do you remember me? Please do sit down." He turned to Jill, "My apologies, madam. Am I spoiling your dinner?"

"Of course not. Do join us, coffee is on its way."

The German pulled out a chair and it creaked under his weight. "I must get back to my friends. But I simply had to say hello to my old friend, Inspector Shaw. Have you placed me yet?"

"Jürgen Kern. You were very helpful to us. I was going to call on you in the morning."

Kern waved a hand. "You would not have found me at Police Headquarters. I retired six months ago. Enjoying my leisure. I did not think you were here on holiday: who would come here, I ask you? You look well, and your lovely . . .?"

"I'm not his wife," interceded Jill, "nor even his girlfriend. I'm his nurse."

"Really? This is true?" Kern laughed. "You pull my leg, I understand."

Jill was smiling wickedly at Shaw's fury; he wanted nothing complicated here. He said nothing to add to the confusion but inadvertently increased it by not explaining. "Who should I see in your place?" he asked quickly.

"Oh, that depends on what you want. It is obviously a police matter or I would offer to help."

"You might still be able to," said Shaw, shooting Jill a look to kill. He took out his wallet and produced the mug shot of Hugo Klatt. He passed it across. "This man was supposed to be born here. I can't vouch for it. His name is Hugo Klatt. I was going to call at Police HQ to see if they have him on their files."

Kern held the copy of the police photograph in a hand that did not waver. The humour had left his pleasant features and little sweat beads began to form on his lip. "Where did this come from?"

"England. It was taken there. He's in prison for car theft. I believe he will be released quite soon."

"Keep him there. In prison. This man is a monster and his name is not Hugo Klatt." The hand was trembling now and the photograph was wavering. Kern used his other hand to steady it. "His name is Wilhelm Maas. If I was to pass this picture around everyone here they would recognise it although some would say they did not and it would be those you must not turn your back to." He gazed at it again. "He's older in this, as you would expect, but there is no mistake. Once you know this man you never forget."

Kern was hypnotised by the photo, not wanting to let it go. "Why do you come here when you already have him?"

"I'm here to find out what I can about him. I didn't think Klatt was his real name."

"And you are right. Maas was head of the Stasi murder squads here. He employed common criminals to go round killing people. So that's where he is. We've searched everywhere for him. We would like to get him back."

"He's been in Britain for a few years, he's naturalised now. It won't be easy."

"It does not matter how long he has been there. Ten, twenty years, one never forgets such a man." Kern raised his heavy head. "Stealing cars, you say? I dare say he had many sidelines, but this one I do not know about. The Poles are the ones for stealing cars. They are highly organised and find Berlin a rich picking ground. Then they take them back.

137

Do you know how many cars were stolen from West Germany last year?"

Shaw did not really want to know and felt he was being side-tracked. Kern was going to tell him anyway, so he said, "No. How many?"

"Eighty-seven thousand. That is a lot of cars. An enormous amount of black market money. If Maas was tied up in it I do not know. I had not heard so." He gave Shaw a long look of warning. "You were lucky I saw you first. Don't go flashing that photograph around here, Inspector. You'd finish up in the Baltic as fish food." He glanced regretfully at Jill. "And so would your lovely companion. Go home, Inspector. As fast as you can."

"I thought that most of the Stasi had been rounded up. Surely there can't be that number on the loose?"

"You show a West European naivety, my friend. Most of them probably have been. But there were an awful lot of them and they cling together for protection." He glanced around the room, beginning to empty now. "And never overlook the informers they used. Many thousands of them. We got a lot but it is impossible to get them all. We are still riddled with them. There are times when we still watch what we say. You find that difficult to believe?"

"No, we don't," Jill replied. "We think it a dreadful situation. Perhaps it will ease with time."

Shaw wanted to get back to what he had come for. "This Maas: was he born here?"

"You want me to show you the house? Will that help? So I have to tell you that it was burned down and has never been rebuilt as a lesson to some of the others. The only regret many of us have is that Maas was not in it at the time. If that sounds terrible it is no less true. We would like to have seen him alive in it as it burned. To hear the screams for mercy he so frequently forced out of others."

Kern was sweating freely now from recollections that were difficult for Shaw and Jill to comprehend. Someone called across from the table he had left and he turned to say he would not be long.

"Where can I find you?" asked Shaw.

138

"To ask more questions about Maas? I think I have already said enough. He will still have support here. In the woodwork, of course, but we want the whole situation to die down and for us to get on with lives we are only just beginning to understand. What else could you possibly want to know?"

"He took over the identity of Hugo Klatt who escaped over the Wall. Did you know the real Klatt?"

"Not that I remember. You could try looking for detail in the town hall records. If Maas took over his identity then Klatt is dead and I would not waste time on trying to trace him."

Shaw felt Jill tap him on the hand. When he looked at her she was silently appealing to him not to push too far. They had already done well and more quickly than they could hope for. But they had come a long way and he had to use the time he had. He tried his coffee to find it cold and put it down again.

"Will you bear with me just a little longer?" he begged. Out of the corner of his eye he had spotted someone waving to Kern, trying to attract his attention again. "Is there any organisation for getting ex-Stasi out of the country?"

Kern laughed, a deep rumbling sound. "That's very funny," he said. "Most of them ran like rats. They were what you call foot soldiers? The higher up the tree the more organised the escape plans. It all happened very quickly, of course, and many were caught, but after the initial shock they went to earth and laid their plans. Why does it matter to you? It is really obvious."

"Because I believe Maas came to Britain for a reason. And I think he had help of some kind in Britain. I think he's still having help, or at least useful advice. I'm just trying to find out what it's all about."

"On your own? With your nurse?" Kern was quietly mocking, eyes twinkling. "You would need the unison of all the security agencies, and the police forces, to dig that deep. This isn't a simple record you can look up, this is organised evil. I do not exaggerate. Maas is evil. Whatever you have seen of him, you have seen nothing or you would not be enquiring. I warn you both again, you got here, you have yet to get back. There is no protection I can give you and the police would not thank you for coming. Go home. Tonight if you can. Sooner, if possible."

13

Shaw let Kern go with the greatest reluctance. He had saved a lot of time by meeting him in this way. Before he left Kern expressed the wish to be left alone from now on and hoped that Shaw would honour that wish. He had no regrets about what he had already told Shaw, and indeed was glad to have had the opportunity to warn him; he still had a guilty conscience about losing Shaw his IRA suspects those few years ago.

Shaw and Jill went to their rooms, refusing the lift. At her door he said, "Can I come in?"

At once she saw that he was not asking her as a woman but as someone to listen to what he had to say. "Of course," she replied, opening the door wider.

It was a simple room, far from luxurious, but roomy with artificial beams running across the ceiling to match the genuine ones downstairs. She sat on the edge of the bed while he tried the solitary chair. "It's been a long day, Laurie."

He suddenly realised how tired she was. "I'm sorry." He rose. "It can wait."

"Don't go. Tell me."

"Kern has given us important information but there is much more to be had. I'm sure of it. Now if you prefer to go back I will understand perfectly. You can take the car or we can check on what sort of air services they might have here. But I must stay and do some more digging."

"In spite of the danger he talked about?"

"I've worked in Northern Ireland. It was pretty dangerous there."

"Don't try to compare the two; there is no cavalry here

141

who might come charging to your rescue. This thing has got to you. It's become an obsession. That's when you forget to look over your shoulder."

He glared at her. "Don't let's ever forget that this is about my brother being murdered."

"Bullshit."

He stared unbelievingly. It was not so much what she had said but that she should have said it at all. It was not her kind of language; which made it the more effective.

While he was still under shock, Jill added, "It started out like that. But you are satisfied who killed Terry. Now you're on to something else. You now know who Klatt is – we'd better still call him that or we'll confuse ourselves – but you want much more. You are now trying to solve a quite different issue."

"It's tied up," he insisted. "And some of the answers are in this town."

"Then let them stay here. We've got enough to take back and to insist on an enquiry. We have evidence that Klatt is not who he says he is and entered Britain under false pretences, later to become naturalised. We have all this as we are both witness to what Kern said. It's enough to raise a lot of hackles and to find out who let him in. Isn't that what you want?"

"I want him sent down for life."

"Who better to do that than the Germans themselves? Kern says they want him, which means extradition, and once he's been exposed it all should be a matter of form. I think he would suffer more in their hands than in ours."

"I also want whoever put him up to it and whoever is protecting him now. And I want to know why. All we've really established is that Klatt is a Stasi murderer. Have you ever considered why he should steal a car which landed him a jail sentence? It's crazy. He must have had previous form or he would have got a suspended sentence. Yet I can find no evidence of it. Incidentally he has only two more months to serve. It was an eighteen-month sentence, which is only a year with good behaviour." Shaw almost choked on the last words. "I thought we wanted the same thing," he finished lamely.

"We do. I'm just backing Kern up on the dangers. I'm your bodyguard, don't forget. Where thou goest, go I."

His tension eased a little. He smiled. "Some bodyguard. I thought you were my nurse; you never told him why."

"I would have said you are dying from some rare disease." She suddenly sneezed and groped for a handkerchief. When she couldn't find one he reached for her handbag which was near him on the dressing-table. "Is there one in here? Or would you like one of mine?" He was trying to mask his feelings as he felt something hard in the bag. He took the bag over to her and she sneezed again as she took it from him.

"Thanks. It must be the dust in here."

He stood over her. "I've waffled too much. Let's see how we feel in the morning."

She pulled a tissue from her bag and dabbed her nose. "Sorry about that."

"That's all right. Shall I put the bag back for you?"

"No, thanks. I need it anyway. I'll sleep on what you've said and we'll discuss it tomorrow."

He went to the door, opened it, looked back. "Don't forget to make sure it's properly locked when I've gone. If you need me, bang on the wall."

He went into his room wondering how she had got a gun through a security check at London Airport, and through customs this end. He could not be absolutely sure that it was a gun without looking inside the handbag. There was only one way to find out.

As tired as he was, at half-past-two he roused himself. It was a trick he had learned over the years, waking at any hour without an alarm. He pulled himself round with the greatest difficulty and left his room after collecting his pencil torch and removing the key from the lock. He went to the bathroom at the end of the corridor. He splashed cold water over his face and crept back to Jill's room. He put an ear to her door before crouching down to peer through her keyhole.

Never leave a key in a lock. Any burglar will tell you. It can be turned with the right instrument. Shaw produced his own key and inserted it to find no obstruction. He was working on the premise that this was a very old hotel in an area of a low crime rate; political crime had been another matter. He was banking on most of the locks being the same; they were all old and solid, but one key might open a lot of doors. He turned it very carefully. Halfway the tumblers decided to give and the amount of noise made him cringe.

He waited so long he was forced to straighten and he heard someone moving about downstairs. Nobody came up the stairs and he slowly turned the old-fashioned door knob. He pushed gently only to find resistance. He pushed again and heard something creak the other side of the door. He stopped at once, stepped to one side and leaned against the wall, puffing out his cheeks and thinking that Jill had removed her key but had then wedged the chair under the inner door knob.

Shaw positioned himself again and slowly turned the key, moving away quickly once he heard the tumblers make their heavy sound. He returned to his room frustrated and tired. He could not accuse Jill of lack of security. She had taken the danger warning seriously.

When he went down for breakfast next morning Jill was already there and much brighter than he. There were few people in the dining-room and those that were there gave them formal nods of greeting.

"Have I smudged my lipstick? Got egg on my face?"

"I'm sorry," responded Shaw. "Was I staring at you?"

"Enough to notice. Not a friendly stare either. More of a 'what have you been up to' stare. Didn't you sleep well?"

"No. Intermittent. Feel dreadful."

"Neither did I. Someone tried to break into my room last night."

"You're not serious?"

"Used a key to open the lock but I had a chair pushed under the handle. He was obviously an amateur. And not a very good one at that."

Was she mocking him? "Are you sure? Maybe you dreamed it."

"The tumblers made a hell of a racket. Old locks. Noisy but solid. Of course, once opened he had to lock the door again to give the impression that nobody had tried. What a berk."

Shaw swallowed on that, convinced that she knew. "What would you have done had he come in?"

Jill's eyes were bright as she replied, "He would have had the surprise of his life. He wouldn't have enjoyed it."

"How do you know it was a he?"

"A woman wouldn't have been so stupid. She'd have known that a foreign woman on her own in a strange town, in an old-fashioned hotel where the locks were likely to be the same, would have wedged something against the door, if only to protect her honour."

Now he knew she was getting back at him. But it was no laughing matter. Had she got a gun or not? He could not think what else it could be. "You'd better report it to the management," he said.

"There's no need for that. Are we going back today?"

"I'd like at least one more day here. You can go back if you like."

Jill placed the huge, heavily starched napkin on the table. She finished her coffee and pushed back her chair. She reached down and retrieved her handbag from the floor. Shaw found it difficult to take his gaze from it until he thought she was watching him, when he said, "So what are you going to do?"

"You must have had a worse night than you realise. We've already decided that. I stay with you. This is a very old port. There must be some interest here."

"I wouldn't call it a tourist attraction and I don't intend a sight-seeing tour. In spite of what Kern said I shall call at the main police station and see if there is anything else to find out about Klatt." They were hedging with each other again as if neither wanted the other to know precisely what they had in mind. Mistrust had taken another turn.

"You seem fascinated by my bag," Jill observed as she

pushed her chair back under the table. The bag was now over her arm.

"My girlfriend had one very similar. Is it snake or croc?"

"You can't tell the difference?"

"I haven't had a really good look at it. Croc then."

"And you are right. I'm going back to my room. I'll meet you in the lobby."

After she left, Shaw went out to the cobbled car park at the rear of the hotel. Most of the cars had already gone but the Volkswagen was still over by the corner, dust- and rain-soaked by now, and he decided to give it a wipe down. He opened the boot to look for something to clean it with and went cold as he realised that here of all places he had forgotten his usual routine. It was the difference between being in or out of the force. Or of being confused by Jill Palmer.

He lowered himself to look under the car and saw the bomb almost at once. It had been strapped directly under the front passenger seats. He had no equipment to dismantle it and was reluctant to open any of the doors or the bonnet for fear of triggering it. As far as he could see it was a professional job, neat, compact, deadly.

He rolled on to his back. The bomb might have a use. He climbed to his feet, brushed himself down and went back into the hotel. At the desk he asked the receptionist to get him the police. When she hesitated, he said, "There is a bomb under my car, tell them to bring someone capable of removing it." He did not trouble to keep his voice down and a few heads turned as he spoke.

The startled receptionist still was not sure. "A bomb?" Then she saw he was not joking and went to the phone, keeping an eye on him, hoping he would not run off to leave her to manage the situation on her own. A bomb. The message poured out down the phone and now those already in the lobby were on their feet wondering what they should do. Shouldn't the hotel be evacuated?

If the car had not been in the far corner of the car park Shaw would have suggested just that. That side of the hotel

146

could be damaged but there was no point in starting a panic. He had achieved what he wanted, everyone would now know; the word would be passed round like wild fire. "Just make certain nobody goes into the car park. Rope it off and post a danger sign at the entrances."

The police arrived quite quickly; the sound of their approach must have been heard through the town. And with the police, sirens wailing, came a fire engine. Three men wearing heavy flak jackets rushed in, and the receptionist referred them to the waiting Shaw. It was at this stage, having heard the sirens, that Jill came down the stairs to find out what had happened. At the foot of the stairs she heard Shaw explain about the bomb and remained where she was. Her German was not as good as his but good enough to realise what he had found.

The police and Shaw went out to the car park and Shaw showed them the bomb under his hired car. The police did what Shaw had tried to avoid and insisted that the hotel be cleared. Guests filed into the street the far side of the hotel and onlookers swelled their numbers by the minute. A bomb had been planted under a car; the word went round and the area was buzzing.

The police brought equipment from one of their vans and gingerly jacked up the car at the front. It was not a process Shaw would have favoured but it was out of his hands. A bomb expert crawled under the car, poked out an arm to give a thumbs-up to indicate he had everything in hand, and shortly afterwards reappeared, moving slowly on his back, the bomb held carefully in both hands, the adhesive strips trailing. Once clear of the car, he placed it on the ground and produced from a plastic bag the detonator he had detached.

With the bomb dismantled the danger was over. The bomb was then taken to a special van which moved off in a small convoy. Some onlookers clapped, some gave feeble cheers, relief was evident and guests began to move back into the hotel.

"Herr Shaw?" The features were genial. Shaw had seen similar expressions on similar policemen just before an arrest.

"I am Werner Scherer. I am with the police department here. You've frightened half the town, I am bound to say. A bomb under your car. How did you find it?"

"I looked. I was a policeman myself not long ago. Special Branch, possibly like yourself. Worked for a while in Northern Ireland. Habit dies hard, Herr Scherer. And that was all it was. Force of habit."

"Why would someone do that to you here? Perhaps it was more than habit. Perhaps you were expecting it?"

"Not particularly. I intended to call at police headquarters this morning. I'm trying to get information on a man who was born here. I believe he was a member of the Stasi before going to West Germany, prior to unification, and then to England where he still is."

"If he belonged to the Stasi, quite a few people would be looking for him, so why should someone pick on you to put a bomb under your car?" Scherer was more than interested and not just for his report. "Would you like to talk about it here or down at HQ?"

"Let's go into the bar. It should be empty at this time."

Shaw led the way. Scherer was a tall man, polite in attitude, the eyes soft and probably misleading. Shaw had not asked his rank but was confident that he was senior enough and was probably in State Security, bearing in mind the nature of the event and that a foreigner was involved.

On the way Shaw noticed Jill standing with others in the lobby but ignored her and she made no attempt to speak to him. They went into the bar and apart from a cleaner and a young barman polishing glasses, there was nobody else there. Shaw did not see the sign of dismissal but suddenly the barman disappeared and the cleaner turned off her vacuum and left the room. The two men were now alone. They selected a table as far from the door as possible and sat down. It was a strange sensation to be in a bar so lifeless.

Shaw told his story without prompting and when he had finished, Scherer said, "I congratulate you on your German. Very good indeed. You have a photo of this man?"

Shaw produced the mug shot. He had not mentioned his

meeting with Kern. He did not want to compromise the retired policeman but instinct also held him back.

"I don't recognise him at all," Scherer said thoughtfully. He laid the mug shot on the table between them and facing himself. "But then at the time you are talking about I was stationed in Rostock. That's my home town," he added with a smile. "Three times bigger than here and twice as busy." He smiled ruefully. "Perhaps I did the right thing in moving; the Neo-Nazis are now burning the homes of the immigrants there. There will be plenty more trouble."

"The Baltic's largest port, I believe." Shaw did not ask why Scherer had moved to Greifswald. Perhaps he had been given promotion; or the opposite?

"It is obvious that someone here knows you are looking into this man's background and has given you a warning."

"A warning? The bomb expert said it was wired to the ignition. He tried to kill me."

"I did not intend to play it down but whoever did it might know of your vigilance."

Shaw was beginning to wonder where Scherer's sympathies lay. "I might have had an off-day," he replied bitterly. "Meanwhile, where do we go from here?"

"You have no known enemies here? Clearly someone knows of you. Now why would you be considered to be a danger?"

"I think I already explained that."

"But you say this man who calls himself Klatt has been gone so long. And you have him locked up anyway. There has to be much more than you have told me."

Shaw nodded agreement. "There has to be, but I don't know the answer. Put in the context of what has happened, Klatt's part is minor in all this. But in some way he is still the key. Have you anyone on the force who can give me more detail about him?"

Scherer's expression was resigned as he said, "You mean more than you have already been told by Jürgen Kern?"

Shaw's estimation of Scherer rose. The eyes were still full of kindness and compassion but they clearly hid a lot more about the man.

"Did he tell you we met here in the hotel?"

"Does it matter? I think I know somebody who might know more about Klatt. I don't know where it will take you. As I see it the solution to your problems lie in England. That is where Klatt is and surely the answers?"

"Someone here doesn't think so. And whoever that is has gone to extreme lengths to stop me enquiring. So there must be something to learn here."

Scherer glanced towards the bar. "It's unnatural to sit here like this without a drink when there is so much beckoning. Let's go have one."

Scherer went behind the bar as if completely familiar with its layout, and poured two large schnapps. Shaw perched himself on a bar stool and they now faced each other like a barman and customer.

"*Prost!*"

"Cheers."

It was early for a drink but neither seemed to notice it.

"Will you be here this evening? I'll send a man round who might be able to help."

Klatt was not mentioned again. The two men talked away quite comfortably and ostensibly at ease with each other, but Shaw's mind was still on Klatt and he had the feeling that so was Scherer's. Half an hour later Scherer said he had to leave, shook hands with Shaw and left the bar.

Shaw suddenly felt lonely, and guilty about the drink. Scherer had left no IOU and Shaw decided to pay for the drinks himself. He left the bar.

The lobby was now back to normal but there was no sign of Jill. He informed the receptionist about the drinks and then went upstairs to Jill's room. He knocked on the door and when there was no reply tried to open it. She was obviously out, but where? He went down to the lobby again and asked the receptionist if she had seen Jill. She had but she had left the hotel some time ago with a man.

This made Shaw wary; so far as he knew Jill knew nobody here. He went out into the car park again. A small group of people were looking at his car which had become a centre of attraction. When they saw him they drifted away sheepishly but Jill was not among them.

He walked towards the docks, some little distance away as the hotel was on the other side of town. Various historical features were still visible but that it was predominantly an active port was borne out by the rumble of articulated trucks moving to and from the docks. He kept to the busiest streets aware that he was taking risks walking on his own.

As he neared the docks the usual strong tang of sea was less than he would expect before he remembered that the Baltic was almost land-locked, linked to the North Sea only by narrow straits between Denmark and the Scandinavian peninsula.

Shaw suddenly stopped. Did he think he could find Jill by walking the streets and offering himself as such an easy target? He turned round and headed back towards the hotel. Why the hell hadn't she left a note? He began to get angry. Gone off with a man? That worried him for all sorts of reasons. Jill was not stupid.

He reached the hotel again and checked the public rooms to find he had become an object of curiosity. Heads turned as soon as he put in an appearance. He went up to her room again and back to check with reception. Yes, she had been seen going up the stairs about half an hour ago. But he had just been up there. Shaw checked the time; he had been wandering the streets for much longer than he realised. He raced up the stairs again, taking two at a time, tried her room again. It was still locked and he rattled the door. If she had come upstairs, where had she gone? He tried the bathroom knowing it to be futile as she had her own bath. He inserted the key into his own door lock to find it already unlocked. He opened the door carefully. Jill was face down on his bed.

14

Shaw stood in the open doorway at first thinking the worst. Then he noticed her shoes were off. She moved slightly and he caught the slightest sound of breathing. He stepped into the room and closed the door quietly behind him. He felt relief at seeing her there then curiosity when he noticed her handbag on his dressing-table. The temptation was too strong.

He moved towards the dressing-table, his gaze on her rather than the bag, and when he reached it turned so that he was facing her with the bag behind him. He stretched his hand back, groped blindly, found the bag, and pressed his hand down on it. The gun had gone. He began to believe he had imagined it in the first place. But he had not and she had now removed it. It raised a lot of questions about her.

He stepped towards the bed and leaned on the old-fashioned footboard. Jill seemed to be fast asleep. He stepped round the bed and the next moment was facing the gun he had been searching for. Jill was suddenly on one elbow and the gun was levelled straight at him. He froze immediately.

She relaxed as she recognised him and lowered the gun. "Don't ever creep up on me like that again."

"Christ, you nearly shot me. Who needs bombers with you around? And where did you get the bloody gun?"

She swung her legs over the side of the bed and groped for her shoes, slipped into them and stood up. "I'm tired out," she said. "I couldn't find you. I knocked on your door, no reply, so let myself in with my own key. I knew you'd pitch up some time so lay down and must have dozed off."

"Face down with a gun in your hand?"

"I invariably sleep face down. And the gun is a harmless

replica, but useful against people who do not know that." She held it in the palm of her hand and moved towards the dressing-table.

"Let's have a look."

She ignored him and put the gun in her handbag and pressed the catch. "There," she said. "Little Laurie won't be scared again."

He supposed he had asked for that but could not let her get away with it. "You certainly know how to handle a replica," he commented. "Wrist in line with the barrel; arm level. Pointing at the right spot and not a waver. Great stuff. But you are not getting away with it, Jill. A replica shows up on X-ray just the same as the real thing, so how did you get it here?"

She was examining herself in the mirror, wiping away some smudged lipstick. "I have my ways."

"That's not good enough. And that's no replica."

"It is and that's all you're going to get."

"I thought we had no secrets between us. You are raising suspicions."

"If we had no secrets between us life would be dull. And you've always been suspicious of me. Nothing has really changed. Do you want to know what happened to me or not?"

"It had better be good."

She slipped her handbag over her arm and faced him. "You could have told me about the car bomb, you bastard. I had to overhear while you were telling everybody else. I was worried sick."

"So was I. It was me who found it."

There was an uneasy silence and then she said, "I'm sorry. I suppose you were trying to protect me."

He ignored that and said, "I'm still not satisfied about the gun."

She shrugged and sat on the edge of the bed. "We might as well talk here as anywhere." She glanced at the door and Shaw crept over to it and suddenly opened it. There was nobody there.

"When you went into the bar with Scherer, who belongs

153

to the Ministry of State Security as you probably guessed, I was approached by a man who called himself Joachim Tag, who knew we were here together and had come to make enquiries about Klatt. I suppose the whole town knows by now. He said he had plucked up courage to approach me because you were occupying Scherer. He told me to tell you not to trust Scherer, and that he knew something of Klatt's background which might interest us. He's a weasel of a man. He didn't want to be seen talking to me by Scherer so we went for a walk. I thought it worth the risk."

"And you had your replica with you."

"I didn't know what to make of it. How did he hear of us and know that we are interested in Klatt? Kern was the only person we spoke to; perhaps he's not as solid as he seems. Just who are our enemies?"

Shaw was thinking the same thing. They were on unfamiliar soil, in a country which had suffered under an oppressive regime, and like all such countries, had used the back-up of a secret police. Suspicion was a way of life. Murder squads were old hat but a sickening reality just the same. When it had ended its effects were still there and mistrust would take a long time to die. Until the disparity between East and West Germany was finally resolved and one country became a reality in every sense, problems would remain with festering suspicion. Jill was right; who were their enemies? Just how many were involved with Klatt and what was Klatt involved in anyway, except his Stasi past? Maybe that was enough. But Shaw found that too simple an answer. These thoughts flashed through his mind and he snapped from the reverie as he saw Jill's questioning look.

"Are you back with me?" she asked.

"Weasel-face took you for a walk."

"He said he knew Klatt. It took me a little time to realise that he meant the real Klatt. The real Hugo Klatt was a local hero, one of the few who made it over the Berlin Wall. That he started out from a Baltic port made his escape even more remarkable. Tag thought I wanted to know about his disappearance, which in part I did. He reckoned that Klatt was murdered and disposed of by the Stasi using a hit squad in West Berlin. When I showed him the copy mug shot of our Klatt he recognised him at once. And that frightened him, but also confirmed what he had suspected all along: Maas had either killed or had had killed the original Klatt and taken his place.

"Tag was also in the Stasi. He had worked with our Klatt for a while. But the interesting point was that he claims that Klatt was back in Greifswald less than two years ago."

"How come that Tag, ex-Stasi, is roaming free and loose?"

"He claims his roll was minor and, anyway, he turned State evidence. He got a sentence of three years but was paroled after six months. I suppose all this could be corroborated."

"Do you believe him about seeing Klatt?"

"If he had been in the Stasi he would have a mind trained to deceive. So it's difficult to say. He's willing to see us both. He says he has some information on Klatt's activities here but that walking the streets was not the place to trot them out. Anyway he had to get back in case any of Scherer's men saw him with me. He was in a highly nervous state throughout. Tag came to the hotel on spec; he had no idea about the bomb and was surprised to see Scherer there. I've got a number to ring so that we can fix a meeting. He had to be very careful, he says." She had saved the best till last. "One thing tends to support him: Tag says Klatt was with a redhead."

It had the effect on Shaw Jill had expected but she did not anticipate his reply.

"You're a redhead."

"So I am. But it wasn't me and I believe this one was older."

"Was he close enough to hear them speak?"

"Not to hear precisely what they were saying, but enough to decide that the woman was German. At first he thought she might be a foreigner. It was in an out-of-town beer garden but it was cold and they were inside in separate cubicles. It was sheer chance that he saw Klatt. That's the way it often happens."

Shaw was silent for so long that Jill said, "You're thinking it might be Molly Winters?"

"As far as I could make out, Molly Winters was English, or spoke English with a southern accent. Max Fuller remembers her visiting while he was still inside, and he said they spoke in English. Do you think Tag is having us on?"

"What for? It would be a hell of a coincidence for him to choose a redhead as Klatt's companion."

"Unless he was told to say that?"

"You think he merely wants us to arrange a meet in order to get rid of us?"

"Don't you? We'd need more than a replica gun."

Jill would not be drawn. But she was uncertain and it was with a little trepidation that she said, "I suppose there is only one way to find out."

"Yes." Shaw stood, hands in pockets. "Have you considered that Tag might be the one who planted the bomb? An ex-Stasi man would be well qualified. When he saw he had failed he went to plan B. Otherwise, just why is he willing to help us if it's so risky?"

"It's for money. He wants £5,000 sterling. We'd have to decide whether it is worth it. Isn't this the sort of thing Terry left his money for? I think we have to meet him. Otherwise we bury our heads in the sand and go home."

"We'd be going in blind. You do realise the risks?"

"Yes, of course. It has to be done."

Shaw stared long and hard at her. Was she more attractive than when they first met, or was he late in appreciating her looks? He really knew so little about her that she herself could be an enemy. She was certainly facing the risk of a meeting with Tag squarely and that in itself raised a few questions. And there was still the gun. Shaw had the strange feeling that he was speaking for himself, facing his own dangers, when he said, "Okay, ring the number and arrange a meet."

They decided to have lunch in the hotel before Jill telephoned, which they had decided it would be best to do from outside the hotel. There was a tension between them which was difficult to explain. Shaw thought they

156

might have different motives for meeting Tag. The feeling was there and perhaps Jill sensed it. Yet it was virtually impossible to go their own ways. For whatever reason they were bound together at the moment and a new kind of unease had arisen between them.

Over lunch they were ostensibly friendly but there was a vague coldness about it as if they were putting on an act for the spectators who would not stop glancing their way. Shaw was glad when the meal was over, for it had been getting increasingly uncomfortable between them.

Eventually Jill said, "We are not going to get very far if we go on like this. We'll be too busy watching each other instead of the enemy."

"And why do you think we are like this?"

"You don't trust me. You're wondering if I'm setting you up."

"Would you prefer it if I went on my own?"

"If I said yes you'd be convinced that I had. So I'll come with you and you'll have to wait to see who your friends are."

"It's not my friends I'm worried about. Come on, let's get out of this fish bowl and make that call."

Veida Ash was summoned to the office of Sir Charles Melville and as it was almost six in the evening, he offered her a drink. She chose a gin and tonic and sat opposite him. She knew Sir Charles quite well, having worked with him abroad before he was appointed to his present post of Director-General of MI6.

Sir Charles did not represent a typical civil servant image. He had a florid face which could appear inane at times, and he wore outrageous ties. Some said he was colour blind, others that he should be if he was not. Veida stared at the mesmeric mass of harsh and scrambled colours across the desk and finally managed to reach his deceptive eyes.

"Shaw," Melville announced, coming straight to the point. "What are you up to?"

"Have you been speaking to Judith Walker? She took me

to lunch the other day when I thought she should really have been taking you."

"I was spared that but I've had a word with her since. You can't go around begging favours of MI5 unless I know about it. Not on that scale, anyway. In any event I'm not too keen, they invariably want one back. Answer."

"I explained it all to her, well, the basis. Although the court found it to be suicide, I'm convinced that Shaw's brother was murdered in prison and that Laurie Shaw, the elder brother, late SB, has been getting in the way ever since in order to prove the murder. There is an ex-Stasi called Klatt in prison for minor crime. He was running an escape route for the Stasi which we would like to know more about as I'm convinced that a few have come here. I'm not doing this just because they are ex-Stasi but because some of them carry an awful lot of useful information we would like to lay our hands on. And one or two were helping us before the Wall crumbled. I want to know where they've gone. Many of their most delicate files were destroyed by them. Klatt had refused to see us officially, probably suspecting a trap, and we weren't too keen to meet him officially anyway. We needed to be in a position to deny it. We put Terry Shaw in with him to make contact and to make him certain offers, possibly immunity and money if the return was good enough."

"Shouldn't Judith Walker's crowd be handling that?"

Veida was not fooled by Melville's sloppy grin. "It all stems from abroad and will finish abroad. It's our property. This is not danger against the State but information to be obtained, and shared with our 'friends' in the States. We need these men for all sorts of reasons; some can be induced to work for us."

"Would we want them, Veida?"

Veida appeared surprised. "We want anyone who can help our cause and they had inroads into a lot of places, not only in Germany. They also hold information on many West Germans if there is such a distinction these days. I don't want Shaw trampling all over fertile ground and forcing people like Klatt into silence."

"Where is Shaw now?"

"Stirring it up in Germany. He can do irreparable damage. I wish I could get him back. He's travelling with a girl called Jill Palmer, a girlfriend of Terry. I find it difficult to raise anything on her. As far as I can see she's a fairly wealthy layabout with too much time on her hands and probably thinks she is helping Shaw. I can only hope she is a distraction to him."

When Melville made no immediate response, Veida added, "I did not give Judith Walker the account I am now giving you. I simply gave her the bones. Anyway, I no longer have help from MI5. Which has made it more difficult for me."

Melville was bland, fingering his tie as if it held some hypnotic power, which it sometimes did. "Keep me in touch. You can't spend forever on it." He hesitated. "I'm well aware of your record, long before I came here, as you well know. It's second to none, but sometimes even a genius can be wrong. Call it a day in, say, a couple of weeks' time." Melville looked at his calendar. "As from now."

Veida went back to her own office. When Gerald Ratcliffe showed his face round the door she snapped at him and he withdrew quickly; he walked away thinking that Boadicea had lost her chariot.

Veida was annoyed with herself for showing her irritation like that. She rued the day that Laurie Shaw had come on the scene. How could one man cause so much trouble? Nothing too serious had happened yet, but it could. And he had to be dealt with more effectively than hitherto.

When Veida had left, Melville was thoughtful for some time before reaching for his scrambler. He tapped in the brief number of a direct line. "Judith! I thought you might have gone."

"I'm always here. Have a bed made up. Are you ringing from home?"

Melville smiled at the quip. "Of course. I have several scramblers there, all different colours. I'm worried about Shaw and the girl."

"So am I. Deeply. Would it help if we forced another

enquiry into the death of his brother? It might bring Shaw home if we can get a message to him."

"I think it's too late for that. It's our fault that we supported the suicide findings and applied some pressure to it. We apparently had our reasons."

"Yes, of course." There was no conviction in her tone.

"Have you any ideas?"

"Really, Charles. What on earth can we do out there? That's your province."

"Out where, Judith? How do you know where he is?"

"With little else to do these days we keep an eye on your crowd. I'm sure I heard it from one of your sources."

Melville chuckled, it was his turn to be unconvinced but he said nothing to contradict her. "It looks as if the poor chap is on his own. I find that very sad. I think he needs help."

"Then give it to him. Talk some sense into Veida. She should be in a strong position to help."

So Judith Walker refused to be forthcoming. Melville had rather hoped she would. "It looks like the only thing to do," he agreed.

"Charles, why have you phoned me about this? My only part was to stop Veida from using our services as if she owned them."

"I'm getting senile," he said. "Forget I ever did. Although it sometimes helps to talk to someone outside our own organisation without breaking the Official Secrets Act. A brainstorm, my dear. Goodnight."

Brainstorm my eye. Judith Walker put down the phone and said aloud to herself, "You're getting nothing out of me, you crafty old devil."

It was late evening, just after dark, when they took the Volkswagen, with Shaw doing his usual bomb check before moving off, a precaution which seemed to worry Jill. And they drove towards the docks. Shaw remembered some of the layout but it had been a long time since he had driven in this city with Sandy Taylor. The circumstances had been quite different too.

160

So he was nervous at the wheel, particularly as he was trying a circuitous route. They had given themselves plenty of time in hand so he took them through the wide shopping streets, now with far more goods on sale at horrific prices to people not yet adjusted to the ways of free Europe. The main streets were a blaze of light but traffic was thin and Jill urged Shaw to take to the darker areas.

"I'm just trying to lay a false trail," he replied.

He swung away from the shopping districts and eventually entered a twilight zone of badly lit streets. There was poverty here in what had been an idealistic State, and after a while it became depressing. All towns have districts like it, anywhere in the world, and he had to remind himself of it. Perhaps he had chosen an unfortunate route, but suddenly he felt threatened and he thought that Jill felt it too.

Shaw frequently checked his rear-view mirror. He felt Jill glancing at him and he pretended not to notice. They both experienced relief when, above the dark irregular shape of a squat building line, they could see the overhang of giant cranes, lights fixed at the top to focus on cargoes below. Pockets of light haze hung over the docks like illuminated clouds.

"Can you remember where to go?" asked Jill who had not spoken for some time.

"I can remember what you told me after you phoned Tag. We've got to get to the end of the docks first, anyway. When the lights peter out we start looking." He noticed Jill draw her handbag closer.

Docks are the same the world over. Rail and crane tracks, ships' cargoes, dull lights and blazing lights, depending on the activity. This Baltic port was not as busy as its sister, Rostock, which was the biggest of them and to the west, but it was busy enough.

Shaw managed to keep on a parallel route behind the docks on an erratic course which dissected the avenue taken by the massive carrier trucks rumbling away when loaded and battened down, and often in small convoys. He kept driving, glad of the lights and the action about them until he steered into a no-man's-land of deserted, and sometimes, derelict, warehouses. The lights dimmed; there were no active cranes here, they had virtually petered out altogether.

Shaw turned and approached the dockside itself, crossing the tracks and then running beside them before passing through old, disused gates. He pulled up and climbed out to look back. He could just discern the stern of a large cargo ship, the deck lights a faint blur, but it was far too dark to make out the name of the ship. There was a dull glow on the slightly heaving water beneath the curving stern.

"Eerie," Jill observed now standing beside Shaw. "I shall be glad to get out of here."

"You said Tag mentioned the third empty warehouse along; the one with a couple of rusted rail trolleys outside. We'd better get back in the car and keep our eyes skinned."

They climbed back into the car and Shaw doused their lights as he drove on, taking his direction from the faint glow of the tracks. He could just about see them but it was crucial that he did with the sea a black smudge only feet away to their right. He almost drove into the first rail trolley and was forced to brake hard, forcing a gasp from Jill. He backed away, then veered round the trolley to see a second one in front of it. To their left was a derelict warehouse, gaping black holes where the front used to be. They had each brought a flashlight and now produced them. As they climbed out the whole structure appeared distinctly unsafe. Shaw located the faint reflection of a car tucked far into the interior.

As he moved forward Jill grabbed his arm and he knew she was as nervous as he. He whispered, "I think you'd better stay in the car."

"No. I'd be more afraid there than with you. Besides I've got the replica."

He raised his flashlight but did not want to switch it on until they were inside the framework of the derelict building. The car was now more distinct and facing them, the glass on the headlights picking out what little light there was.

"He should be waiting for us, but why hasn't he shown?

We'd better look inside." He turned to see how tense she was and hoped it was for the right reasons. "Are you ready?" It had to be done.

"Let's go."

15

They approached at an angle, the silence unnerving. From the distance came the busy sound of port activity but that was from another world, disconnected completely from where they were. The gap became a cavern as they drew nearer, the car acting like a beacon to focus upon.

They entered the dark interior and now it was worse than before, all light shut off, but they could still pick out the dull outline of the car. When they reached it Shaw recognised it as an Opel and insisted that Jill got down flat while he shone his flashlight into the car interior.

The beam reflected off the windows but penetrated sufficiently to show the car was empty. Shaw whispered to Jill to remain down while he shone his flashlight round the huge interior of the derelict building. There were empty tea chests strewn across the vast floor space. Newspapers lay screwed up like pathetic footballs. Litter was everywhere. Nothing stirred.

Shaw called out softly, "Tag! Tag!" The name came back in various forms as the strange acoustics bounced it around the deserted warehouse. Why was the Opel there? It was bound to act as an attraction. "Shine your light under the car, Jill."

She did so and said at once, "There's something fixed underneath."

Shaw pulled her to her feet. "Run," he urged, and grabbed her hand. He dragged her to the right of the building to run along the front of the structure next to it. After a while they stopped to get their breath and leaned against a steel support, struggling for air.

"I don't understand it," he gasped. Shaw was holding on

to the rusted steel column, bent almost double. "They could have picked us off easily enough, why arm the car?"

"You think someone is in there waiting for us?" Jill straightened before Shaw and seemed to be in pain.

"I don't know. We've yet to get back to our own car." He peered at her in the gloom. "You all right?"

"I am now. But I don't understand what they are up to."

"For one thing they've got us on the run." He pushed himself away from the steel support and ventured out on to the near barren dock. The Volkswagen was still there, planted in front of the two rail trolleys. Nothing had changed. But he did not like the idea of their car being plumb in front of the warehouse where the Opel stood, apparently with explosive strapped to its under belly.

"What do we do?" asked Jill, her voice quite calm again.

"I think we were expected to try the car doors to see if there was anything inside. And that would have been that."

"Or to see what might be in the boot," Jill suggested.

"Are you thinking that Tag's body is in the boot? We'd better get back to our car bloody quick. There won't be anyone waiting in the warehouse if they were expecting the Opel to be blown to bits; the boot will be packed with explosive too. Come on."

They took a long looping route back to the Volkswagen and then came along the extreme edge of the docks, passing a row of solid wooden battens with their rope fenders, half rotten by now.

They separated, Shaw taking the lead, and crouched low as they neared the Volkswagen. When they reached it they made sure that it was between them and the warehouse. The Opel still faced them, dull and uninviting, and like a bad dream repeating itself.

"I should have turned the car round to face the way we came. I'll have to get in first." He climbed in and slid across to the driver's seat and Jill was soon beside him. He switched on and once round pulled away as fast as he could. "So much for Tag," he said as he put his foot down.

"We had to try. At least we know what we're up against. We'd better get home as fast as we can."

"If they'll let us. I have a gut feeling that they are going to seal us in tight."

She made no comment but he could feel her concern. And he could not fault her support, and then he had the terrible doubt that there might not have been explosive under the Opel at all.

He should have been concentrating more on his driving, for Jill let out a yell as she saw a huge container truck coming straight at them. Suddenly the truck was ablaze with lights beaming down at them and blinding Shaw completely. He veered towards the line of warehouses but the oncoming truck did the same and there was virtually no room to pass. He swung out the other way towards the sea and the truck swung over to follow, the gap closing with frightening speed. It was all a matter of seconds and now the truck was almost on them and it was finally clear that it intended to crush them.

Jill screamed and Shaw shouted at the top of his voice, "For Christ's sake jump. JUMP, damn you." He did not know whether she did or not as he made one more swerve, this time heading straight for the edge of the docks. There was no way he could get past and the truck, now massive behind the barrage of blinding lights, was right on top of them like some grotesque crushing machine.

As Shaw tried to open his door the truck struck the Volkswagen side-on at its rear. There was a crunching of metal, the car took an enormous jolt and was sent spinning along the docks as if on an axis. There was a terrible grinding and the crash of shattered glass and the Volkswagen came to an uneasy halt as it hovered halfway over the dockside before finally tipping over into the sea. Shaw had passed out on the initial impact. The truck thundered past and took a slip road further along to rejoin the regular route into town.

The water revived Shaw as the Volkswagen plunged and gurgled, huge pockets of air bursting on the surface. He fought for his life not really knowing what he was doing. He was suffering some terrible nightmare and struggled to

166

wake from it. The car, which had at first nose-dived, turned turtle as it hit the water, and as it sank, turned slowly on its side leaving Shaw's door pointing upwards, taking some of the lower water pressure from it. But there was little time.

Because the night was balmy the window was wide open and while this let in the sea it also provided an escape hatch. Not knowing what he was doing he lunged out with his right arm to where Jill had been sitting, found nothing there and then managed to get his left arm out of the open window. It was a move that enabled him to squeeze through the small gap. Once half out he was able to use both arms to apply pressure against the car. Suddenly he popped out like a cork.

He surfaced against the slime-ridden side of the dock wall, half conscious and trying to spew out filthy water. He could find nothing to cling to and tried to get purchase with the flat of his hands. But he kept bobbing under and the swell was lifting and hurling him against the wall until he had the sense to roll on to his back and use one arm as a protective fender. He had neither the consciousness nor the strength to swim, and he had never been very good at it.

He floated and was bady bruised from each incoming swell. The constant motion was making him sick. He did not know which way he was going but as long as he could feel the dock wall he would fight to keep afloat. He drifted in and out of consciousness. Eventually he felt he did not have to struggle any more, the sea, instead of buffeting, was now comforting. After a while he felt cosy and warm. He was content to drift and when he lost touch with the wall no longer cared. He was being carried away and the strength of the swell was not enough to cover his face and he could go along with that, riding on a water bed forever.

He had reached an extreme sensation of comfort from which he would undoubtedly drown when he received another massive shock to his system. A terrible pain shot through his leg to shatter his cosy dream. It was drastic treatment but it felt as though his leg was being severed. He opened his eyes and cried out in pain, and it all came back to him and he fought for his life as never before.

167

He received another terrific jolt, this time on his body, and he managed to turn over to see a gigantic canopy hanging over him like a cloud of doom and through that cloud he hazily made out the word *Odense* at the top of the stern. Pain brought him to his senses and he quickly saw in the difficult light that he had struck the rudder of a ship. He felt he had been chopped by a massive guillotine.

As the swell raised him for another crashing blow he grabbed desperately at the rudder, could not get a grip, suffered a gruelling body blow which almost put him out again, and was then cast away ready to be heaved up by the next swell.

He was more prepared next time. Knowing it was now or never as he was hurled towards the huge blade, he swung his body sideways so that he was swept forward and he managed to grab the rudder with both hands. He thought his arms would come out of their sockets. He clung desperately until the swell subsided and then, before the next one came, slipped into the narrow channel between the ship's hull and the dockside.

By now he had recovered sufficiently to know he could be committing a gruesome suicide to be crushed against the dock wall by the enormous steel hull of the ship. He also knew there was no other course. He could not have held on to the rudder for any longer and there were no convenient ropes dangling by which he could pull himself up.

It was terrifying to be between the hull and the wall. Both rose up above him like a narrow canyon and at once he believed he had made a fatal mistake. He could just see the slit of sky above his head and it was this faint glimmer of hope that kept him going.

He was still being buffeted, for there was barely room for him to move between ship and dock, but it was quieter in the gap though claustrophobic. As far as he could determine, nothing was happening above him. Whether the ship had already been loaded or unloaded or was waiting its turn he could not tell but there was no activity he could see or hear.

He resisted the temptation to call out. Jill had said it; who

168

were their enemies? He edged his way along the rusting steel side using both ship and wall to make progress, until he came to the first of the huge rope fenders suspended from one of the wooden bollards to protect the ship's hull. The gap between ship and wall was at its narrowest here. He reached up but, even when taking advantage of a rising swell, could not reach the fender.

Pressing his back against the bollard and stretching out his hands and feet to reach the hull, he tried to climb as a mountaineer would in a narrow fissure. At the first attempt he dropped straight back into the sea and lacerated his knees against the hull. He tried again knowing it was now or never; his strength was almost drained. In tortuous moves, pausing now and again to ease the tremendous strain on his legs, he reached the fender and clung to it.

His problems were far from over, for he had to mount the curve of the fender, initially using only the strength of his arms. Once able to get a toe grip it became a little easier and he was soon standing on top of the fender, relieved and gasping for breath.

Shaw clung on grimly, water filling his eyes and cascading down his drenched body, but he got a hold on the rope from which the fender was suspended and it was his life-line. His position was precarious, the rope slippery under his wet hands. He started to climb.

The nearer he got to the top the closer the rope was to the bollard and the more difficult it was to get his hands round it. He slipped and suffered rope burn. Then he continued to climb, using his feet more until he was able to get a hand on the top and pull himself up, finally to get an arm over and heave himself until he could raise a leg and get better purchase. Once he had both arms over he made that extra effort which brought him to safety.

Shaw lay prone on the top of the dockside, wet and shivering and never had anything like the hard, dirty surface beneath him felt so sweet. When he got his breath back and could absorb the fact that at present he was safe, he scanned in both directions and was relieved that nobody appeared to be near.

The next ship was a little distance away and busy, lighted cranes were operating, stevedores moving around, and beyond that point there was a mass of activity. Shaw was glad that he had emerged at the neglected end of the docks. He lifted himself to his knees and was immediately sick. After that he rolled over and could not move for a while. Eventually he managed to get to his feet and stood swaying like a stick insect. With relative safety came memory and the sickening possibilities of what might have happened to Jill. He must go back.

He clung to the nearest support, an iron bollard from which a rope trailed up to the deck of the Danish registered ship. He staggered towards the building line; these were functional warehouses at present locked. Tag had known what he was doing when he had told Jill where they should meet.

The distance back was much further than he realised. It was easy to keep to the shadows along the row of warehouses but his feet squelched and he could not forget how he had got into this situation. The nearer he got to the point where he had gone over the edge the more nervous he became. For the very first time he wished he was armed.

He stopped when he was about thirty yards from the point of impact with the truck. He found it difficult to go on, and it was only concern for what might have happened to Jill that drove him forward. She might still have been in the car and when he considered that he hurried on, fears for himself receding.

He now started to scan every deep shadow. He moved unwillingly towards the dock edge. This was roughly the point where he had been tipped into the sea and Jill, if she was around at all, should be somewhere near this spot. If she had jumped.

He traversed the whole area. There was no sign of her. He walked on, aware that he was drawing uncomfortably close to the derelict warehouse where the Opel was. It gave him the sensation of putting himself up as a slowly moving target as he drew nearer. He reached the nearest opening and peered round the rusting framework. The Opel was

170

still there, like a dull insect in hibernation, waiting to be activated.

He rolled round the stanchion which helped to hold up a gaping roof, and crept into the cavity. It was difficult to take his gaze off the Opel, knowing it to be a waiting bomb, and he was nearer to it than he would have liked. He walked past it, and went deeper into the interior.

He backed into a crate, instinctively reached for his flashlight and realised it must have gone down with the car. He heard something move and stayed still. Every movement was difficult and great waves of nausea kept gushing through him.

He heard it again; an uneven sort of shuffling. He couldn't see anything. As he stood he became suddenly aware of the pain in his hands and knees.

He became bolder and stepped out more obviously. He could make out most of the steel supports disappearing into the roof cavity, and some of the lighter coloured debris, but he could see nobody and then he heard movement again. He went towards the sound convinced that whatever it was seemed unaffected by his own movements.

He saw a figure swaying, wandering, following no obvious route and he was at once certain it was Jill. He ran then, and almost collapsed under the pain from his knees. He kept on, limping but mobile and as he drew near he recognised her. She was wandering in a highly dazed state clearly unaware of where she was or what she was doing.

He hobbled forward calling her name out softly. When he reached her she was barely aware anyone was there. He took hold of her gently and held her to him realising she was probably concussed or in a state of shock. She collapsed in his arms. He picked her up and carried her to the entrance of the warehouse where he carefully put her down with her back against a girder. Even in the dim light he could see she was in a bad way. Clothes were torn and her hands and face were lacerated, congealed blood making a huge blister on one side. To add to this was the incongruous fact that she still had her handbag looped over her arm as if it was part of her.

171

When he tried to slip the handbag off her arm she resisted, holding it closer without knowing what she was doing. He pulled it off and she gazed at him without recognition as if he had violated her in some way. And then her eyes closed and her head fell forward. As he put the handbag aside he realised the chance to examine the gun had never been better, but now that he was able to he found he could not do it, as though he would betray a trust. And yet over the gun there had been no trust.

He tried to revive her, talking to her, at first gently patting her face and then slapping it more firmly. He thought she might not want to revive, afraid of what she might find if she did, so his chatter became louder and he began to shake her, not knowing whether he was doing the right thing.

She began to groan a little and he then shook her more vigorously until she made a garbled protest and her eyes began to flicker and finally opened. She stared straight at him with no recognition and then her expression changed and her gaze focused unsteadily on him squatting before her. Her lips moved. "I thought you were de . . ." The words were barely audible.

"I'm battered but far from dead."

She revived more quickly at that, concentration growing, and she stirred. Then she stared as if seeing his ghost, and flung her arms round his neck, crying softly.

He held her there for some time until she pushed herself away as if she had just committed a terrible sin. "You're alive," she said at last as if still in doubt.

"Just about. I'm not a good swimmer but in the event it didn't matter. I wasn't sure you had got out."

"I jumped when you bawled at me. I remember rolling, but must have hit my head against something, for after that I was so dazed I had no idea of what was happening. Did you find me or did I find you? God, my head aches." She was exploring at the back of her head.

They told their stories and it helped bring Jill round. She had no idea why she had gone back to the warehouse and had no recollection of it at all. She suddenly spotted the handbag lying beside her and put a hand out to it.

She said listlessly, "I suppose you now know the gun is real?"

He was glad then that he had not opened the bag. "Would I do that to you while you were unconscious?"

"You mean you didn't look? Well, you would have before this happened."

"Can you stand?"

"If I was wandering around I must be able to."

"We're far from out of this yet. They won't leave the Opel here." He helped her to her feet but she was still very groggy and he had to support her against the roof stanchion.

"God, just look at us," she said as he steadied her. She was beginning to worry about her appearance and Shaw thought that a good sign. "We can't go back to the hotel looking like this."

He could just see dark wet stains down her front where they had clung together. He started to shiver in his saturated clothes. His trousers were ripped open and his exposed knees were covered in blood. It was difficult to know what to do except to get away from this place as fast as they could. Where to go was another matter.

"Do you sleep with that thing?" Shaw was alluding to the handbag now looped over her arm again.

She did not answer and as she moved away from the stanchion, swayed on her feet. He caught her by the arm just as they heard the approach of a car. They instinctively drew back into the interior to watch the headlights bounce along the dockside drawing closer.

"Give me the gun," Shaw demanded.

But the shock of hearing the car approach revived Jill like a hard slap in the face. She already had it in her hand and did not intend to hand it over.

In any event it was too late. The car drew up outside and the lights were doused. Two men got out. They did not use flashlights until they were inside the warehouse and the beams were directed at the Opel. One of them carried what appeared to be a car-jack.

Shaw held Jill's arm and gently tugged her back deeper into the shadows until they could go no further. There was a

173

danger that they might be seen on the peripheries of the light beams. It was clear to Shaw what was about to happen.

One man put the flashlight down, directing it between the front wheels of the Opel while the other jacked up the car. Then one eased himself under the car while the other went to the rear, mounted his flashlight and started to work on the boot. So explosives had been packed there as well as under the car.

"Can you reach their car outside on your own?" Shaw whispered into Jill's ear. She squeezed his arm as an affirmative.

They moved very slowly towards the entrance. Shaw knew that disarming the bombs was not a job that could be rushed no matter how expert the men might be, particularly the one under the car which was in an awkward place. They had to operate with extreme care and total concentration. There would never be a better moment. Shaw urged Jill forward more quickly.

It was never going to be easy. Jill was still shaky and no matter how much he tried Shaw could not stop his shoes from squelching; the floor was too gritty for him to risk walking in stockinged feet. They kept going, reached the entrance and were seen by the man at the rear of the Opel as they made for the car the men had arrived in. The man shouted, stepped out from behind and reached inside his jacket as the other man rolled out from under the car.

To Shaw's amazement Jill turned and fired, not at either of the men but at the front of the Opel. The bullet went straight through the body and hit the engine with a clang. The two men were frozen, petrified she might hit the bomb. She fired again and they fled to the rear of the warehouse, flinging themselves flat as Shaw managed to open the other car door. He gave a shout as he found the keys in the ignition which would save him time. He called out to Jill to get in but she was still standing there with gun raised.

Shaw bawled at the top of his voice, "We're too near. Get in before you blow up the whole bloody lot of us."

Jill didn't react at once, acting as if the warning had not been understood, and then she was running round the car to the passenger seat while Shaw drove off before her door was closed. The car was parked too centrally on the dockside to do a U-turn so he drove forward not knowing where it would lead. He had to use the headlights to see. When he found a gap between two warehouses he took it and hoped for the best.

Jill was looking back to see if the men emerged and when they did not before Shaw took the turn, gave a little shout of triumph. She had earned the feeling of satisfaction, so he kept quiet about what would happen next; the two bombs would be dismantled and the Opel would be used to give chase. Another thing worried Shaw: there was a car phone in the Opel. It had not meant anything at the time he saw it. Now it did. He had not the heart to tell Jill. They were sealed in more than ever and he was certain that the intention was that they should not get back to England. He took another turn and found they were in a dead end, the headlights chasing their own reflection as they closed in on white painted timber gates.

16

Shaw almost crashed into the gates, braked in time, reversed straight back, the dead-end being too narrow for a quick turn, skidded round the corner and drove on no wiser as to general direction. All he wanted to do was get them into a part of town where they would be reasonably safe.

He took turn after turn and his only consolation was that Jill, recognising the problem, was not critical. The roads were not improving until quite unexpectedly he burst on to a main street. He could not recall ever getting satisfaction from seeing so much traffic. He still had no idea in which part of town they were but began to pick up road signs and gain some idea of position. When he drove into the main shopping area, even with most shops now closed, it was with immense relief that he was at last able to ask, "Where did you learn to shoot like that?"

"So we are back to the suspicions. Anyone can hit a car."

"You knew what you were firing at if not the result had you hit it. So who taught you?"

"It runs through the family. My father used to shoot at Bisley. So have I, without much success."

Only the best shots in the world fire at Bisley. So why hadn't Bob Reedy at New Scotland Yard picked up this little piece of information. "You got us out of a jam," he acknowledged. "Are you going to tell me how you got the gun here?" He felt safe at the moment but they still had to decide what to do.

"I didn't bring it out of the country. I picked it up here."

He glanced at her. "That takes arranging. I didn't see it happen."

"You weren't supposed to."

Shaw saw a space and pulled in; it was late for them to be booked for illegal parking. He switched off and the silence reminded them too much of the docks. "There's a hell of a lot you're not telling me, Jill. That's been more than half the problem."

"And you've told me everything you know, have you? Nothing left out? You've given me the bare bones, no more. And you've checked up on me."

"I was bound to the way you were carrying on." He touched his eye. "I can still feel it. How did you know I ran a check?"

"I have a relative quite high up in Scotland Yard. It would not be fair to give his name."

"Of course not." Another bit of information Bob Reedy had neglected to tell him. "His name isn't Reedy, by any chance?"

"You mean Detective Superintendent Robert Reedy? No, he's the man you got to check on me."

They were at it again, reflected Shaw. They had been through hell, had barely survived, had embraced, helped each other, and now they were back on course for a war of words. "Your relative must be very high up indeed. It didn't stop you coming with me."

"I'm just trying to explain the trust angle. Neither of us was sure if we could trust the other."

"And we can now?"

"You say you didn't look in my handbag. If that's true I have to trust you."

He was being put on the defensive again. "I think we'd better get back to the hotel and see what happens from there."

He took the odd wrong turn but once familiar with the layout drove carefully. He pulled up a little distance from the hotel and switched off. The hotel lay further along the street, white paint peeling from the old-fashioned front entrance pillars, very much part of the old town. They sat there staring ahead until Shaw said, "Isn't that the Opel that was at the docks?"

Jill craned forward, suddenly tense. "It could be. As far as I can see it's the same colour but it's tucked in and is too far away."

The Opel was facing them in a row of parked cars beyond the hotel and on the opposite side of the street. Only part of it could be seen.

"If it's the same car they must have decided to head straight back to the hotel and wait for us here. Now what do we do?" Shaw was suffering the discomfort of wet clothes and was shivering.

"You need a bath and a change of clothing," said Jill, not knowing what else to say.

"We both do. But how do we get into the hotel if that is the Opel? And how do we get in looking like this?"

Neither of them had suggested calling the police and neither found it strange. It would put them on view and a centre of attraction which was the last thing they wanted.

"We can't stay here. Is there a back way into the hotel?"

"Through the kitchens but that could cause just as much stir."

They were so engrossed in keeping the Opel in view that they neglected their backs. The rear door was wrenched open and before Jill could undo her handbag a gun was rammed into Shaw's neck as the other door opened and a second person jumped in.

"It's all right," said the man with the gun. "It's me, Tag. I had to be careful; I didn't want one of you taking a snap shot. It's my car you're looking at up there. I've brought along a friend." The gun was lowered. Shaw and Jill turned to see Tag, whom Shaw had not yet met but whom Jill recognised, and a bigger man seated beside him, his gaze darting everywhere. "This is Frederik," said Tag as if that explained everything. "He has more to tell you than I. But he, too, will want paying."

"Hold on," said Shaw. "We nearly got killed because of you; you'd better make it a good story. What happened?"

"Can we drive somewhere else first? We've seen the Opel, the men in it might see us."

Shaw glanced at Jill not knowing whether to trust these

178

men, and accepted her faint nod. He drove off and followed the directions Tag gave him until they were out of sight of the hotel in a fairly quiet side street. He switched off. None of them were in the most comfortable of positions and Tag, who put his hand on Shaw's shoulder said, "My God, you're soaked through. What happened?"

"What happened was that we arrived at the warehouse, could see no sign of you nor get a response to our calls, saw the Opel inside, found it wired up, shot off fast only to be dumped in the sea by a container truck. It was no accident. So how did the Opel get there?"

"I drove it there. Frederik was with me. We were very early; that's routine to recce the place. Once parked we got right at the back of the warehouse as far from the car as possible. I think we must have been followed for, shortly after, two men arrived, shone flashlights around, but we were well dug in and had a gap to run through if they came for us. But they seemed more interested in the car. When we saw what they were up to we crept out the far end and headed back to town damned quick."

"You mean you pushed off knowing we were coming and left us to it?"

"What else could we do? There were two of them and for all we knew they had back-up. Neither of us was armed and they were bound to be; I picked up this pistol since. We had no way to warn you; telephones are not exactly thick on the ground up there. And you must have been on your way by then. They may not have known what to expect. We thought they probably wanted to blow us up and when we returned to the car that would have happened. We were lucky to see them."

Shaw exchanged glances with Jill. It was impossible to know if Tag was lying. "So what did you do next?"

"We walked for miles and decided the best thing to do was to go to your hotel and wait. If all went well, angry or not, you would return there. We weren't willing to check on the car until tomorrow in daylight, with a few more friends around us. We were right, weren't we? Here you are."

"We are lucky to be here."

"So are we. You say a container truck pushed you into the sea, that proves our point: there was back-up. Just what could we have done about it?"

"Don't you think you're taking a hell of a risk coming back to the hotel?"

"No more risk than you. Our best escape is to West Germany. But that calls for money and we don't have enough. We need sufficient to tide us over there but to go without any cash would be hopeless. Your arrival here was a godsend. You offered five thousand sterling to me, Frederik here has even more information you may want. So you should pay us ten thousand sterling. Our lives are on the line; it is cheap."

"It seems that your lives are on the line anyway." Shaw reflected that informers' lives invariably are. "We didn't offer five thousand, you asked for it. In any event the most we have at the moment is two thousand in travellers' cheques. We could arrange the rest in cash tomorrow through a local bank. Can you get into the hotel without causing a stir?"

"For what purpose?" Tag sounded uneasy.

"We need dry clothes. And our passports and travellers' cheques are in our rooms. We can't go in like this without raising questions. You go to our rooms and bring out what we tell you and we'll discuss terms for your service."

"You have no travellers' cheques with you?"

"I have some in my pocket but they're soaked through. There are more upstairs. Can you get in or not?"

The two men conversed rapidly. It was the first time Frederik had spoken at all but now it was clear that he was quick-witted and intelligent, belying Shaw's first impression. "You can give us the room keys?"

"They are with reception. Is that a problem? When Tag shook his head Shaw added, "There's a grip in my room you can bundle things into and my friend has a suitcase. We'll each need a full change of clothing."

"Getting in will be no problem; there is a service door at the back next to the kitchens. Coming out with your stuff might be more difficult. We'll try."

"It's the only way you'll get paid. Just one thing more:

180

don't try running off with the cheques. If you don't come back I'll put a stop on them and you won't be able to use them and you'll have lost out all round. Okay?"

"We are not common thieves. Give us your room numbers. As your keys are with reception we'll have to manage without them." Shaw and Jill told them the room numbers and Tag and Frederik climbed out once satisfied the car was not under observation. When they had gone it was uncomfortably quiet in the car. It had been a strange experience and neither knew what to make of it. Shaw switched on the ignition.

"Why have you done that?" Jill was edgy.

"So that I can take off at the first sign of trouble."

"Do you think we've done the right thing in trusting those two?"

"What else could we do? We need clothes. We can settle the hotel bill some other time."

"What about paying Tag?"

"Terry's money or not, there's no way they're going to get ten thousand quid from us. They are risking their lives but not entirely due to us. How will we know they'll not spill us a load of bull?"

"You're an ex-copper, you're trained to spot the lie."

He shot her a quick look not sure which way to take the remark but it was hardly the time for joking.

With the engine on, the car started to steam up so he put on the fan and they sat in complete misery as if waiting for their execution, and the possibility was not lost on either. For some reason Shaw began to feel increasingly uneasy. Leaving the engine running he climbed out and took a good look round. The street did not boast the best of lighting but it was far from deserted. The hotel was not in sight from here, and the street was quite short and not exactly fashionable. With the two men waiting in the Opel near the hotel he knew Tag and Frederik were taking a big risk, but like themselves, were in a tight corner.

"I'm just as unhappy as you are about it." Jill had climbed out to stand beside him, keeping her kerbside door open. "This is a crazy situation to be in. We've put ourselves in the hands of two informers, possibly crooks or even killers.

We know Tag is ex-Stasi and have only his word for it that he played a minor role. If Frederik is a mine of information he must have served with them too."

"You started it," said Shaw without rancour. "When you're dealing with someone like Klatt you're not suddenly going to find yourself dealing with the nice guys."

A couple went past and turned their heads before continuing on. "We'd better get back in the car," Jill said. "We've forgotten what we look like. People aren't used to seeing bleeding knobbly knees and torn trousers, not to mention pulped shoes."

It was the best part of another hour before the two Germans appeared. Tag carried a grip and Frederik a suitcase. "We had to find and pack the stuff and then had to wait before it was safe to leave the service entrance. We ran into the night shift arriving."

The only place to change was in the car itself and that would be difficult enough. Tag had included a bath towel which they could use in turn. The Germans agreed to wait outside the car while Jill used the rear seat and Shaw the front as changing rooms.

They changed as fast as they could. Jill was the first to emerge in jeans and shirt with a light cardigan, and flat-heeled shoes. Shaw finally climbed out also in jeans, shirt and pullover, stout shoes, and his wallet and travellers' cheques.

"Thanks very much," he said. "My God, it feels good to be dry." He took stock of the two Germans who were uneasily looking up and down the street. "Is there somewhere we can go and talk? The car is too cramped and might be seen by the Opel crowd."

Tag said, "That's no problem. Let me drive to save giving instructions." He gazed around again and it was clear that he could not get away fast enough. Shaw wondered if anything had happened in the hotel they had not been told about. There was no point in raising it.

"Are you sure this restaurant is safe?" Shaw began to wonder if they should not have stayed in the car. They were seated in a vine-covered L-shaped terrace. Attractive greenery climbed up trellis and there were several arbours which partitioned the place off into intimate pockets. Fairy lights twinkled among the foliage. Somehow the two Germans did not seem to fit in here and he realised he might have provided his own answer.

Frederik smiled, his huge frame relaxed. "We can't afford such a place. We would not be expected here. But as you are paying we can manage." It must have been a joke, for Tag burst out laughing before saying, "It does not close until midnight."

It was now after 10.30. They settled for a simple dish of sauerkraut and frankfurters. Tag had been selective in his choice of table: they were tucked away and because of the time and the fact that it was now chilly the garden restaurant was less than half full.

"So tell us what you know and to avoid confusion, we've grown used to thinking of Maas as Hugo Klatt. Let's keep it that way."

"We have yet to agree a fee." Tag was as practical as ever. "The travellers' cheques now and the rest in cash tomorrow. Say, here at this time."

"Ten thousand is a ridiculous amount. We don't yet know whether you have information to justify anything."

"Ten thousand will just about help the two of us to find a place in the west and to sort ourselves out from there. We are not the lucky ones with false papers; we've been living on our wits." Tag leaned forward to peer at Shaw and to tap the table to make his point. "To you it might be a large sum, to us it will be pitifully little with which to establish ourselves."

Shaw had not discussed it with Jill since telling her he would not pay that amount. He now looked at her for guidance.

She replied before he could ask her the question. "It depends on what Terry is worth to you. You'll have to decide whether what we hear takes us any further forward in that direction. That's all you're here for, isn't it? And it is his money."

183

Shaw knew that it was not all he was here for. His policeman's instincts had taken him well beyond that point and he wanted to know why, and who had driven Klatt to it, at the same time feeling there was something much bigger behind the whole affair. Tag was right, it was pitifully little but both men should be in jail if they were Stasi.

"Okay," he said at last. "But it will depend on our assessment of what we hear. We'll have to trust each other."

The Germans seemed to be satisfied with that, perhaps realising they had no option. Tag gave Frederik a nod and it was he who started once they had finished their meal and had schnapps and coffee before them. He chose his words thoughtfully and at first addressed Jill.

"Joachim was right when he told you that Klatt was a killer but he did it by proxy. Klatt belonged to a Stasi unit called Department VIII, which was known as H8. This was a killer organisation. The hierarchy of the Stasi, and Klatt was one locally, never soiled their own hands by killing. It would never have surprised me if Klatt was an exception, for he was quite capable and would probably enjoy it. But officially it was deemed to be beneath their dignity."

While Frederik talked, his concentration on Shaw and Jill, Tag on the other hand took no obvious interest but acted as look-out, his gaze constantly travelling the terrace and it was clear that he was listening intently to dialogue beyond his own table.

"So H8 employed criminals to do their killing for them. So far as I know, there were nineteen assassins under the control of H8. The amounts paid would vary but £3,500 in your money would be around the average for a killing. There were also other privileges, like sleeping with a victim's wife to get a key impression of her front door while she was afterwards taking a bath. They had stupid code-names, like Karate, and Racing Driver, a whole lot of crazy names." Frederik, certain now that he had their attention, added, "But Klatt's interests went beyond that. Of his own accord he was into crime. And there was a mass of it in the Warsaw Pact countries. It was the only way a lot of people could live."

"How do you know this unless you were involved with Klatt?"

"Did I say I wasn't?" Frederik was not put out by the question. "You have to make up your own minds whether or not I'm telling the truth."

"Would the truth come easily from an ex-Stasi?"

Jill gave Shaw a warning kick under the table, thinking the question provocative. Tag and Frederik were unknowns and therefore unpredictable.

Frederik clearly did not like it but he shrugged it off and even managed a wry smile. "There are times," he said, "when I find it difficult to get used to being out of the Stasi. Suddenly the power has gone. Overnight. And I have to endure that sort of challenge which before would have been dealt with so easily."

For a moment Shaw felt the chill of the threat until he realised that it was wishful thinking from Frederik; that was how things had been, now it was very different and must take a lot of getting used to. "I'm only being practical," Shaw said. "You want money for what you are telling us but it is we who have to gauge the authenticity of what you are saying."

Frederik inclined his head. "As it is clear that you want information that would damage Klatt – you are not here as his friend – I could have told you the exact opposite and whitewashed him. It might be safer if I did that. Department VIII can be checked out. And, I would guess, so could the number they employed and perhaps even some idea of the number of killings. Klatt himself carries much of this information if you can get him to talk."

"What about the ordinary crimes?"

Frederik lowered his head, then glanced at Tag but Tag was checking on some new arrivals. "He was involved with the Poles on car thefts in Germany."

"Poles? Where do they come in?"

Frederik smiled, shaking his head. There were aspects about him that Shaw liked but he concentrated on what the German was saying.

"I thought everybody knew that the Poles ran the car

185

theft industry. Mostly from what was West Germany, quality cars, taken over the border where there is a huge black market."

"You do surprise me." But Shaw made no mention that Kern had already told them.

"That's the trouble with you British. You have little conception of what is happening beyond your own little island. Crime here is nationalised. The Yugoslavs, even now, run the prostitution and gambling rackets, the Russians lead the way in fencing ex-army weapons and also control most of the protection rackets, the Romanians cater for babies and children from adoption to child pornography and the Poles I've just told you about. You would never have made a policeman if you do not know of these things."

Shaw noticed a faint smile from Jill; he did not think that Frederik knew he had been a policeman. "Are you suggesting that Klatt was tied up in all these rackets?"

"I did not say that. Car theft I knew about although not the extent. Perhaps he just played at it."

"Do you know if he did any of this on his own or was he helped?"

"He would have to have been helped."

"Do you think he controlled what he did or was he being controlled?"

"He was controlled by his superiors in the Stasi, but not in stealing cars, I imagine. He would not be the first to have little side rackets. But I don't think that is the answer you wanted."

Jill had not made a response to any of this and repeated glances from Shaw to see which way she was taking it got him nowhere. His knees were hurting where the skin had been ripped off and he had the feeling that he was receiving interesting information but getting nowhere in his enquiries. "What about the redhead?"

Frederik nudged Tag who turned his attention to them. He seemed to be increasingly nervous. "I know no more than I have already told you. Klatt was in Greifswald about twenty months ago having lunch with a redhead. I wasn't going to get near enough for him to recognise me."

"Supposing you made a mistake?"

Tag and Frederik exchanged glances and secret smiles. "Nobody forgets Maas, I mean Klatt, particularly when having worked under him. Nor would those who had suffered by him forget. He is not a man to forget in any way."

Shaw was forced to agree; Klatt was not a likely figure to forget. "Do you know who she is?"

"No. Her back was to me and fortunately she shielded Klatt from sight of me. But I had already identified him. I have no idea what they were saying or planning but whatever it was it was very serious or perhaps I would have been seen."

Shaw felt he would not get much further. "Was Klatt involved in any organisation for the escape of the Stasi?"

They replied in unison but Tag let Frederik continue. "The collapse happened too quickly. Virtually overnight. It was every man for himself. Only later, when things settled down a little, did some form of organisation evolve. But that would be for the hierarchy, not the hoi polloi like ourselves. Klatt himself obviously escaped but we don't know whether he was helped by an underground movement or managed it on his own. He may have had help from the criminals he knew and whom he could finger if it came to it."

They finished their schnapps and ordered more coffee and drank largely in silence. Shaw was not at all certain where all this had got him and he received no help from Jill who seemed to be lost in her own thoughts.

"Have we earned our money?"

"You told us a lot but little about the main issue. We wanted to know Klatt's contacts here and the identity of the redhead."

"You would have to get that from others. We know no more. We have identified Klatt as a member of a death squad in the Stasi and that he was here fairly recently and that he was in at least part of the stolen car racket; what else could you possibly expect?"

Jill put in a rare word: "Pay them the two thousand and

we'll hand over the rest tomorrow, here at this time as you suggested."

"In that case it's lucky I have hundred pound cheques." Shaw pulled out his travellers' cheques and while he started to sign them asked, "We can't go back to the hotel; can you recommend somewhere where we can safely stay?"

"Stay nowhere. Get the hell out of the country as soon as we have the rest of the money."

"That's easier said than done. We need help."

Frederik nodded as Tag rose, still gazing around the terrace. "We all need help."

Shaw handed over the travellers' cheques to Tag who snatched them and headed for the exit without saying a word. He had become increasingly agitated, almost losing interest in what was going on at the table, and now he wanted to get away as fast as possible. Because Tag had all the money, Frederik uttered a quick apology and a "thank you" for Tag and hurried after him.

Shaw and Jill had risen, surprised by the hasty exit and perhaps thinking that they had been conned, when there was a plop like a cork withdrawn from one of the sparkling wine bottles. Tag staggered back awkwardly, threw out his arms as there was another plop, and crashed back into a table at which sat two men and a woman who jumped up startled and frightened, trying to avoid the flying food and drink. The woman screamed when she saw the blood oozing from Tag's chest as he sprawled face up across their shattered table, dead eyes staring into space.

17

The restaurant was suddenly in turmoil. Diners rushed for the exit, most not knowing exactly what was going on and guided by those closer to the crime who were horrified. The woman who had first screamed continued and the panic spread. Staff who tried to calm things down failed and finally decided to get out into the street themselves as two hooded men approached through the terror-stricken diners, guns sweeping as they advanced.

Frederik stood absolutely still, afraid of what he saw and knowing his opportunity to escape was waning. Shaw and Jill who knew why the killing had happened, kept their heads and as Shaw pulled Jill down below table level he called to Frederik to do the same as he saw the two men at the far end of the terrace, one of them standing over Tag's arched body to make sure he was dead.

Frederik was caught in two minds. Instinct told him to escape, to run for it and to jump the nearby trellised wall which ran along a side street. Common sense told him there was no escape without the money Tag still had on him. A gun was already in his hand as he dived sideways, knocking over a table but finishing up behind another. There was another plop and a bullet passed straight through the table where Frederik crouched. He raised his head and fired back, his unsilenced gun like a cannon shot.

Frederik ran from table to table, none of which offered protection from a high velocity bullet but they did hide him from view. The approach of the gunmen was relentless and they spread out to come at him from different directions.

The restaurant was now empty of diners and the sudden silence after the screams and general panic was equally unnerving. The commotion in the street outside was from another dimension. There was a period of stand-off during which Frederik could not be seen and the gunmen were still.

Shaw dragged Jill back to as near to the wall as possible but was operating blind, relying solely on hearing. Jill had managed to open her handbag to produce her pistol and it was one time when Shaw made no argument. They would be top of the agenda for killing and only Tag's abrupt attempt to leave and now Frederik's desperate attempt to take on a fight he could hardly win had kept them till last. They had to get out but that meant showing themselves for the wall was the only route left open to them.

Crouched under one of the tables, by unspoken consent they both eased themselves to a prone position. There were too many table and chair legs to get an unrestricted view, and with two of the tables down it was even worse. But when someone moved it drew attention and they each picked out a pair of legs on which to concentrate. They could only see two pairs and one might be Frederik's.

Why hadn't the police been alerted? The thought flashed through Shaw's mind and gave no comfort. So far little time had passed, the initial shooting lasting but seconds, but how long were the gunmen willing to spend? It was as if his thoughts were transmitted, for the next moment there was a rush of feet, tables and chairs smashed aside as the two gunmen burst forward to finish off Frederik, seeing him as the immediate danger as the man with a gun.

The plop of silenced guns was unreal, but the rending of splintered wood and plastic as Frederik raced from table to table brought back the terrifying truth.

Before he could stop her Jill was on her feet and Shaw was shouting at her to get down and trying to pull at her. At the same time Frederik decided to shoot it out, made one further run and then rose to fire at the nearest man. The gun roared again and one hooded gunman was whipped back off his feet, arms flailing. Before he hit the ground the second man fired and killed Frederik with two quick shots just a fraction before Jill fired at him. He pivoted

190

round, eyes grotesque in the holes of the mask, half raised his gun but dropped sideways as Jill was about to fire again. Meanwhile Frederik had fallen forward across a table which surprisingly held his weight.

By this time Shaw was on his feet. He immediately grasped the outcome of the shoot-out, was about to follow Jill who was already racing for the wall, and dashed towards the dead Tag, recovered the travellers' cheques and scooped up Frederik's gun on the way back. Jill was almost at the top of the trellis when he reached the base of the wall. As he started to climb, the belated sound of police sirens cut through the babble of the crowd still clustered at the front of the restaurant waiting for the police to arrive.

By the time Shaw rolled over the top of the wall and let himself fall, Jill was already waiting for him. They ran as fast as they could in the opposite direction to the shriek of the sirens.

They ran until Jill began to lag and Shaw slowed down to help her. They seemed to be in a respectable area of middle-class houses, in a tree-lined street. They almost collapsed at the foot of a small wall with a hedge sprouting behind it which ran along the front of one of the houses. The street was empty.

They eventually raised themselves to sit on the wall itself, the hedge prickling their backs, while they pondered on what to do. The run had taken it out of them and it was some time before they were breathing normally.

"You killed him," Shaw said eventually. "You bloody well got him with one shot. How many more have you done?"

"They were going to kill us, for God's sake."

"I know. I know." He put an arm round her shoulder as he felt her shiver. "I'm not complaining. You could have warned me first."

"Asked your permission, you mean? God forbid."

"No, not asked my permission, but warned me you were going to do it with one shot. He was a fair distance." He started to laugh light-headedly.

Jill joined him and they sat laughing until she suddenly turned her head to bury it on his shoulder and quietly cried. He held her, rocking her gently like a baby until she stopped.

"What the hell happens now? They won't let us find out anything more here, and they'll work their guts out to stop us using what we've got." Jill spoke softly, almost to herself.

Shaw said, "We're not dealing with a couple of trigger-happy junkies. We're up against an organisation the strength of which we haven't really touched. I said it before: they have us hemmed in."

Jill said, "Thanks for the shoulder to cry on. But this isn't about Klatt, is it?"

"No. This is about what Klatt knows. It has to be, doesn't it? We've got to find this bloody redhead."

Jill failed to respond to that. She said, "Tag and Frederik are dead because Tag lost his nerve in the end. They both had guns and they might have survived."

"I got the cheques back. I had to, they have my signature."

"We can't stay here, Laurie. And we can't go back to the hotel. Did you pick up Frederik's gun?"

"Yes." He still had his arm round her shoulder as he suggested, "I thought about trying to board that Danish container ship. We've plenty enough to bribe anyone for a passage back to a Danish port."

"I'm not keen," Jill replied quickly. "Once on a ship you are trapped. And haven't you the feeling that even though Terry's money is a large sum, whoever we're up against has a bottomless pit of money? What we have is petty cash."

Shaw turned to face her, holding her by both arms. "Right from the beginning I've had the feeling that you know something about all this that you're keeping to yourself. It's only one step from that idea to thinking you are in some way involved and I'm not convinced on which side."

"You really feel that?"

"At times, yes."

"Then you'd better watch your back."

"I'm already doing that."

She ignored that. "Aren't you worried why the police took so long?"

"The telephone wires must have been cut which might mean there was a third man. The restaurant is on the fringe of town so it would take the police a little longer in any case."

"We'd better move on. God knows where." Jill pushed herself away from the wall.

Shaw pulled out the pistol. "It's an old Mauser." He slipped the magazine catch and ran a finger up the side of the magazine to count the rounds. He slammed the magazine back in and checked there was a round in the breech. "Ten shots," he said. "How many have you got?"

Jill did not answer but demanded, "Are you coming?"

Shaw eased himself off the wall. "Have you got a long nail-file in that bag of yours?"

Jill noticed a change had come over him as if he had made up his mind about something. "What do you want it for?"

"To steal a car. I once knew a villain who could teach Klatt a thing or two about breaking into cars. Actually it's very simple."

There were plenty of cars on the street and they chose a Mercedes for no other reason than that the door was unlocked. Jill put her nail-file away. It took Shaw a little time to sort out the wiring but by the time they pulled away it was still not midnight.

"Do you know where you're going?" asked Jill.

"South-west."

She felt better when they were on the move. Only then did she say, "I shot to wound."

She saw his faint smile in the gloom and smiled with him; he would never know for sure.

Beside her Shaw reflected that they were joking about killing people yet for some reason he had no problem living with it. Perhaps it was the only way to maintain their sanity against the attempts on their lives.

"What's happened to you?" asked Jill. "You've changed."

"I've woken up to the fact that I'll dig my own grave if I carry on acting like a policeman. There's no fair way of solving this or even of surviving. Why? Because Terry was murdered or because of why he was murdered? There are

193

so many shadows, so much hidden power that we're being forced back more and more into ourselves. Do we know anyone whom we sufficiently trust to turn to for help?"

"You could start by trusting me."

"I will as soon as you come up front."

They drove as far as Gustrow, about a hundred miles north-west of Berlin. They passed a classic range of sixteenth-century buildings and, in the dead of night, it created a time-warp as if they were going back in history. Shaw had driven south-west instead of directly south, which would have got them to Berlin much sooner, because it was by far the least obvious route. There was nothing much in the way of towns between Gustrow and Berlin. The only noticeable place of which Shaw was aware en route to Berlin was Ravensbrück which had been the site of a Nazi concentration camp for women during the war.

Once beyond Gustrow he swung on to a country lane, turned the car round ready for a quick exit and said, "If you want to sleep, this is as good a place as any. It's too risky to try a hotel in Gustrow."

"Couldn't we drive on to Berlin? It might be easier to lose ourselves there."

"I want to avoid the main roads and autobahns where the car is more likely to be picked up once reported stolen. I don't know the country roads and could get us hopelessly lost at night. And we haven't too much petrol."

Jill sat thinking. "We're not likely to find a gas station at this time of night and if we did we'd be noticed. So if you don't mind I'll take the back seat."

"Gas station?"

"Sure. Petrol. Gas. Fuel."

"That's an American expression."

"So it is. What are you trying to work out now?"

"Gas is what you put a match to. Are you a bloody American?"

"With my accent? You're going whacko, Laurie. I'm going for a walk. Cool down while I'm away."

She was gone ten minutes which seemed like an hour to Shaw. He could not make up his mind whether she

194

deliberately baited him or was just being herself. If he had too many reservations about her she could only blame herself. He wondered how Terry got on with her, a thought which he was beginning to find a barrier; Terry's slap-happy way had probably suited her better.

She opened the rear door and climbed in. "The sooner we get to Berlin the sooner we can get a change of clothing," she said as she spread herself on the rear seat.

"This isn't a bloody shopping spree. The sooner we're in Berlin the sooner our trail will be picked up." It was some time before he tried to get comfortable. He hated sleeping in cars, it reminded him too much of endless hours of surveillance when it was difficult to keep awake. Now he was tired out and beyond sleep.

He must have dozed off, for when he woke dawn was creeping in, his neck and back were stiff and he was at a difficult angle. When he straightened he looked round to find Jill curled up, her head supported on one of the arm rests at an awkward angle. The strap of her handbag was still looped through an arm. He opened his door as quietly as possible and, leaving it open, took a walk up the lane which probably led to a farm.

Farmers rose early, and as confirmation he believed he heard a tractor start up. It was some distance away and he was not sure. He hurried back to find Jill awake and using her vanity mirror to touch up her face.

"We must leave," he said. The first hard shafts of sunlight lifted in wavering spikes above the horizon.

"You won't find a gas station open at this time."

Shaw felt she was deliberately goading him. "You're right," he said. "But we might find some petrol even if we nick it."

"Give me five minutes."

"Sure." While she was gone he tried to calculate how much petrol they had. He was not sure how many gallons the car held, but he did know they had only one quarter of a tank left. He lowered the window right down; it was quite chilly but refreshing at this time of day. Now he was sure he could hear a tractor. The sound grew louder and nearer and then he was not at all sure that it was a tractor. He was suddenly wary and waited with increasing impatience for Jill to return. When she did come she was running.

"Do you hear that?" she gasped as she climbed in.

"The tractor?"

"Tractor, my aunt Fanny. That's a helicopter."

It's not loud enough, thought Shaw. But she was right; it was not a tractor. He switched on and eased the car down the track towards the road and swung south-east. There was no road map in the car but Shaw vaguely recalled there were lakes around Mecklenburg, which they had avoided by their direct route on the way up.

At the moment they were in featureless farm country, roughly divided between the wheat, sugarbeet and maize of the east, and the rye and potato areas of the less fertile west. All Shaw could do was to keep driving but as he did Jill was craning her head to search the skies.

"Helicopters don't buzz like that, they're damned noisy. Stop worrying."

"I can still hear it," she asserted. "Can't you?"

"I can only hear the car engine, and that's not exactly loud." He didn't want to argue again.

They drove on in silence for a while. It was still very early morning, the road so far empty and he managed without using the lights. Then he thought he heard something of the sound Jill had picked up. It was intermittent but definitely not a helicopter or a tractor. He pulled in and climbed out to scan behind them.

The light was improving in spite of an encroaching high ceiling of cloud. They could see nothing. Both picked up the sound of approaching trucks, heavy and ponderous and fairly unmistakable, advancing from the south. They drove off again and Shaw hit the accelerator.

"I thought we were short of fuel? Aren't you burning it up?"

"It's sod's law," he explained. "We need cover as quickly as we can get it. At the moment it's like driving through a desert. It's a gamble but there must be a petrol station somewhere."

196

Two enormous trucks thundered past a few minutes later with headlights on and Shaw saw them disappear in the rear-view mirror. No brake lights came on and he was relieved. They could not expect the roads to remain this empty for much longer. They were putting distance between themselves and Greifswald but safety was something they could no longer believe in.

The buzz became much more distinct just a few minutes later and still they could see nothing until Jill suddenly yelled, "He's right behind us."

Shaw caught just a glimpse in his mirror and then it was gone and now he knew what the buzzing was. A microlight was following almost at ground level, and when he heard a more distinct sound directly above, realised there were two.

There was nothing he could do but motor on. At first he thought it might be the police, then he reasoned that they would use a helicopter with its greater range and speed. The micros suddenly dropped away and out of sight and a little later the reason was clear as another truck thundered up and went past causing a wind blast that rocked the car. When the truck was out of sight the micros reappeared and Shaw simply kept driving on refusing to be intimidated.

When the impact of the first burst of shots striking the rear of the car forced him to swerve they at last knew what they were up against.

Jill kept quiet while Shaw began to zig-zag across the road to make it awkward for them. Another burst pitted the road just in front of them, sending up spurts of dust which disappeared under their wheels.

"I'm going to drive off the road," Shaw yelled. "It's our only chance. As soon as I pull up dive out and get behind the body of the car."

He gave Jill a few seconds to answer, to suggest something better, and when she did not he did some spectacular zig-zagging which threw her around the car, before pulling hard over to his right into the roadside scrub, the tail of the car swinging round in a huge cloud of dust. He heard Jill's door open and as the car stopped he jumped out to crouch behind it, trying to pick out the micros beyond the settling dust cloud.

He was hardly aware of Jill crouching beside him; they could hear the micros without actually seeing them and then there was a terrible thumping the other side of the car as high velocity bullets were pumped into the metal. There was nowhere to run but open country.

The sound of the busy little engines disappeared again and a car flashed past, travelling south, and obviously either did not see them or did not want to. Silence again, followed by the persistent buzz as the micros closed in.

Shaw glanced at Jill's automatic pistol held so expertly. But it was pathetic against a mobile target and at least machine-pistols being used against them. He was holding Frederik's 9 mm but that seemed totally inadequate too. He crept towards the rear of the car and Jill followed, probably reading his mind.

"Shall we go for it?"

She nodded, head tilted to pick up the sound of the micros. Jill said, "Wait until they stop firing and get them as they go past. But only if they're low enough. Otherwise we'll have to sweat it out and wait for the next time."

Shaw swallowed his surprise; she was always surprising him. "They'll keep it up until there's no more bloody car to protect us, for God's sake. It's now or never. Hark at them."

The micros were homing in and they could be seen through the car windows, coming in at almost ground level one behind the other to avoid collision and in order to give sustained fire in two consecutive bursts.

Before they reached the car one micro banked away and Shaw guessed what would happen. "We're being flanked," he bawled. "Get under the car."

They flattened and squeezed under as much as possible while one machine flew at an angle so the pilot could get better aim as he approached, and the other came round the rear of the car. One burst hit the Mercedes flank-on, a door falling half off, and the boot flew up from the burst from second micro. It was a marvel the petrol tank escaped.

It was now or never. They scrambled to their knees as the flanking micro was still turning in order to avoid the first. For just a couple of seconds the machine was side-on to them, the pilot quite visible and, having fired, was momentarily correcting his direction. Shaw and Jill fired repeatedly until the micro swerved away again, and they held their fire to watch. The first machine was circling back to come at them from this side and the second headed straight at it.

The first pilot took immediate evasive action by banking away and the second simply kept going until the micro suddenly dipped and was lost from sight. Neither Shaw nor Jill heard it land but assumed that it had and this opinion was confirmed by the first micro swinging round once again and then circling like an eagle over its prey.

"He'll be back. We'd better stand our ground." Shaw knew they could have few rounds left between them.

The solitary micro turned as if operating on its own, for the pilot could not be seen. It came straight at the two kneeling figures with guns raised straight out by the car. It would have to turn for the pilot to fire accurately at them and they waited for this to happen.

As the micro headed straight at them it rose about thirty yards out to soar over their heads like an angry, giant insect. The pilot fired but it was impossible to get direction from that angle and the shots struck far from the car. As it continued to rise and they turned to watch, a stream of cars came from the north and hummed past. None stopped.

"We've scared him but he'll be back. We must have brought down the other micro." Shaw straightened to watch.

They waited for some time, seeing the micro disappear until it was nothing but a speck and then nothing at all. The buzz could just be heard and then, that too, was gone. They looked at each other uncertainly, unable to believe it.

"Do you think he chickened out?" Shaw was still staring at where the spot had finally vanished.

"Or has gone to get help?"

They ran towards the area where the other micro had presumably come down. "Be careful," Shaw panted, "the pilot might still be alive."

They were now running through what they thought might be fields of young rye. Neither knew anything about farming. Looking for the micro was not easy from ground level but they roughly knew the direction in which it had disappeared and that distances could be deceptive.

It was the taller Shaw who first saw what he thought was the tipped-up wing of the micro and they veered slightly towards it. The shot exploded when they were about twenty yards from it and they threw themselves to the ground.

18

Lying down they could not see a thing. Shaw crawled forward, the hairs rising at the nape of his neck. He signalled to Jill to stay where she was. He thought he was heading in the right direction and simply kept going forward on knees that crucified him. When the micro did not come into view he stopped, considered his options and reluctantly rose, just a little, to get sight of the machine.

He picked out what he had thought to be a tilted wing but could now see was the tailplane sticking up like a sail, almost directly to his right, so his direction had been awry. He continued forward, trying to ignore the pain in his knees and concentrate on the dangers. He was still on all fours when he reached the micro. He veered to come up behind it.

The machine was a crumpled wreck, the tailplane the only part immediately recognisable. The nose was buried into the ground and the momentum from the impact had crushed the pilot with it. He lay head forward and as Shaw crept carefully towards him he felt sick. The face was a mass of blood. The legs were smashed, almost severed, as was one arm. A pistol dangled from one hand and Shaw managed to reach over to take it. The barrel was warm. A few feet away a machine-pistol, thrown out on impact, lay almost hidden on the ground. Overriding everything was the strong smell of fuel and it was amazing that the micro had not burst into flame.

He searched for some reason for the shot and when he could not satisfy himself, called out for Jill to come. He met her just before she reached the plane and suggested she went no further. "He's a mess. There's no point in you seeing him. I think the shot must have been some kind of a reflex action. We'll never know. He's dead and an ugly sight so stay away while I go through his pockets. We might find some ammunition."

While he went back to the micro Jill wandered over to recover the machine-pistol. She, too, could smell the petrol. She gazed back towards the road but it was well out of sight from this distance. She turned back to watch Shaw forage around the bloody mess that had once been the pilot. It was difficult to feel compassion.

Shaw was almost sick as he delicately went through the dead pilot's pockets. It was made more difficult because he had been mashed up with the machine and Shaw had to pull pieces of metal away before he could make a reasonable search.

Jill was growing increasingly nervous. They were out in the open with no protection, for the crashed machine offered none. She expected the other micro to return with help. She called out to Shaw to hurry but he either did not hear or ignored her. When he did finally approach she saw the blood oozing through his jeans at knee level and felt for him.

He looked grim by the time he reached her. "He's too smashed up for me to see whether or not we hit him. There are no obvious signs of shots. If we got him in the legs or arm then only a pathologist will be able to sort it out. The same with the machine; most of the front is buried in the soil. But we must have hit him or the machine somewhere."

Jill let him talk on to release the shock of what he had seen. And then everything changed as he continued.

"Two spare clips for his pistol. They will be useful. The rounds are 9 mm and might fit yours as well. I think the machine-pistol is too difficult to carry around although we need it. But this is the real find." He handed her two pieces of paper which he tried to straighten out for her.

Jill threw the machine-pistol down and then took the pieces of paper from him. For a while she could only stare. They were prints of their faces, and clearly had been taken recently. She looked up at him. "These are faxes."

"Bang on. Faxes with the fax code removed. You can see

202

where they have been cut." Jill did not seem so surprised as he thought she should be, so he added, "Doesn't this mean anything to you?"

"It means someone wants us really bad."

"We knew that already. This indicates the extent. If we didn't know before we know now that a whole network is after us. Which means we're trying to investigate a whole network, not just Klatt and his murderous capers. This is much bigger than we thought, Jill. I knew we were up against it but not to this extent. Faxes? Of our mug shots? That's not a shot of me I have had taken myself; that's been taken without my knowledge."

"The same here. The only difference between us is that I'm not surprised. Look, we'd better get away from here quick. Can you manage with those knees?"

"Sure. But the car's a write-off."

"Then we'll have to hitch."

They hurried back to the road which was now busier, mainly trucks operating in both directions. Shaw examined the car; there were holes punched all over it. Two of the tyres were flat and there was no hope of getting it going.

"Where were these faxes sent to?" asked Shaw. "Maybe we should go back to Greifswald. They must have been sent there."

They were walking south as Shaw made the suggestion and he hesitated. Jill took his arm and forced him forward. "You're losing your marbles. Look what happened to us in Greifswald. The final answer lies in England. It always has. We were forced to come here to pick up bits and pieces. And we have. It's time to get back, Laurie."

"When did you take over?" He felt inadequate and aggrieved. "You're confirming what I've thought all along: you're holding back, as you have all the time."

"You're forgetting I came as your bodyguard. You thought it was a joke. I don't think I've done a bad job, do you?" She kept looking back for an approaching car or truck.

"Do you ever answer a bloody question?" he stormed. "Just for once give me a straight answer, damn you."

"What was the question? You've made some stupid accusations. And you're swearing too bloody much."

He started to laugh at that. "God, you're the limit. How Terry ever put up with you I don't know." Mentioning his brother quelled an urge for him to put his arm round her. It was a feeling that was happening too often for comfort.

She tucked an arm through his and smiled as if that would satisfy him. A truck thundered up behind and they thumbed it to stop but it continued on, a huge moving bulk disappearing south. Neither mentioned it but both knew that the chances of getting back to England alive were increasingly slim. The faxes all too clearly showed the intent and the extent against them. Their banter was a form of armour, a relief against the odds facing them.

"Is there any way we can find out where those faxes came from? That would solve a few problems."

"Not from these mug shots. The answer to that might lie in Greifswald but we might as well shoot ourselves to save them the trouble if we go back. Anyway, they could have been sent to Berlin or anywhere else and sent on from there."

She knew he was in pain but he showed no sign of it. They kept walking, at the side of the road, signalling as each vehicle went by, and accepting that the truck drivers were probably forbidden to pick up passengers. The sun continued to rise, and their shadows shortened, and they simply kept plodding on because there was nothing else they could do. The banter stopped after a few miles and Jill had long since slipped her arm away from Shaw's. It was not the distance alone that wore them down but the certainty that there would be nothing at the end of it. When a car did pull up beside them neither had signalled. It restored suspicion.

Two men were in the car, a Volkswagen like the one Shaw had almost drowned in. They were moderately dressed, in their forties, and offered a lift. The one in the passenger seat climbed out after seeing the blood stains around Shaw's knees. "You had better get in the front," he said. "More room for your legs." He smiled. "The lady can come in the back with me."

204

Shaw got in the front, thanked them for their kindness and Jill got in the back with the other man. There was nothing extraordinary about either man, one lean-featured with sparse hair, the other more firmly built and heavier with a round face and a thick, wild head of hair. Shaw took them to be farmers but kept his hand over the bulk of his pistol just the same. In the back, Jill had placed her handbag on the blind side of her companion, had her hand in it and her gun pointing straight at the back of the driver.

As he pulled away, the driver said, "You look as if you've had an accident."

"Our car ran off the road. The steering went. We've been trying to hitch for the last two hours."

"Engländer? You are English? From the UK?"

"I thought my German was better than that. Yes, we're English. Over to see some old friends."

"Your German is better than my English. But I spent a little time in England. I thought I detected just a trace of accent." He glanced over his shoulder. "Your wife? She is beautiful."

"Yes. We've only been married for a few months."

"So? Good." He grinned at Jill over his shoulder. "You speak German too?"

"Enough to understand what my husband said but not as well as he." They seemed harmless enough but she was uneasy and they had not asked where they wanted to go.

"We're going to East Berlin," said the man beside her as if on cue. "How far do you want to go?"

"That would be fine," said Jill. "We can make arrangements from there."

"You are going back to England? Flying back?"

"We don't know yet. We might stay on for a while. We'll see how it goes." Jill was annoyed that Shaw was leaving most of the explaining to her and felt he was doing it deliberately.

"But you have no luggage," said the driver with a chuckle.

"We had to leave it in the car. It was far too heavy to carry. We'll get someone to collect it."

"Of course." The driver suddenly broke into passable English. "Rotten luck is what you English say, isn't it? What a shame." They all laughed and he slipped back into German. "Was that your Merc off the road about eight miles back? Looked a wreck."

"Probably." Shaw decided to chip in. "Unless someone else has crashed."

"Not often the steering goes on those. Where had you come from?"

There were too many questions, reflected Shaw. "Gustrow."

"Ah! Pretty place. Good time of year before the tourists really build up. And then on to the lakes?"

"Possibly. We hadn't decided." Shaw wanted to be quiet, to have time to size things up.

They drove on in silence for some time but both Shaw and Jill remained wide awake and alert. The man beside Jill fidgeted quite a lot and each small movement brought him closer to her. She would edge away until there was nowhere further to go. Finally she said, "I'm afraid you're cramping me, I have a sore leg."

This produced a tirade from the driver whose benign personality changed in a moment. He spoke fast and harshly and it was not in German. The man beside Jill quickly moved to his side of the car, glaring balefully at the back of the driver's head.

"Do you speak Dutch?" The driver asked Shaw.

"Was that Dutch? No. German is my limit. But you are not Dutch, are you?"

The driver kept his eyes on the road. He laughed a little but it was an effort; he was still clearly annoyed with his companion. "No. But my friend is. I practise on him from time to time. I'm getting quite good." He laughed nervously and lapsed into English again, "I like to bawl him out now and again. Good practice for quick speech."

The tirade had hardly been practice. Shaw tried to get a better view of the driver by half turning in his seat. The driver became aware of the scrutiny and was distinctly uncomfortable.

On the rear seat, Jill sensed something was going to

206

happen. When she turned her head to watch the man beside her, it was at once clear that he was brooding, probably resentful of the driver's forceful comments. He felt her watching him and turned to glare, leaning forward so that she would not miss his surly expression; he obviously believed she had got him into trouble. It also meant that the driver was the man with the authority and of what use would that be between friends? There was something even more convincing: as the man had leaned forward his jacket had opened slightly and she saw the barest glimpse of a gun butt.

She pulled out her pistol and levelled it at the man beside her at the same time saying in English, "They're armed. Tell him to stop the car."

Shaw had the advantage of having both hands free. He produced his gun and told the driver to stop. The extraordinary thing was that the driver made no attempt to argue and expressed anger rather than surprise or fear. The man beside Jill made no move at all as if waiting for her to make the slightest mistake.

The car was pulled in off the road and Shaw backed out first, followed by Jill, both leaving the doors open and guns levelled.

"Get out," said Shaw. "This side."

"Do you want money? We haven't much. We're poor farmers." The driver spoke as he eased his way across and climbed out by the passenger door.

"It's too late for that crap," Shaw said. "And you're not good at it."

The man in the rear followed and somehow looked more dangerous. He stood surly and brooding, eyes roaming quickly, seeking the half-chance. He showed no surprise and no alarm as if he had suffered it all before.

"Someone passing will see your guns," said the driver. "They will call the police."

"Nobody's stopped yet," Shaw observed, making certain his back was to the road and the gun held in front of his body, making it difficult for passing motorists to see what he was doing. He said to Jill, "Disarm them."

She went round the back of them, made them raise their arms sideways and quickly removed two silenced automatics, stuffing them in her waistband.

"Now turn round and start walking," Shaw ordered.

Only then did the two men appear concerned. It was clear that they expected to be shot.

"Move or I'll blow your kneecaps off."

They turned unwillingly and crossed the farmland with Shaw and Jill not too close behind them. When they started to drift towards each other Shaw made them separate again. "That's far enough," Shaw said at last. "Now sit down and take off your shoes."

When Shaw was satisfied, he came up behind one man and Jill behind the other. "Now take your trousers off."

When they protested Shaw said indifferently, "You can die here and now or thumb a lift with your trousers off. It means nothing to us one way or the other. We're giving you a chance. You have five seconds."

They struggled with their trousers because Shaw forbade them to stand. When they were finally off, Shaw told them to stand. "Now walk away from the road until I tell you to stop. And don't look back."

It was then that the real animosity came out. They had been made to look ridiculous and at some time would have to explain to their masters. They stood where they were, defiant and fuming.

Shaw asked Jill for one of the silenced guns and fired between the driver's legs. His aim was not so good and the bullet tore through the dangling shirt and clearly went too close to the crotch. The driver turned white and spun round to hobble over the field as fast as he could, his companion going with him.

As quickly as they could Shaw and Jill gathered up the trousers and shoes and hurried back to the car. They climbed in, took a last look at the hobbling figures, bare legs mostly covered by the crop, and drove off. Three miles further on Shaw pulled in and flung the clothes far into the fields.

They had not spoken until then, wanting only to put

distance between the men and themselves. "We're building up quite an arsenal." Shaw had tried to be flippant but it fell flat as they accepted that they were moving from crisis to crisis.

Without discussing it, they recognised that each attempt on their lives had the hallmarks of haste, one following another without real co-ordination. That had to be a result of their enquiries starting immediately on arrival, leaving little time for competent planning against them. But it was a situation that could not last as repeated failure would increase the pressure against them to end it quickly. At last Jill said, "I don't know how long we can keep this up."

"We'll be all right once we get back home."

"You think that?"

He glanced at her. "I don't know what to think. I'm not sure what we're doing any more. I'm beginning to lose sight of what it's all about."

"Terry."

He shook his head. "I thought that once. This isn't about Terry. I think I'm in over my head. Whoever wants us killed is far cleverer than us, with what seems to be infinite resources. What could be so bloody important to induce these extremes? What danger could we possibly be? And above all what the hell have we wandered into?"

"If we do get home our troubles will just begin. I think you really know that."

Shaw showed his despair as he tried to keep his gaze on the road. "Yes, I do know. I would like to sort out Terry's murder but I don't think we'll ever do it to our satisfaction."

"This is not a situation from which you just retire, Laurie. That won't be allowed to happen."

"I know that too. Why is it you're able to keep so bloody level-headed about it, Jill?"

"Level-headed?" She had trouble keeping her voice steady. "You think I'm some pistol-packing momma? I'm a bundle of nerves. I'm just about holding on."

"Well, you're making a damned good job of it. If you knew it was likely to develop like this why the hell did you come?"

She hesitated for a long time and when she finally spoke

her reluctance was clear. "Because I was told to. And because I really do want to know about Terry."

He did not answer immediately. He sat driving quietly, giving the impression of controlled calm while his mind felt as if it had exploded. "Told to?" It was all he could manage and lacked the incredulity he felt.

"You must have sussed something out. From the moment you saw the gun you knew I wasn't your average girlfriend trying to do right by her man."

"I think I would have been tipped off by one of my SB friends if you were with the Security Service. You can't be with MI5 because they're domestic. Six? Are you with them?"

"No. Nor the police, nor private. I'd rather you just accepted things as they are. It's not just a matter of secrecy; other people are involved and it could cause complications for them if I went public."

"Christ! Telling me is going public?"

The monotonous farmland had disappeared as they entered the long tunnel of pine forests and suddenly it was darker, more brooding.

"You were in SB and should know the form. They can't squeeze out of you what you don't know."

"But they can squeeze it out of you."

There were now far more cars about and the first glimpse of a lake sparkled through the trees as they took a slow bend over rising ground.

"That reduces the chances by fifty per cent."

"My God! You've been brain-washed. Is it that important?"

"If you don't know that yet, you're thicker than I realised. Leave it until later."

"If there is a later. I've a pretty good idea anyway. But I'm not bloody happy about it."

"Nor am I."

They drove on in silence again, the vagaries of the road calling for Shaw's attention. They entered an open area of lake, sunlight, people and picnics, continued on and were swallowed by forests once more.

He thought he heard her sobbing and turned briefly but she was staring straight ahead, eyes screwed up as if the light hurt them, but the light was dull under the continual shadow of the pines; he suddenly felt for her.

"I never slept with him, you know."

It was so unexpected that at first he was not sure about whom she was talking. When he did grasp it, he pulled too hard on the steering wheel and had to make a correction. His mouth was dry and he knew that whatever he said would be the wrong thing so he said nothing.

"He was never my boyfriend."

He could feel her looking at him but kept his gaze on the road. They were living one crazy life after another and he felt he could not cope. Nor could he believe. He made no response at all, his mind numbed as he struggled to concentrate on the driving. He simply did not know what to make of her and that distressed him too.

"Do you believe me?" she asked when he showed no reaction.

He did not know what to say. He wanted to call her a liar, other names that would hurt. From their first meeting there had been nothing straightforward about her.

"You're hurt," she said.

That was something he understood. "You could say that. Just a tiny bit."

"I'm sorry. Really sorry. I don't want to hurt you."

"But you'll do it just the same." Suddenly he did not want to know. "Drop it," he snapped. "Just drop it. As long as I can rely on you to help get us back, that's all I want from you. We need each other for that so let's leave it at that."

Again the silence during which he could feel her shooting him occasional glances. The mood was the worst he could recall. They had endured their ups and downs, she had blacked his eye, still sore and slightly discoloured, they had argued, but they had always finally seemed to finish up fighting on the same side. He had been unsure of certain of her actions and had made allowances for them even when not entirely sure he was doing the right thing. And he had grown fond of her although avoiding the issue, pushing it

211

from his mind with the utmost difficulty. Now he did not know where he stood with her and he was afraid to ask her more about her association with Terry in case he did not like the answers.

He was so screwed up, and so too must Jill have been, or they would have seen the danger long before it was on them. Traffic had thickened and they had run into odd patches of tailback; nothing apparently serious, just a few cars at a time. Because the road was undulating, creeping round lakes and forests, the reason for these minor delays was not obvious.

They continued on, saying nothing more, and the atmosphere heavy between them. At the next hold-up Jill put her hand out to touch his, quickly withdrew it and said, "It's because we're in such trouble that I told you. Just in case I didn't get another chance."

Before he could answer armed police burst from the shelter of the trees and one leaned down to the driver's window to say, "You are both under arrest. Pull over there and keep your hands where we can see them."

19

When they eased over to the side, surrounded by a small army of police, they were ordered to get out, face the car and put their hands on their heads. As if from nowhere police cars now blocked their car front and rear. They were searched and disarmed, and it must have appeared to the police as if they were about to start a minor war. Five pistols in all were collected. They were then separated without getting a chance to speak to each other first.

Because the place they had been stopped at had been thoughtfully chosen a crowd was avoided and motorists were soon on their way. As Shaw was hustled off to a police car he desperately sought for sight of Jill but she seemed to have disappeared. Someone forced his head down as he climbed in. He was furious at his lapse; he should have picked up the signs instead of wallowing in his own emotions. What was particularly galling was that they were less than sixty miles from the outskirts of Berlin. Another hour and they might have lost themselves in the city.

Shaw sat between two policemen, one of whom spoke a little English and insisted on improving it at Shaw's expense until his colleague, who spoke none, told him to shut up. The road still crept through the forests until they began to slip away to their right and fifteen minutes later they entered a small country town with wide streets and a market square. The police station was just off the square and the convoy of police cars brought the sleepy little town to life. Nothing like it had been seen since the Stasi had disappeared.

Nevertheless, the size of the Police HQ in relation to the size of the town was totally disproportionate and smacked of the past. He was taken down to a cell and locked in. There was a toilet the other side of the bed. For what had been East Germany with its ultra harsh regime he supposed he had been given luxury class, yet there was a deep melancholy about the place.

There was constant movement outside the cell: footsteps, voices, sometimes the sound of clinking metal he could not place. What a mess. There was nothing he could do but sit on the edge of the bed and wait to be interviewed but they might not be in a hurry to do that, preferring him to sweat it out and make up a story that would not match Jill's.

They brought him a meal which was not at all bad and he realised how hungry he was. He was beginning to be more than thankful that Germany was now reunited and the treatment he would receive would be that of the West, by intent if not by deed.

Shaw was there for almost two hours before two policemen came to take him to an interview room upstairs at ground level. He had seen so many police interview rooms in differing circumstances that it was almost impossible for him to get used to being the wrong side of the table and to answer questions instead of asking them. The pleasant-looking plainclothes detective who came in, offered him a cigarette which he declined, pulled up his chair to straddle it, giving his subordinate a nod to switch on the tape, could have been himself; he knew every move, even to the uniformed man blocking the closed door.

The usual introductions were made for the sake of the tape and then, "I'm sorry you've had to wait so long but it took the locals a little time to dig me out. My name is Rumer, and my rank is the equivalent of one of your chief inspectors'. If it will be easier for you to speak in English, then, as you can see, I can accommodate you." Rumer had spoken in very good colloquial English which surprised Shaw.

Observing this surprise Rumer added, "I was in Intelligence for a long time. English was always useful. Still is. I've also visited Scotland Yard and Hendon. Wouldn't have missed either." He glanced at his companion. "My subordinate does not speak English. Which is unfortunate if your German is not fluent enough to cope with answering some very serious questions."

The hint could not be broader. Shaw took the German to be about ten years older than himself. There was a curious innocence about his quite good-looking features. A head of fair hair was brushed straight back, blue eyes were steady under pale brows. He had not explained which intelligence force he had been in, east or west, and Shaw was loath to ask, thinking it might be a mistake. "My German is rusty," he replied. "It would be easier for me to speak in English." He noticed Rumer's thin smile of satisfaction and guessed he was well aware of Shaw's fluency in German. Rumer wanted to speak in English and not for practice. Shaw added, "I used to hold the same rank at Scotland Yard."

"I know you did." Rumer pulled the chair round and sat down properly to face Shaw squarely. "Which is why I know this case is far from simple. What would an ex-Special Branch officer be doing with five guns in Germany? Having been part of a shoot-out in a well-known restaurant in Greifswald, after which he stole a Merc and shot down a microlight killing the pilot. It's been all go, Mr Shaw. What a way to spend a holiday visiting friends. You going to tell me about it?"

"I didn't mention I was in Special Branch. And I entered this country completely unarmed."

"I agree with you on both counts. Do you find it difficult being at the wrong end of these questions?" The blue eyes were smiling.

Shaw almost fell for a ploy he had often used himself. The German was portraying himself as an understanding friend, one reluctantly forced to do his duty. "I've found it increasingly difficult ever since I arrived here. We just want to get back home." And then, "You're very comfortable with English, aren't you? And very good indeed."

"I love it. Could live there easily. Pity you can't play soccer as well as us. And it will make it easier for me to get at the truth. So we both feel comfortable. What about some straight answers? One copper to another?"

During the two-hour wait Shaw had debated what to say

215

under interrogation; it depended on the interrogator and now he was not quite sure. Rumer already seemed to know a lot and he wondered if he had questioned Jill. He tried to imagine what she would say, but with great gaps in his knowledge of her it was impossible to guess.

"Do you intend to say nothing? That would not be too clever."

"It's such a long story I'm wondering if it can be condensed. Have you spoken to my friend?"

"Yes. It was part reason for my delay. But I'm not going to tell you what she said. You know the form."

"And then there's the question of how much I can trust you, not as a policeman, in that respect you are simply doing your duty, but as a German. There is still a lot of the old regime in the woodwork of this part of Germany."

"Quit stalling, Mr Shaw. There is nothing I can say to convince you on that score. You don't know me well enough and I might lie through my teeth. Hedging won't help you at all and will merely prolong your agony." Rumer toyed with the packet of cigarettes he had offered Shaw. "At the moment the evidence against you both, for murder, car theft and causing an affray, is so clear, at the same time so bizarre, that I tend to lean towards the possibility that none of what happened is as simple as it seems; one does not just go round shooting micro pilots. But without your co-operation my attitude can change. I'm giving you a more than fair chance. If I wanted an easy conviction then I already have one. What about meeting me halfway?"

"Okay." Shaw told him the story from the time of Terry's murder, well aware that if Rumer was part of the organisation against him he was digging his own grave. It seemed to be the lesser risk as those trying to kill Jill and himself must already know most of what he was saying. If Rumer was straight then it might just possibly help. He condensed it down, left certain things out, portrayed Jill as a zany helping hand who got in the way and knew nothing of the real issues, but by and large covered the body of the affair so that it made some sort of sense.

Rumer made no interruptions and his features gave nothing away as he just sat back and listened. When Shaw had finished, Rumer ordered coffee and, when it arrived, pushed a mug over to Shaw, then sat back thinking. After a while he said, "Are you suggesting that this is all about an escape route for ex-Stasi on the run?"

"That's only part of it. Perhaps a minor part. They have a lot to lose and a mass of enemies and very few friends. What else can they do but run and hope to get false papers?"

"But from what you say they are extremely well-organised and that is what sticks in my gullet. Those capable of being well-organised have either already gone or have been arrested and are serving time. Those who remain are going to an awful lot of trouble to stop you. There is your flaw. You are talking of an international network for a relatively minor problem."

"Not all your compatriots would consider it minor. A good many of the Nazis managed it." Shaw had not wanted to mention the Nazis, knowing the Germans to be sensitive about them.

Rumer suddenly tossed the cigarettes aside. "I don't even smoke the things." He was obviously not satisfied. "Forgive me for saying this, but I can understand your brother being murdered if he discovered something about this man Klatt, who seems to be the Stasi murderer Maas, that could get him extradited and sent back here to serve a life sentence. That I understand. But I doubt that Klatt would have the backing of the type of resources you are talking about."

"I agree. There is someone behind Klatt."

"For what purpose? I think the escape route is too thin."

"If I knew for what purpose I'd have got the hell out of here by now."

"Isn't that what you are trying to do? And if your story has any credence at all, someone is trying to stop you. Do you think the answer to your question lies here in Germany?"

"The physical side. I think that has been proved. There is definitely an organisation only too ready to kill to protect whatever it stands for. But having found out what little we have I think the rest lies in England."

Rumer studied the table, looked up, eyed Shaw quizzically and said, "It's so crazy a story I'm inclined to believe it. You understand that there is no way I can release you. You have to be tried for the crimes committed and self-defence will have to be established. You have no alternative but to go through the courts. It might cheer you to know that we found the dead pilot's machine-pistol where either you hurled it or it was thrown on impact. We think we can raise prints from the corpse and have already raised some from the gun. I hope they are not yours."

"We both handled it. But if it was ours we'd hardly leave it there."

"Again, that's for the courts to decide. There is one aspect which will not please you at all. Greifswald police are sending someone down to collect you. That's where the shoot-out occurred, the first crime, and that's where you'll stand trial."

Shaw felt paralysed. For a moment he could not think at all. It had not occurred to him that they might be returned to Greifswald; he should have considered it, that's what would have happened at home. He had concentrated so much on making Rumer believe him that he had not had time to see beyond that. Of course they had to go back. And he found the probability devastating. "Is there no way round it?"

"You don't trust the police there? Is that what you are suggesting?"

"No. I'm not sure what I'm suggesting except that once back there we'll be buried and not publicly."

Rumer sipped his coffee, wrinkling his nose as he found it nearly cold. "You'd better drink that before it becomes iced coffee." He shook his head. "I don't much like it either but there is nothing I can do, as you well know. Gustrow might make a claim as being nearer to the micro but I don't think they'll get anywhere and I don't think it would help if they did. I'm not absolutely sure what you're worried about. You'd be in police hands."

"Our experience is that there are more powerful forces

than the police. We had been warned by one of the men murdered at the restaurant not to trust a certain member of your State Security."

Rumer grinned. "Nobody trusts members of the State Security. I was one myself for a spell. Care to name him?"

Shaw hesitated but their lives were on the line and he said, "Werner Scherer, though I have to admit he was quite reasonable with me when he interviewed me about the bomb under our car."

Rumer sat forward sharply. "You are paying the cost of generalising. What bomb? Nobody mentioned a bomb."

Shaw got satisfaction from telling him, realising he should have given more actual detail about the attacks on them. "Doesn't that prove my point?" He sipped his coffee. "This is as bad as ours used to be."

Rumer nodded, clearly unhappy at not being advised about the bomb. "I'll do what I can. I'll use one of your expressions that has always amused me: I'll be flogging a dead horse. But I'll try."

"Is it possible to see my friend?" He did not want to use her name not knowing what she might have told them.

Rumer pushed his chair back and rose. "No, you can't see Miss Palmer but you can use her name quite freely now. And you know why. I must keep you apart for the time being." He gave a signal to his subordinate to wind up officially and switch off the tape, then eased the chair under the table and leaned on its back. "You know, I don't like any of what I've heard this afternoon. It's almost as if the clock has been put back and we don't want that. We've cleaned up a lot here but nobody is perfect. I still think you have some way to go and I would rather you did not do this on German soil. If I could prove your story I would apply for your expulsion, but you're in the hands of the law and that must be followed through. I'm simply warning you how it will look to a jury. But I think you know that. I might see you again."

When Shaw was taken back to his cell he felt desperate. Rumer had been as helpful as any man in his position could possibly be. He had conducted the whole interview in English so that Shaw would feel at ease and not intimidated by the presence of the other police officers, but in the end, helpful or not, he had to follow the dictates of procedure even if he accepted Shaw's fears about returning to Greifswald in custody. He supposed Jill had been told the same and wondered how she felt.

From this point time really dragged and his concern switched more and more to Jill. She was extremely capable in an emergency, handled a gun like a pro and in a way that suggested this sort of thing was not entirely new to her, if not the degree. But she was cut off as was he, the difference being he knew about police procedure, what to expect. He should have asked Rumer if she had been warned about returning to Greifswald.

They brought him a meal about eight but by now he had no inclination to eat. He was powerless. He knew what was against him and that in court his story, even if substantiated by Jill, would take a lot of believing. They needed help but he could not see from where it might come. So after nine o'clock, while the protected cell lights were still on, he was surprised when a smiling Rumer came in accompanied by a uniformed officer, and said, "I have good news for you. We have just received instructions from our bosses in Berlin to escort you out of the country. You can stay the night here and tomorrow we'll take you to the airport to catch the first flight to London. You seem to have very powerful friends."

It took a while to sink in. Powerful friends?

An hour later, after the night shift had taken over, four armed police headed by a sergeant arrived to collect the two prisoners. They had come from Greifswald and presented the necessary documentation.

The desk sergeant was confused. He had been advised that the two English prisoners were being returned to the UK as soon as possible the following day. He had nothing in writing as the matter was straightforward, and Rumer had gone home as had others involved. The brief left to the night duty was that the English prisoners would stay overnight. Had someone forgotten to advise Greifswald or, as it appeared, was the escort well on its way and out of police radio control at the time it happened? The sergeant acknowledged the authenticity of the documents but decided to buzz his inspector who was upstairs.

When he had finished he put down the phone and explained to the waiting escort that Greifswald Police had been advised to cancel, and in view of the fact that at that time the police escort was nearer to their point of arrival than departure, would matters please be explained and the escort returned? They were not to take advantage and stay the night.

The desk sergeant explained this in a very pleasant way to the fellow policemen and was therefore astounded when four guns were suddenly pointed at him and the sergeant-in-charge told the desk sergeant to release the prisoners into his care or get his head blown off. Meanwhile, one of the other armed men went round the desk and behind the screen at the rear of it to keep the telephone operator quiet with a sharp blow to the head with his gun.

The desk sergeant did not like the empty expressions facing him. Three men escorted him to get the cell keys, then one stayed with him while the other two went down to unlock the cells.

When Shaw saw a policeman with raised gun ordering him out of his cell he was confused and nervous. "What's going on? We're supposed to stay here the night?"

"There's been a change of plan. You're being returned to Greifswald."

Shaw's heart sank. He thought he knew what had happened and that would explain the raised gun. "I want to see Chief Inspector Rumer. I'm not leaving here until I do."

"You'll leave here feet first if you don't move. So make up your mind which way you want to go."

Shaw stepped out of the cell as a second uniformed gunman came into view with Jill. They smiled nervously. It was the first time they had seen each other since their arrest.

They were taken to the front desk where the desk sergeant was being held at bay well clear of the counter. It was clear that the desk sergeant was waiting for an opportunity to press the alarm and equally clear that the man with him would

221

kill him if he tried. During this time nobody had entered, which was perhaps lucky for them as the four armed men were clearly quite willing to blast their way out. The desk sergeant was told to turn round, and, expecting a bullet in the back, dived for the alarm and received a crack on his skull which put him down and left him bleeding on the floor behind the counter.

There was a general rush for the door, Shaw and Jill being bundled roughly down the steps to two waiting police cars. They were still kept separated as they were pushed into different cars which sped away with a scream of tyres before the doors were properly closed. As Shaw sat there in an awkward position he knew that they would not reach Greifswald and would be taken to some pre-selected place where they would be killed and probably buried.

20

They did not even bother to tie him and they had handcuffs they could have used. One man sat next to him on the rear seat, a gun pointed at Shaw's middle. The driver drove out of town as fast as he could.

Shaw felt so depleted he could have wept. And then he considered how Jill must feel. This was disaster at a time when things had turned in their favour. He looked at the blank-eyed man beside him. They would only shoot him in the car if he tried to escape; cars had a habit of retaining forensic evidence. So he said, "Did you murder the real police? Lay an ambush?" He did not expect a reply but merely wanted to test the man. He wondered how Jill was coping. This was a time when they needed to be together.

It seemed to Shaw that they must have been travelling for well over an hour before the trees closed round them and they were in a dark tunnel, the headlights cascading off the greenery on either side. It was eerie, the more so because neither man spoke and it was claustrophobic in the car with the dark pines rising on either side. The driver was in such a hurry that he refused to dip his headlights on the approach of other vehicles. It reached a point where the driving was becoming reckless and the rear wheels were skidding on the bends. But the man beside Shaw remained unperturbed.

There had to be a turn-off point because Shaw realised there must be a limited time they could safely stay on the main road. It was with this in mind that he prepared himself to take a chance and leap. It would depend on how sharply the driver took the turn.

The turn came without warning. The driver did not slow down but pulled on the steering wheel which made the car lurch on two wheels and Shaw thought they were going to turn over. The gunman next to Shaw was as surprised by the crazy motion as Shaw himself and the effect was to throw him straight at his hostage. Shaw made a grab at where he thought the gun might be, found it and the next moment the two men were wrestling madly.

The driver suddenly slammed on his brakes as a battery of lights made a bizarre film set of the whole scene. The car skidded round in a half-circle, and was rammed by the following car carrying Jill. Shaw hung on grimly to the gun knowing it meant life or death. There was no sound from the driver who had smashed his head against the dashboard.

There were strange, echoing voices from outside the car which Shaw, still having a frenetic struggle with the gunman, realised was someone using a loud-hailer. Something must have communicated itself to the gunman, for he suddenly let go of the gun, slithered over the front seat and opened the passenger door, dived out and ran. There were warning shouts and then a burst of shots as Shaw climbed out on his side. It was then that he could see that the rear door on the gunman's side was still locked to the front of the following car.

There seemed to be police all over the place; in fact he was later to discover there were only six including Rumer and the floodlights were two judiciously placed police cars with headlights on. But it was far from over.

The gunman who had run from Shaw's car lay prone with two police officers standing over him. The driver of the second car was wandering about in a daze and was easily picked up. The gunman who had been sitting with Jill was standing beside his car dazed but cunning enough to point his gun into the car and to shout, "Keep away or I'll blow her brains out."

Everything came to a standstill. It would be relatively easy for the police to pick him off, but he was very close to the car and his gun hand was now through the open window. Shooting him might set off a reflex action and his trigger finger could tighten sufficiently to fire.

"I'll change places with her," Shaw said evenly. He

had pocketed the gun. "I'm the one you want, in any case."

The gunman made no reply to that. He was in a highly nervous state and unpredictable. His only plan was immediate escape. "I want one of the cars," he snapped. "And tear the radio out of the other." He was now beginning to think.

It was at this point that Shaw saw Rumer standing behind the police cars with their headlights on; just a dark shadow, quite motionless. But he took no apparent part as one of the police answered, "Take which one you like. It's up to you."

The gunman felt a trap. "You get in it and drive it past this pile-up, and face the main road."

It was then that Rumer intervened. "So far you have killed nobody. Whatever else you have done you have avoided the really serious crime. Don't step over the line and be a fool. The police you ambushed are all right. We had a call from Greifswald which is why we know this and why we are here. One of them got free and managed to get to a phone. So you see, you did not seriously injure any of them. Now be sensible and keep it like that. Let the woman go."

Shaw was standing in the full floodlight from the cars and could be seen by the gunman. He was still standing near the crashed car and, without moving his feet, simply sunk down out of view. The driver, bloodied head still against the dashboard, started to groan and Shaw reflected there was little time. He crawled along the side of the car.

When he reached the rear he was able to creep round to the second car which had rammed them and still lay entangled. It faced him at right angles and the gunman was now very close but the other side of the car. The two locked cars formed a screen against the police headlights. Shaw kept moving in the shadow of the car hoping he would not be seen. He had drawn the gun and groped for the safety-catch to find it already off.

It was dark behind the car, the headlights throwing a huge image of the pile-up against the backcloth of trees. He came up alongside and raised his head slightly until he could see

225

the arm through the open window the other side and could just detect the gun. He could see no sign of Jill, who might be on the floor. He could see part of the rear seat but not all, so she could be curled up on that.

"You'd better get that car down here quick or she's had it."

The voice, so near, startled Shaw. He tried to evade the thought but had to consider if Jill was still alive. There was absolutely no movement in the car. He heard a policeman moving up towards one of the road block cars but taking his time and he raised his head again to try to get a better view of the interior. The policeman made so much noise that the gunman got suspicious and started to look about him. The darkness behind the locked cars held good and Shaw tried to get himself in a position to aim and realised it was far too risky to fire through a closed car window and there was still the possibility of the man's gun going off in a reflex action. Paradoxically, he now needed more light. He decided to creep round the car and come up behind the gunman who was still facing the police.

The policeman must have reached his car, for there was sudden silence. Nobody moved and everybody was strung out waiting for something to happen and surprised when it did. Instead of creeping round Shaw remained still, for otherwise he would be heard. Then an engine started up and the driver deliberately revved loudly to confuse the issue and, covered by the noise, Shaw opened the door his side to find no sign of Jill.

He felt sick. He withdrew his head from the car, kept down and bawled out at the top of his voice, "She's not in the car."

The police driver was still revving but the gunman heard the call and fired repeatedly into the car through the open window knowing his bluff had been called. The shots came tearing through the metal as Shaw dived flat. The revving stopped, there was a ragged volley of shots and the gunman fell against the side of the car and slithered down, remaining propped up against it when he stopped moving.

There was a rush of footsteps through the bracken and

along the road, a lot of shouting and the next moment Shaw was being helped to his feet and he was asking repeatedly, "Where is she?" They fanned out, the police using their powerful flashlights, and started to search. Logically she would have been pushed out or had jumped on the way up the slope.

It took almost an hour to find her. She was unconscious, clothes torn by the undergrowth off the road, small lacerations to hands and face, but alive. She must have rolled after falling out. She struggled but Shaw calmed her down and told her she was safe. Only then did she open her eyes fully and cling to him.

Four police remained behind with one of the cars to wait for an ambulance and a police wagon, two others took the front seat of the second car and Jill, Shaw and Rumer squeezed in on the rear seat.

On the way back there was no sign of euphoria as Rumer explained what had happened. The original escort had been waylaid about forty miles from Greifswald. There had been two cars with two police in each. They had all been bound and gagged and bundled well off the road and their cars taken. Two of them had worked together to untie each other's bonds, one ran to the road to flag down a car which had a radio phone. Their luck changed from that point.

This had all taken time and by the time the town police station was contacted and there was no reply it was quickly realised that the phone had been cut or the station was under siege. The Chief of Police was contacted and he in turn contacted Rumer who managed to raise two police patrol cars. Some of the ambushed police, including the one who had flagged down the passing car, had heard some of the dialogue between the gunmen, two of whom had talked carelessly under stress. They learned what was to happen but, crucially, they also learned the description of where the final act might take place.

Rumer decided it was too late to go to the station and he reasoned that he would need more men if he did. There was no time. He knew the short cuts through the forests and took his chance. He arrived just a few minutes before the gunmen. In the end it had been everybody's lucky day.

Yet nobody really believed it. It had all been too close. When they reached the police station again Rumer decided to stay for the rest of the night and had a camp bed made up in his office. And it was in his office where the three of them sat talking.

Nobody really wanted to sleep. The cells were still available to Shaw and Jill but they showed no eagerness to return to them. And Rumer made no move to pressure them. Shaw had been disarmed again but Rumer now wore a holstered pistol and had an SMG on his desk, the first time any of his men could recall having seen one in his office.

Coffee was constantly available and they must already have drunk several cups when Rumer said, "We're doing a check on the kidnappers. We should have results on some of them tonight. Okay, so we are a comparatively small station but I don't think the size would have made a difference. They would have still done the job. What particularly worries me is that police uniforms were so readily available. They took no chance on taking the ambushed officers' uniforms and hoping they would fit. They were streamlined for the event. They must have a stock of them. Ready for what?"

He looked at Shaw and shook his head. "You talked of an organisation, now I have to believe. They were able to act very quickly and that is impressive. Their lines of communication must be excellent." He pulled out another packet of cigarettes which he never opened, and fiddled with it. "With no disrespect, I was hoping to get rid of you two and that would have been that. Now I'm landed with the problem after you have gone." He turned to Jill who had largely been silent. "Are you all right?"

"Shaky," said Jill. "That's the second time recently that I've dived from a moving car. I don't think I'm up to it."

"Oh, but you look wonderful. The doctor has done a good job on you, the scratches are hardly visible." Rumer was exuding charm. He waved a dismissive hand. "If the clothes are a little torn they can be replaced as soon as you reach London, but really you bring anything you wear into fashion."

Shaw felt chagrin as he listened, wondering why he could never pour on the oil in the same convincing way.

Rumer had not yet finished. "That was a very important call you made to London. It certainly pulled some strings in the highest places."

"What call?" demanded Shaw, feeling left out.

"But I told you," Rumer replied. "Didn't I say you had friends in high places when I told you you were being released?"

"I made a call to London," Jill chipped in. "I made the point to Herr Rumer that I was surely entitled to one telephone call."

Still feeling left out Shaw said, "Whom did you call?"

"Auntie," said Jill with an enigmatic smile. "She has some really powerful friends."

Shaw did not reply. She was baiting him again and he was not going to rise to it in front of Rumer. She had not taken long to recover.

They talked on, and Rumer produced some schnapps to go with the coffee. They were at a stage when they were so tired they could not sleep. At 2.45 in the morning a sergeant brought Rumer two faxes which he laid on the desk and left. Rumer wearily picked them up, rubbed his eyes and read them. When he had finished he put them down, the expression on his drawn face blank.

"Common criminals," he pronounced. "We have news on three of the men who kidnapped you. One is a released extortionist, the other two have been in crime all their lives as far as I can see. They all have long records but there is something in common with all three, apart from their crimes. None have been arrested in the past three years as though they had all started to lead blameless lives. But we know the lie to that, don't we? So have they been more careful or have they had protection?"

"Police protection?"

Rumer found the reply too distasteful to voice. He sat staring at the sheets, then read them again. He said,

"This really complicates things. I was hoping that this whole business was somehow political, but it does not seem to be."

He turned to Jill again and Shaw thought, here comes the smarm, but Rumer said, "You were unconscious at the time but I think you should know that your friend here offered to take your place when we all believed there was a gun at your head. That's a pleasant thought to take back to London with you."

The police escort was lined up as if they were royalty. An outrider on each side and a car in front and behind. Rumer had taken the threat to their lives seriously, because, at last, Shaw felt that someone accepted the feasibility of a powerful organisation which he and Jill somehow threatened. They had picked up information in Germany and had obviously trodden heavily on some toes, but whom those toes belonged to was quite a different matter and in this respect Shaw considered that they had not got too far.

What had really got to Rumer, and what the other two already knew to their detriment, were the lengths to which the opposition would go. Not just murder but murder on the front doorstep of the judiciary. These people were not afraid of any given situation or, alternatively, were made offers they simply could not refuse. In any event they were very sure of themselves.

At the airport Rumer shook hands and spoiled it a little when he said, "The outriders were merely to impress. I wanted whoever might be concerned to know that we are now on a war footing. Force with force. It is as well they know."

They thanked him for everything for, without him, they would surely not be catching a flight home. They were escorted past all controls and straight on to the aircraft. Rumer came aboard and told them that security officers would be standing by the boarding points to scrutinise passengers. They were leaving him with a big problem but he would now have national help. That the machinery of German security could be so roused was impressive and somewhat frightening.

After Rumer left the aircraft and Shaw and Jill sat side by side they felt as if a protective shield had been removed. Before they realised what had actually happened they were fiercely holding hands and did not want to let go. They had arrived on their own and were now departing on their own. But a lot had happened in the interim and they knew that at times they had been very lucky.

Once they took off, illogically, they felt more exposed as if they were surrounded by the enemy and there was no possible escape. It might have been a reaction to what they had already suffered but they were unsure of themselves. Shaw found he was unable to ask any of the many questions which had crossed his mind about Jill's part in all this. He was afraid of upsetting the contact and the obvious need of each other that had developed. They held hands most of the way back, breaking away only to eat or drink.

When they bumped over the English coast, now in deep cloud, they were still holding hands, even hurting each other by the tightness of their grip. They had to do up their safety-belts and when their hands crept back into each other's grip, they were still tense, and on landing, remained seated while everyone else hustled to get off.

When they did finally emerge from the aircraft they were still holding on grimly to each other and relaxed only when a police escort closed in on them and took them away from the usual formalities. There was a split second of panic on seeing the police, remembering the escort which had come for them only the previous day, but it was over the moment Jill recognised a man Shaw last recalled seeing with her at the Coroner's Court during Terry's inquest; he was obviously in charge of the security arrangements.

The scale of precaution was as impressive as the one in Germany but it made Shaw realise that another factor had come on the scene. Police protection now made them official and that turn-round could only have taken shape from the moment of Jill's phone call to London. And that made her official too. It also illustrated only too clearly that they were far from being out of danger.

On the drive into London it was not easy for them to speak while a plainclothes man sat in the back of the Daimler limousine with them, and two in the front. Shaw began to feel uneasy again but for reasons far divorced from a sense of danger. He began to feel inadequate, that he knew less about this affair than anyone else. Worse than that, he now had the strong feeling that he had been used.

He had no intention of starting a row in the car but he at least expected to be taken home. Instead they were taken to a house in one of the old squares in North Kensington, close to the Portobello Road, and escorted inside, and only then were they left alone.

"What's going on?" Shaw demanded even before they had entered the pleasantly furnished lounge. "I've been taken over."

"We're being protected. We'll be quite safe here."

"As safe as being locked in a prison cell? That was bloody safe, wasn't it? I want some answers, Jill; I'm tired of being the monkey."

She went into a very modern kitchen and put the kettle on. "That doesn't sound like the man who offered to take my place because he thought I was going to be shot."

He followed her in. "I was in shock at the time. Didn't know what I was saying."

She had filled the kettle, switched it on and reached for some cups on wooden pegs. "Tea or coffee?"

"Answers. Without milk."

She turned to find him close behind her and the next moment they were embracing as if trying to crush the life out of each other. They clung for a long time, kissing and murmuring but Shaw still felt the obstacle of his dead brother even in the depth of passion. Sensing his resistance Jill whispered, "I was his bodyguard like I was yours. But they tucked him away where I couldn't get at him. I'm sorry, Laurie. So sorry. But we were never lovers or even close to it."

As he carried her from the kitchen for once he wanted no further explanations. They could wait forever.

Later they both bathed and then she cooked him a meal. There was an array of clothes in respective built-in wardrobes and they clad themselves comfortably. When they had finished eating they put the crockery in the dishwasher and went back to the lounge to relax. But although they sat side by side with arms around each other, they knew that this was no longer the time to relax.

Shaw examined his feelings which had done a complete turnabout. He no longer wanted her to explain anything, feeling that if she did he would lose her forever, that her replies would put a tremendous barrier between them which he could never break down. It had taken the openness of their passion and love to tear away the old squabbles and place everything on a different footing. In its way it was a new kind of torture but one he was willing to endure. He did not want to lose her and she had shown that she felt the same.

Matters could not be swept under the carpet. They had to be explained. Jill said, "My aunt should be here some time this evening. Let's leave it till then." She did not have to explain what she meant.

He expressed his only surprise by saying, "There really is an aunt?"

"Oh, yes. You'll know her when you see her."

The doorbell rang about half an hour later. Shaw broke away, "I'll get it."

"Come back," said Jill, hastily tidying herself. "The security boys will take care of it. Whoever it is must be screened."

"We're in a goldfish bowl," he ejected in some frustration.

"Are you complaining?" Jill smiled. When she heard the special rap on the door, she said, "This is her. Brace yourself."

As Shaw watched her cross the floor he could only marvel at the dramatic change in their relationship. At the door Jill looked back nervously, blew him a quick kiss, and opened it.

21

She was a tall elegant woman, with an intelligent, rather than an attractive face and Shaw recognised her at once. In the manner she greeted Jill it was obvious to Shaw that she was well capable of deep emotional feeling; there was huge relief in the way she embraced Jill. And then she was holding out a gloved hand to Shaw and saying, "I'm so very grateful to you for looking after her. I can never thank you enough."

Shaw's immediate reaction was not that he was shaking hands with the head of MI5 but that it appeared she really was Jill's aunt. "She denied ever being with the Security Service," he said, for the moment at a loss for any sensible words.

"Well, she's not really. Shall we say she is affiliated, doing her old aunt a favour. Not for the first time, I might add."

Old aunt? That was the least impression Judith Walker gave. But it was clear that Jill was employed by the service in some way.

"Do you play rugby, Mr Shaw?"

"Back in the dark ages. Do please sit down."

"You are that old? Well, you will understand if I describe Jill as one of my loose heads. Special operations like her father before her. As you can see it runs in the family. There was an anxious moment when we wondered if you might remember her in some past operation or other; you did know a good many people in the department when you were with Special Branch."

"She would not have been someone I would forget."

"I hope not. Could I please have a drink? A neat strong malt would do nicely."

Jill got the drinks, seeming to know where everything was. When they were all seated Judith Walker, having critically tasted her malt, said to Shaw, "We really do owe you the most profound apology but we had to wait and see just how far you would go with this thing. A good many people want to avenge for one reason or another but do not often go the whole way, certainly not enough to put their own lives on the line. You have done that rather splendidly."

Shaw was trying to keep his gaze away from Jill and she helped him by riveting her attention on their visitor. The effort on both their parts did not go unnoticed.

"It helped that you were convinced your brother was murdered. He was, of course, but we were not sure of exactly why, though we could guess, and why exactly he agreed to go to prison."

"Agreed? You mean he committed no crime?"

"None that we know of. It is far from the first time that implants have been used to suss out information from another prisoner. But we were more than halfway to believing that, while that might have been the reason for asking him to do the job, he was actually put there to be killed. He knew something that he might not have realised he knew or he would probably not have fallen for it. We shall never know for sure. But I'm convinced that Klatt was ordered to kill him, for whatever reason, and that Klatt insisted that he needed help; which I am sure he did. It might even have been an extreme measure to keep Klatt himself in line as it seemed that he was getting careless and resorting to old pastimes probably just for a perverted pleasure. We would need to know the inside of the mind that planned it but I doubt we will ever have that privilege."

"Privilege, Miss Walker?" Shaw was shattered by the assessment.

"Privilege, Laurie. A mind as cunning, as astute, as sharp and variable as any mind can be in our business; a brilliant mind. We have more than a good idea of who this person is; let's not be coy, we know who it is and we have for some time. I will go so far as to tell you, because by now

235

you must have guessed, if not before, that the person is a member of SIS. And an excellent one too. It is a flaw in the make-up that has created a disease which has spread God knows where. I am not exaggerating. You have experienced some of its effect. And I am sure you will see no cause to argue."

Shaw sat with one leg resting on the other, drink in hand, ostensibly relaxed, but inwardly harbouring a combination of incredulity, anger and hopelessness. "Why has nothing been done?"

"You call what you and Jill have been through, nothing?"

"Two people? You head a whole organisation."

"I could not use recognised operators. I dared not. It only needed the odd inter-departmental word for the thing to collapse. The person concerned knows a good many of our people, top people, including me. There was also a problem with MI6 who do not like it suggested that one of their members is unsafe. It was an opinion that had to be kept from the administrators there, in the event of them closing ranks. So far as I know only one person there knows and he is not at all happy. It had to be attempted on a small, limited scale which would attract nothing but derision and at first that happened. And then, with Jill's assistance, you became too successful and they tried to do to you what they had already done to your brother. The difference was that he had nowhere to run."

Shaw looked to Jill for help but her gaze was elsewhere as if she knew of his torment. "Are you saying that MI6 would close ranks on a traitor?"

"I didn't mention traitor. That is not the problem. Don't push that issue any further at the moment. There are still things to do."

"Can't it be wrung out of Klatt?"

Judith Walker shrugged. She finished her drink and looked to Jill to provide another. "I doubt that anything would ever have been obtained from Klatt. He was crude, tough, hard as nails and had far too much to incriminate him for him to confess to any of it."

"Was?"

236

"He passed on yesterday. He had violent stomach pains and died in agony in his cell. As it takes a little time to get a visitor's pass his death must have been planned at least some days in advance. Probably something slipped into his tea or coffee at visiting time. The post-mortem will tell us what. Klatt was the ultimate loser. He is of no further help. He killed your brother but was not executed for that."

Shaw sat forward, fingers intertwining. "Does anyone know who the visitor was?"

"Oh, yes. You know of her. She must have been getting desperate to take a risk like that, particularly as I don't think she was in any danger from that quarter. It shows she is not willing to leave anything to chance. But all we've come up with is the name of Molly Winters and an accommodation address. We need far more than that. Knowing is far removed from proving, and in the end remains no more than an opinion."

"What about Johnnie West? He must be feeling very vulnerable by now."

"He has already made application to see the governor. He might feel it safer to confess his part in killing your brother and is now well placed to put as much blame on Klatt as he likes. But West knows nothing. He would have been paid through Klatt who was operating for the woman."

"Obviously Molly Winters is your suspect at MI6. Who is she?"

Judith Walker remained looking at him dispassionately, then turned to Jill who seemed to give the slightest nod of the head. Even then there was delay and the decision was clearly difficult to make. "You understand fully that although you resigned you remain for life under the oath you took for the Official Secrets Act?"

"I do realise that and I don't need to be reminded. As well as Jill's, my life is on the line and we're lucky to be here. My brother's murder was arranged by this woman and if, for one moment, I thought I was being sidelined under the pretext of security I will go public here or abroad."

Jill clapped softly and gave him a wicked smile. Judith

Walker also smiled but was not influenced. "You are forthright, Laurie. No good at all for counter-espionage. It is Veida Ash. I'm telling you because you still have a part to play if you want to nail her for your brother's murder. Did you come across her while you were with SB?"

"Not that I recall. I've never heard of her. Can't we tie her to Molly Winters?"

"She's been too clever. She arranged the implant with the prison authorities and, of course, her reason is quite different from ours and more plausible. The prison can't be staked out permanently and if it was she would soon know through her various contacts. Yet we must close her down."

"You say she's not a traitor?"

"Her intelligence work is probably the best in recent times. She has done splendid work in the European sphere which included the Soviet Union before it cracked up. She was a master of intelligence gathering. As for patriotism she cannot be faulted. Her loyalty to her country is not an issue so far as we know."

"So what's the problem? She sounds like God's gift to SIS."

"Do you think I could have another malt, dear? The last one was on the small side." Judith Walker waited for her drink before replying, "We're not absolutely sure. We stumbled into a bank account that led back to her. At the time we were investigating someone else. It was one of those fortuitous mistakes that sometimes fall the right way. That led to further investigation through the banks, which took a long time, and we produced a possible link again. On the evidence of those two issues, Veida Ash is an immensely wealthy woman. We believe we have barely touched the tip of the iceberg. We are still searching the banks, never an easy thing to do and the world has a lot of banks. We have an idea what she is doing but the ramifications are so vast that we must tread very carefully indeed."

"She must know she's under suspicion. Won't the bird fly?"

"She might. But I don't think she will because she is still silencing those she sees as a threat. And she would see it as an admission of guilt and an affront to her ability." Judith Walker suddenly smiled. "She is so sure of herself that she used us to keep tabs on you. A clever move which suggested she had nothing to hide."

Shaw got up and poured himself a drink. He remained standing, restless now. "She can't be all that bloody clever," he said in frustration. "There must be weak links somewhere."

"There are always weak links. It's a matter of finding them. You two found some. They will turn out to be very useful, in fact they already have in terms of intent. But they are not quite enough."

"You think she sent the faxes of our mug shots to Germany?"

That particular story had not yet been covered and Jill obliged.

Shaw had difficulty in accepting the situation. How could anyone be so efficient as to keep at bay an intelligence chief apparently dedicated to destroying her. It was money, of course. If she was that wealthy, protection could always be bought at a high price. "Why don't you just kill the bitch?"

The two women were not as startled as he thought they might be. Judith said, "We would like to be more sure of the reason."

Shaw could not tell whether she was serious. But anyway she clearly thought she should have no more malt and rose to her feet and stood as steady as a guardsman.

"I'm keeping you two under protection until we either get more information or decide what to do. I have yet to convince my opposite number at MI6. It is not a pill he wants to swallow and he's hampered by not being able to use his own personnel on the case, because our Veida would be likely to hear. Unless we can really get to the bottom of it Veida looks like staying until retirement and that's a very long way off. She clearly relishes her job."

"She needs the job to cover whatever she's doing. And I think you know full well what she's doing."

"That openness again. Well, I must be off. I'll send a

couple of men around some time tomorrow morning, not too early, for a full debriefing." Judith Walker gave her warmest smile yet, looking from one to the other. "Meanwhile I'm sure you will find something to do."

After she had gone Shaw collected the glasses and took them into the kitchen. "How did you actually meet Terry?"

Jill put the glasses in the dishwasher. "Judith picked up some information about him. He had been doing odd jobs for Six, useful at times. I think he must have done something for Veida and it must have rung a bell. He led a wild life, as you know, and knew people he was best away from; it's possible they had a common contact which she learned about and realised he might put two and two together and begin to wonder what she was up to. She didn't give him the chance.

"It took time for me to get friendly with him and it was really already too late. I duplicated the key to his flat, which is why I had such easy access. It had to appear I was his girlfriend. Keeping it platonic was a problem but he had plenty on his mind and we were not together very long, and eventually the problem was solved when he was suddenly arrested, tried and sent to prison with hardly any time in remand. It was clear then it was a set-up. And I'm quite sure it was Veida who put the boot in with the prison authorities to stop me going there. He was plucked and ready for slaughter." Jill put a hand out to him. "I'm sorry, Laurie, I should never have put it like that."

"It was true, though, wasn't it? I'll get that bitch if it kills me."

"It probably will, so don't try. We've had enough. If you think I find it easy to shoot at someone, even to save my life, you should know it takes me all my time not to throw up. The after-effect is dreadful."

They went back into the lounge to sit together. "It's no use, Jill. We've come this far. I can't sit back and let her get away with it. I have a name now. You had it all the time. Okay, I understand there was nothing you could tell me then, particularly the way we were

240

carrying on at the time. But I don't intend to let this go."

"Just what do you think you can do? We've done our bit, more than our bit. Let Judith sort it out from now on."

"She's hampered. She admitted it. Can you see someone like Veida Ash standing trial for whatever it is she is doing? Do you really think there's a chance of tying her to Terry's killing? Do you? Klatt was the only one who could have done that and she's taken care of him like she did Terry."

"Look, I know how you feel. Let's go to bed." She stroked his face tenderly. "Why the hell I feel about you the way I do I'll never know. You're an awkward sod, Laurie. Stubborn and difficult."

He took her hand, kissed it, then reached for the phone. He rang his own number. It was some time before it was answered and when it was the voice was slurred. "Max? Are you going through my bloody whisky?"

"Guv'nor? Guv'nor, is that you? Where the hell have you been?"

"Never mind. Sober yourself up by tomorrow and don't leave the place until you've heard from me."

"There are some bills that need paying. Arrived while you've been jaunting around."

"Then pay them. In lieu of rent. But be fit by tomorrow."

He hung up before Max could ask any more questions.

"Just what do you think you intend to do?" Jill asked cautiously.

"I'm not absolutely sure yet. I have a half-baked idea I'm working on."

"Any half-baked idea will get you killed. Please don't do this to me, Laurie. For God's sake, we've only just found each other."

He took her hands. "Jill, I don't think I'm stupid. I know what I'm up against."

"That's just it, you don't. You don't seem to have learned. She's on home ground. Just think what she managed by remote control in Germany. I know how you feel about Terry, but please let it go now. Please. For me."

241

"Tell me first what you know about Veida Ash."

She was scared. She could temporarily take his mind off the idea but the impulse would return and it was the wrong mood in which to start anything, especially against someone like Veida.

He said gently, "If you don't give me what you know I shall have to find out the hard way and if she's as cunning as everybody seems to think she is, then she'll get to hear of it. If you tell me, she won't."

"I don't know much. Her parents were West German, Bernard and Ingrid Gemund. The two families, life-long friends, escaped from Germany in 1938 and came here. The elder boy and girl of each family were childhood sweethearts and in their late teens when they arrived. The reason he escaped military service in Germany was because he was still at university studying engineering. They married here after the war and returned to Germany to try to do their bit to get Germany back on its feet, found the changes too difficult, and returned here in the early fifties where Veida was born. I think she's in her late thirties.

"Her father died soon after she was born so it was her mother's influence alone that directed her. I believe in her early years they went to Europe, and Germany in particular, quite a lot. Not surprisingly she was very close to her mother who I believe is still alive in a nursing home on the south coast. They have never been short of money. Her mother was a highly successful business woman."

"Well, couldn't that be the source of Veida's wealth?"

"They were well off. Very comfortable. What Judith was talking about was immense wealth. Multi-millionaire status."

"Have you never heard of investment growth? Come on."

"You'd have to take that up with Judith. Does it matter to us?"

"To get things in perspective, certainly it does. Is there a Mister Ash?"

"When she was in her early twenties she married a

242

young stockbroker. They divorced after eighteen months. I understand marriage didn't suit her. Since then she just picks a mate and dumps him once satisfied."

"Like a spider."

"A spider devours."

"Ain't it the same? But you are still talking money, Jill. A stockbroker husband. A wealthy mother. Veida wouldn't have been short, would she?"

"Laurie, I can't tell you any more. I've already broken a confidence in telling what I have. This is vetted information from MI6, and Judith could only have raised that from Sir Charles Melville direct. I'm not an analyst. For God's sake play the game."

"But Judith told you."

"I couldn't fly blind. I had to have some inkling and I've been involved officially before you arrived. None of us were sure of you then."

He was not satisfied. Fortunes can be made out of small, skilfully handled investments over a number of years and it would seem that Veida Ash had already had two bites of the financial cherry. Why shouldn't she be loaded? From an intelligence point of view she was ideal. Financial independence, no marital problems, completely Europeanised, and spoke German like the natives her parents were, and probably other languages as well. No wonder she had been successful.

"There's something about all this that simply does not add up," he said at last. "She must have already been rich, so what the hell is her incentive for more?"

"That's how the very rich operate. They always want more. Money is power. The more money the more power. And power corrupts. You know all this; everybody knows it, so just what are you on about, Laurie? Cool down."

"If it was the accidental stumbling across some of Veida's banking that seemed to have started all this, I can't understand the surprise. And it couldn't have been that well hidden or it would not have been found. I reckon it takes one hell of a lot of unravelling if money is really well hidden. Look at the Mafia money; if anyone can find it."

He suddenly went to the window and looked out. There was nobody on view.

Jill watched him, thought she saw a change come over him. He certainly became more reflective. "I have only been told so much, darling. You must know that as well as anyone."

He turned his back to the window and smiled across at her. "We should be making mad passionate love instead of letting this thing come between us. It's taken it out of us, Jill, we're not reacting as lovers should."

"Most lovers are not suffering the kind of danger we've been through and don't find the necessity for bodyguards outside the house." What was he up to?

"I ought to ring that journalist who helped me, Peter Givens. I owe him a story."

Jill was startled. "You can't tell him anything. Laurie, are you feeling all right?"

"Fine. Look, I must ring Max back. I was rather harsh with him. He was very helpful to me before we went to Germany."

"Go on, then."

"Is there another phone somewhere?"

"You mean you don't want to speak in front of me?" She stood up, hurt and furious.

"Well, it will be men's talk, joking and that. Only be a minute."

She angrily threw a cushion at him and went into the kitchen. But part of her anger was feigned. She ran the tap and then returned to the partly opened door, keeping out of sight.

Shaw stood with hand on receiver for a while. A wild anger was building up in him. He had tried to apply logic when there was really no place for it. When it came down to it the bitch had had Terry killed to protect her own skin and that was something he could not let go. It was his problem, he was not concerned with the ramifications of where her wealth came from or what effect it might have on the Security Service. They could sort out their problems and he would sort out his.

244

His hand was trembling as he dialled, forcing him to re-dial. He said into the phone, keeping his voice as low as possible, "Sober up for God's sake. I want a gun, Max, by tomorrow, and I don't want rubbish. Pay as high as you have to."

22

"Have you finished?" Jill moved back from the door as she heard him put the phone down. She was moving things around, anxious, having picked up his brief, whispered instructions.

"That depends on you." He came into the kitchen. "Where does Veida Ash live?"

She turned to face him, her back against the kitchen counter. "Do you really expect me to know that? And before you ask I don't know what she looks like either."

"You know quite a lot about her, why not her address?"

She was doing her best to hide her anxiety. "Addresses are different. I don't know it. Anyway, what would you do if you had it?"

He did not answer but asked another question. "Do we really have to have bodyguards all the time? I ask you? We've managed without them so far."

"If you haven't noticed, Veida is getting desperate. And we're a prime target. Yes, we do need protection and I'm grateful for it." She was searching his face but there was nothing to glean from his blank expression. She was afraid for him and for herself, because just then she did not think that she mattered to him either. He had just one thought on his mind and it was crippling him.

"I want to go for a walk. Just to get some fresh air."

"There's nothing to stop you. Don't I come too?"

"Bear with me just this once, Jill. I want to think certain things over, clear my head. Of course I want you with me, but you'd be a distraction for all the nicest reasons. I love you. I don't have to tell you. Just give me a few minutes."

"You don't intend to come back, do you? You want revenge even if it breaks us up for life."

"For God's sake, I'll have your goons following me. You think I'd throw you away so lightly? I just want a few minutes alone to sort something out. The last thing I want to do is to hurt you."

"But you already are. You've made up your mind about something and you're excluding me. Don't do that to me, Laurie, not after what we've been through. Whatever it is you have in mind let's do it together."

"Like sorting out Veida Ash?"

"You'd never get near her. And you know it. If you think you can, then you really have flipped. Don't leave me now. Leave it to Judith."

He crossed the kitchen and put his arm round her shoulders but she at once felt his tension. He was trying to appear relaxed when he was anything but.

"I'm sure Judith is extremely capable or she wouldn't have the job. But even if she gets the evidence she needs this thing will never go public; we all know it. Veida will be dealt with, punished, dismissed the service but she'll still not stand in court charged with the murder of my brother."

"It could never be proved. We all know that."

"Okay, let's choose Klatt who deserved what he got but she put him up to it. If not Klatt what about Frederik and Tag and Jody Marsh and God knows how many more? Will she stand trial for them?"

"I don't know. I don't make those sort of decisions."

"You know damn fine, Jill. It will all be swept under the carpet. In the interests of the general public, of course. She'll lose things that mean a lot to her but will still avoid the real punishment. And she'll still be rich. What's happening now? Is a deal already being struck? If the goons are suddenly taken from us we'll know then for sure. If we can't do it, then let the Germans handle it. A lot has happened on their soil. Let them have her; they have enough to put her away for life. All they want is the identity. So let's give it to them."

"You mean you just telephone Rumer and say the person

you want is Veida Ash. There are times when I wonder how you ever became a copper."

"That's been said before. Well, if plan A won't work I'll have to resort to plan B."

He was now trying to make light of it while all the time she knew he was totally occupied in finding a way of making Veida Ash suffer for what she had done.

"I'll take that walk," he said, taking his arm from her shoulder.

"I'll come with you." She went into the hall to get a light jacket.

When she returned she smiled radiantly at him; it took considerable effort. He stared at her, and just for a moment he was almost willing to forget about Terry, then the moment passed and he realised he could never do that. If he had somehow failed his brother in life he could not now fail him in death. Anyway, they had come too far to allow that to happen. "I've changed my mind," he said abruptly. "You're right. Let Judith get on with it."

It was a while before she slipped off the jacket. She did not believe he meant what he said, but felt he had changed his mind for her sake. He did not want to hurt her but it was inevitable that he would, no matter how reluctantly. She doubted that he had yet reached that conclusion. He would wriggle, try to find a way, but in the end his obsession would win simply because it had eaten into him for too long and he was trying to put right what he saw as a personal failure.

She wondered when it would happen. In the event she was fast asleep when it did. They had gone to bed and made love as if it was the last time they would spend together and the thought must have been in both their minds.

When he left the bedroom he looked back at the pale glow of her face, hesitated for a moment as he realised the possibility of not seeing her again, briefly looked to the future and accepted that he would never forgive himself if he let matters ride. He carried his clothes down the stairs and dressed in the hall, made sure he had some money and loose change and went to the front door.

He opened it, surprised by the sudden rush of cool air when it had been so hot during the day. He stood on the steps, closed the door quietly, and then went down them. It was 3 am. The moon shone on windows and cars, giving strange, dull reflections. There was no sound at all, not even from the man following, whom Shaw acknowledged as part of the first team put on to guard them. As he reached the street he said to the shadows, "You might as well come with me instead of trying to keep out of sight. I don't expect to be out long."

A man, shorter than Shaw and moving very quietly slipped in beside him. "Funny time for a walk, isn't it?"

"I'm calling on somebody. Thought it better to do it at night with nobody around." Shaw gazed down at the figure beside him. "It will make your job easier, too. I take it you're not alone."

"One man would be no good. I'm part of a detail. You're a nuisance doing this, because it puts more strain on the rest. I'd better report in so nobody panics." They had already turned a corner when the escort lifted a two-way radio to his lips and at that moment Shaw hit him on the back of the neck, and, as he fell, again on the jaw. He caught him awkwardly and pulled him up the nearest steps to prop him out of sight in the porch. He crushed the radio with his heel, again and again until he was satisfied it was smashed, then searched the escort. He found a Smith and Wesson automatic and a spare clip. He no longer needed a gun from Max Fuller.

He felt sorry for the man, who had no other idea in mind than to protect him. But he was now armed and could protect himself. He did not think his escort was in any danger or he would not have abandoned him. He continued walking, searching for the oasis of light from a call-box. He walked some way before finding one. He rang the home number given to him by Peter Givens.

Givens answered after some time but was not as irate as Shaw expected him to be; perhaps newspapermen were used to early morning calls. When he realised it was Shaw ringing he brushed off the dregs of sleep and was immediately alert. "Where the hell have you been? I thought you must be dead."

"Someone had several goes at it. It's part of the story and will have to wait. Do you know a woman called Veida Ash? Works for Six."

"No. I can try to find out from a colleague who covers intelligence matters, writes books about them. But not tonight. He won't be used to the deadly hour like some of us."

"I want to find out where she lives."

"They don't all live in ivory towers. Have you tried the telephone directories?"

"Supposing she lives outside London? I thought you might have a quick answer. The odds are, though, that this lady will be ex-directory."

"I'll see what I can do tomorrow. Where do I ring you?"

"I was hoping I could stay with you for the rest of the night, maybe for a couple of days." Shaw felt wretched.

"Jesus! I hope my wife isn't listening to this. Are you on the run?"

"In a way. Not from the law."

"I don't want you bringing any danger to this household. What are you up against?"

"Just for the night then. I thought you newspapermen took these things in their stride."

"Sure. But my wife doesn't. That's not a reasonable request, Laurie."

"Okay. I'll sleep rough for the rest of the night. I'll have to ring you, though, because I don't know where I'll be. What will be the best time?"

"You crafty bastard. Okay. You can come here but don't bring anyone with you."

"I've got no wheels, Peter. I don't suppose you can collect me?" Shaw let the question hang and moved the phone well away from his ear.

Shaw hid himself in a small front garden behind the call-box and waited. After half an hour a police patrol car passed by very slowly as if looking for someone. He wondered if his escort had come round and made contact with base. He remained tucked in behind railings and shrubs and hoped Givens would not be too long.

It was the best part of an hour before dimmed headlights appeared at the head of the street but Shaw remained where he was until certain. He did not know Givens' car and realised he should have asked him the model. The car pulled up beside the call-box and Shaw thought he could identify Givens behind the wheel from the light of a street lamp. Givens climbed half out and Shaw put in an appearance.

"My God, real cloak and dagger stuff," Givens commented in disgust. "Get in." And when Shaw had his seat-belt fixed, Givens added, "You're a pain in the arse, Laurie. My wife wanted to call the police. It had better be worth it."

"It's better than I thought. Far better."

"Yes, but will they let me print it?"

"It will be a matter of timing. I have one more hurdle to clear." As he glanced across he noticed Givens' pyjamas poking out from the bottom of his trousers and he had not combed his hair. "I really am sorry to bring you out at this time but I had to slip a bodyguard and I could only do that by clumping him."

Givens handled the car competently and kept to the back streets. "So now we're in for GBH. I'm getting nervous as to what you are landing me in."

"A story like this can't be got without risk. I shall be very surprised indeed if you don't think it worth it. They'll make you editor."

Givens took a corner almost on two wheels. When the car settled he said, "I'd rather be a live journalist than a dead editor." He braked and swung over. "We're here."

The news of Shaw's escape broke before Jill was awake. The ringing telephone woke her and she put out a hand to where Shaw should be lying. When she found him missing she assumed he was in the bathroom and clambered across the bed to answer the phone. It was Judith Walker and it

251

was 5.30 am. When she heard the news Jill sat on the edge of the bed and started to shake.

The escort had recovered and made his way to the rest of the detail who had raised the alarm. Judith kept it brief. "Where would he go, Jill?"

Jill was still trying to get over the shock that he had gone, and the manner in which he had done it; she was barely awake. "He might try going to his apartment; I heard him phone Max Fuller, an old lag who's staying there acting as caretaker. He ordered a gun. Then he'd try to find Veida."

"Does he know where she lives?"

"No. But he'll find out. It might take a little time. We'd better get some people over there or he'll kill her."

"He won't find it that simple. We can't send a detail over. She'd notice straight away. She knows damn fine she's under investigation but she can't know exactly how far we've got. Throw a cordon round and we'll blow the whole thing."

"But Laurie could be walking straight into a trap. She would have laid her plans long since, waiting for the day. We must stop him getting there."

"He'll have to take his chances. He shouldn't have walked out. How anyone can walk out on you, I don't know."

"He thinks he let his brother down and believes Veida will get away with it. He feels he has to settle it. Oh, God, what do we do?"

"Our best. And don't you dare move, Jill. Hear me? Stay put."

After she put the phone down Jill sat on the edge of the bed and buried her head in her hands.

Peter Givens' wife, Patricia, made no pretence at wanting to be introduced to Shaw who meant trouble so far as she was concerned. She was an attractive woman, even in the early hours without make-up. She did not stay in bed, because her night had been ruined, so she made coffee for them and then sat isolated at one end of the lounge, dressing-gown pulled round her, mug of coffee in her hand, hair hanging forward over her face.

252

Shaw did not dare apologise to her, the hostility was almost tangible. Givens was at present more concerned with what Shaw had to say than his wife's justifiable mood. Perhaps it was his indifference to her suffering that made her unapproachable.

What made it worse was that, later, Givens had to go to his office and leave Shaw there. Shaw was hoping that they would let him stay for at least part of the coming night. After Givens had gone the whole house seemed to be full of resentment.

By mid-morning, Patricia now dressed to kill and looking lovely said, "I'm off. I've no doubt you'll find everything you need, but do keep the place tidy and don't steal anything. If you want to sleep use one of the chairs, the beds are made." She turned at the door knowing how well she looked. "Maybe we can make love to pass the time when I get back. That will serve the thoughtless sod right for bringing someone home in the middle of the night."

"Look, I'm awfully . . ."

"Stuff it," said Patricia sweetly. "Don't spoil your image." She slammed the door behind her and Shaw was in the house alone thinking that a search for him would have begun some time ago. He tried to push Jill right out of his mind but found it impossible. There was no point in trying to put the clock back now.

At mid-day the telephone rang and he answered it. It was Givens. "Veida Ash. My colleague thinks she lives outside Coulsdon. He doesn't know the number but you'll find a complete set of London and Home Counties directories in my study. Try the north-east Surrey section. He says she is a very highly-rated operator. Spent a long time in the field. I'll leave you to it."

Coulsdon is in Surrey near Croydon which was now part of metropolitan London. Shaw sat at Givens' small desk in his cramped study and went through the Surrey directory and then the London A to Ls. There were a formidable number of Ashes but not too many Vs. What there were he rang. Most Vs turned out to be Victors but there were no Veidas.

It took some time and he broke off about 2 pm and made a sandwich and coffee, and returned to the study. He did not think he would get anywhere. But he tried again and became convinced of what he suspected all along: Veida was ex-directory. The idea that she might be using her maiden name came after he had actually given up hope.

He could find no V. Gemund in the Surrey directory but he did find an I. Gemund with an address near Coulsdon. At first it did not register, then he considered that the house might belong to her mother, Ingrid.

Patricia returned about four, she was carrying no shopping but Shaw had no intention of passing comment. She was in a better mood. She preened herself in front of a mirror over the mantelpiece and asked him if he wanted tea. And then she apologised for her understandable attitude. When she was seated opposite him with her tea she said, "I found your gun in your jacket pocket when you went to the bathroom to wash and shave. I didn't tell Peter. Does he know you are armed?"

"That was careless of me. I'm sorry. But I've been through a lot and was very tired. I don't think he knows. But I'm not a gangster or a hoodlum or any kind of threat to you or him." He risked a smile and she responded. "The gun is for my own protection, no more." He did not like his own lie. "I'll be away from here as soon as it's dark. And I hope Peter will get a very good story from it."

Shaw left at nine. Peter had not yet come home, but Patricia was apparently used to that. He thanked her, asking her to pass on his gratitude to Givens and left, feeling very sorry for her, for the problems he had caused and the loneliness to which he was leaving her.

As the main car hire companies might have been contacted he stole an old Ford in a quiet street and searched for the main London Road heading south. The quickest route was by train from Victoria but he reasoned that Judith would have a stake out there waiting for him. He had no illusions that his intentions would be anticipated. He had no set plan, for he did not know the area of the house and would have to play it by ear. The car broke down in Brixton and he spent some time in finding a mini-cab to take him on to Croydon. He anticipated that both the local rail stations would be covered by police, so he kept well away from them. He hired a cab in Croydon to take him on to Coulsdon. Now it was tricky because he needed to give the address.

The driver had to pull in to study a street map, because they had entered an area where old houses still existed with grounds. They were in a wide tree-lined avenue where properties lay well back and well separated and smacked of wealth. It was all discreetly opulent.

"Do you know which house it is, guv? Or shall I knock one of them up? I know the area well enough but the houses keep themselves to themselves, if you know what I mean."

"Don't knock anyone up. It can't be far."

"I reckon it's the fifth one on from here on the left. I seem to remember that it's the only one with a number, 27, all the rest have posh names. Let's try."

"Just go past it. Don't stop and don't go too slow. I just want to locate it."

The driver was surprised but kept his counsel and drove on. Shortly after, he called out, "I was right. The number is on the big gate post."

"Drive on," said Shaw quickly. A little later he called out. "Okay, you can stop here."

"It's a long walk back, guv. And dark. Rich area, danger of mugging."

Shaw was not certain whether the driver was serious or not. He had a gun, it did not matter. "It's a nice evening. It'll do me good." He paid the cab off and when it had gone moved quickly to the side of the road.

They would be here somewhere, waiting, looking for him. He stepped on to the nearest drive to find it was shingle and immediately stepped off; it was impossible to move quietly over shingle. The drive of the next house was tarmac and he went down towards the house keeping to the tall hedged boundary to avoid the security lights. Judith Walker, if not

255

Veida Ash, would have someone around waiting for him. From now on he must be extremely careful. It was too late to wish he had Max Fuller with him.

He was on his own and that was how it had started.

23

His clothes were ripped by the hedges but he had to keep as far away from the house as possible. He passed a triple garage and under an arbour connecting the house to the garage having been forced nearer to the main building than he wanted. Once through he went wide again and kept to the edge. A dog barked inside the house but nothing stirred and he continued on without triggering any lights; houses like these would have whatever security measures were available.

He reached the rear boundary and looked back surprised by the distance he had come. A huge leylandii screen faced him. He decided to see what was the other side. He lay flat and dragged himself through, picking up painful scratches on the way. It was deeper than he realised and when he emerged on the other side found himself in a copse.

Clear of the house he worked his way from tree to tree and eventually emerged into open ground. Even in the dark he could feel the space around him and at first thought he must be on a common. Then he realised he had blundered on to a golf course.

It was easier to keep going then, just clear of the erratic tree line. The rough was suddenly paradise. The problem now was to judge at which point to cut back into the garden of no. 27. He could only estimate the distance and there was some way to go. The house whose grounds he had gone through was six dwellings away from no. 27, and the size of the grounds would be variable but he judged that none of them would have less than three-quarters of an acre and most would have far more. That they backed on to a golf course was a bonus. There was a lot of walking to do yet, but at least he was in the open and could make good progress in spite of the total darkness.

He avoided the temptation of too early an entry and kept going until he thought he might have reached the rear boundary of no. 27. It was guesswork coupled with a sense of distance. He cut through the trees and eventually came across a hawthorn hedge, prickly, in bud, and formidable. He followed the line of hawthorn, not easy with the obstruction of trees and undergrowth. The hedge seemed to go on forever and then it met an obstacle of steel mesh about twenty feet high and this continued to run where the hedge left off.

The last time Shaw had seen a mesh this high and as solid was at one of the top security prisons, an inner wall from the traditional brick structure. It was this impression that made him believe, perhaps illogically, that this was the sort of extra protection someone like Veida Ash might have. He found the nearest stanchion to which the mesh was supported, and started to climb.

Reaching the top was not too difficult. Getting over it and trying to evade being impaled by a variety of trees which formed their own formidable barrier was another matter. In the end, just over halfway down, he covered his face with an arm and dropped. It was noisy, extremely painful, and quick. He lay in a heap hoping that he was too far from the house to be heard. When he finally emerged into the open, a fading vista of lawns and trees spread before him, at the top of which, in the far distance, was the dulled white outline of the house, some windows alight.

The faint outline was similar to his impression when passing in the taxi. The only way to be sure was to go the whole distance to the front gates and check on the number. He could not do that. The house would be under some kind of surveillance at the front even if curtailed, and he guessed that the owners of one or two of the opposite properties would have been approached; it was a tricky business to keep such operations secret. If Veida had protection then he guessed it would remain in her own grounds. He started

258

to move up the left-hand boundary which was the furthest from the house.

He kept going towards the garages which were well separated from the house. As he drew nearer he saw the dark shape of a large ornamental pond, reeds poking up and gently waving. There were a couple of loud plops and he ducked instinctively before realising that the pond was probably a Koi pool and the fish were enjoying the balmy weather. He scanned for security lights at the back, usually fixed centrally to give the widest cover, and to pick up the body heat of anyone close to the house. He reached the rear of the garages and leaned against the wall. He felt a wreck but at the same time exhilarated. There were three small windows at the back of the garages and when he peered through could just make out the outline of three cars. One was unmistakably a Rolls-Royce. Would Veida flaunt her money like that? If she could justify it, why not? For a moment, though, he thought he might have the wrong house. He wished he had some way of checking but in the end he could only rely on his own impressions and judgement. It seemed to be ludicrous, particularly to an ex-policeman used to dealing in hard facts, but this *felt* like Veida's house. It was not an instinct, there was a distinct communication. She was in the house. He could only hope that she did not suffer the same sensation.

He decided to back the feeling. There was barely space between the garages and the sturdy hedge growing alongside them. He got down on hands and knees and thrust himself into what felt like a thousand needles and bedded himself down as comfortably as he could. Nobody was likely to come round this side but it would only be safe through the night.

There was no comfort; he did not expect any. He would have to stay the whole night in a tortuous position, clothes torn, hands and face lacerated, knees painful, and he could feel blood trickling down from his hairline, but he was satisfied, even content. He groped for the gun in the darkness, making sure it was easily to hand, and then checked on the magazine clip. He had no flashlight, no comfort except his own will to deal with Veida Ash.

*   *   *

He barely slept, but dozed intermittently. The cold woke him long before dawn. The temperature had dropped and there was a drizzle. He felt dreadful, stiff and wet and had to move because of cramp. He managed to push himself up against the garage wall and sat like that for some time. It was too early for the birds and still pitch black. After a disastrous night he was at his lowest, depressed enough to make him consider giving up.

The first chirp from the trees caught his ear and from then on the dawn chorus swelled like an orchestra. The sheer variety and beauty of it held his attention and enough determination crept back to keep him where he was. It was almost as if the birds knew his plight and made a special effort to salve his spirit. Soon afterwards the drizzle stopped and the first light appeared like a creeping fog under the cloud mass building up above.

He stretched his legs and got cramp again but now he was afraid to move too much. In the distance he heard the first human sounds and the hum of a milk float. He decided his cover still held good and in spite of the conditions continued to stay there. Now he could actually see the birds staking their claim to tenuous positions and chasing each other around the skies and looking for food.

Shaw was damp right through but it no longer mattered. Time dragged heavily but the moment drew closer and this kept him going. The cloud must have lifted, for suddenly it was full daylight and life was showing itself in many forms.

It was 7.30 when someone came towards him; a woman's footsteps. He kept his nerve, realising that she was heading for the garages. The huge door swung up and he guessed it was operated by remote control. He edged out from the side and crawled round the back to lift himself very carefully at the corner of the nearest window.

He was reluctant to take the risk of peering through but in the end found himself doing so, just enough to see a little. A woman was throwing a coat in the back of one of the cars which he could now see was a Jaguar. Was this Veida? Smart, quite good-looking, fair hair and a quiet air of efficiency; a competent woman. If this was Veida she was far more than competent. He caught a glimpse of her eyes. At a time when she thought she was not under scrutiny she did not have to adopt a pose. The eyes worried him; she was as hard as teak. The damp may have caused the shiver which ran down his spine but he did not think so. She climbed into the Jag and backed out, braked, and swept away up the drive, presumably on her way to Century House. He was now completely sure that he had the right house. It was time to move.

He could not avoid the open ground between the garages and the house, but reasoned that the tall front hedges would hide him from the houses opposite which, in any event, were some distance away. He ran to the back of the house, approached patio doors and sidled up to them. Above him he saw one of the siren box alarms. He doubted that the alarm was on; Veida would hardly be the sort to do housework, nor to live alone in a house this size. He waited, then after a while thought he heard someone move and then a motor of some sort. As it grew louder he realised it was a vacuum cleaner.

The patio doors were too big to break, the noise would be heard all over the house. By locating the outlet pipes he found the kitchen. The frames were much smaller but one of the windows was open, and through it came the smell of burned toast. The rest was relatively easy; he put a hand through to lift the window bar and then pushed it open wide. He pulled himself up, stepped through with difficulty and found himself with a foot in each of the twin sinks. He was in. He climbed down and hooked the window back where it had been and wiped his wet footmarks off the floor with the nearest cloth. The kitchen was ultra modern and as big as most drawing-rooms. A search produced a ball of twine and a paring knife; he cut off several lengths and slipped them into a pocket with the knife.

How many were in the house? A maid, certainly. But who else? He placed the sound of the vacuum cleaner upstairs and sidled into the downstairs rooms one by one. The house was huge, the drawing-room almost large enough

261

to hold a ball. There was a grand piano at one end and easy chairs were scattered throughout. Marble pedestals supported exquisite sculptures. Furniture was a mixture of new and old, everything of the highest quality. There was a study and a library, a dining-room with Regency fittings and drapes and a table laid out with silver and early Wedgwood like a room in a museum. And that was his impression, the place had the feel of a museum rather than a home; there was no homely warmth. He discovered the swimming pool, the blue reflection of water wavering on the curved Perspex of a canopy which could obviously open like an observatory. He checked each cubicle. Nobody had swum so far that morning.

The house was full of infra-red points and he did not doubt that there were plenty of door and pressure pads as well. What intrigued him was the number of panic buttons, not just by the front and back doors but in the main rooms as well, and judiciously placed around the rooms were remote control boxes, little bigger than a match-box. He slipped one into a pocket.

He returned to the spacious hall. The hoovering stopped and he moved under the shelter of a cantilever staircase. He was satisfied that there was nobody downstairs. He waited some time before deciding to mount the stairs. He wished the vacuum would start up again and obligingly it did. With gun in hand he dashed up the stairs two at a time.

On the landing there were so many doors leading off that he did not know where to start. He backed to the wall between two doors and waited. A door opened and someone came out of a room to his right and entered a room further away from him. He leaned forward to see a vacuum cleaner being dragged in and then it started up again. He hurried along the landing to the room, grateful for the deep pile that muffled his footsteps, and opened the door.

The maid was cleaning around a bed with her back to him. He crossed the floor in long strides, cupped a hand to her mouth and held the gun to her head. She almost fainted from terror and he had to hold her up. When she calmed down a little he whispered in her ear, "Nothing will happen to you if you do what I say."

She grunted something through his fingers in German. He repeated his warning in German and added, "I'm going to bind your hands as a precaution. I don't intend to do anything to you. If you scream or call out I'll kill you. Nod if you understand."

He bound her wrists behind her back and made her sit on the edge of the bed. The cleaner was still on which made it difficult to converse but he let it run. With his head close to hers, he asked, "Is there anyone else in the house? Lie and it will be your last."

"Carl is in the main bedroom. At the end, facing the garden." She was a woman in her mid-forties, dark and plumping, and at the moment her deep brown eyes were filled with terror.

"You mean he's in bed?"

"He does not usually get up until past nine. What are you going to do?"

"I'm going to gag you but I'll make sure you can breathe, and if that's a bathroom, I'm going to lock you in there. You'll be perfectly safe but it may be for some time. But I promise you I won't harm you if you are sensible. Don't panic. When I've dealt with Carl I'll come back and turn the cleaner off."

Shaw cut strips from the patterned sheet with the paring knife and gagged the woman before helping her to the bathroom. He took a bedroom chair in to make it more comfortable for her then bound her feet together. He took the key out from the inside of the door and locked it from the outside after warning her again to make no noise.

He went along to what he guessed was the main bedroom and quietly opened the door. Carl was apparently still asleep with his face buried in one of the pillows of the gigantic bed. Shaw crept up alongside and hit him hard at the base of the skull with the Smith and Wesson. The fair-haired hunk of manhood was naked under the sheets, and a near perfect physical example; Veida obviously preferred her toy-boys to be muscular.

Shaw tied him up, hands behind the back and then the ankles. He dragged him into the magnificent en-suite bathroom and laid him on the floor and threw a blanket over him. He locked the bathroom door and then searched the bedroom. On a top shelf in one of the built-in wardrobes were three wigs on stands; a brunette, a blonde, and a redhead. He took the redhead off the stand and left the bedroom, locking the door behind him. He then went from room to room. Of the seven bedrooms only one was without a bathroom and all were luxurious. He was now satisfied that the house was empty of all but Carl, the maid and himself. He returned to the lounge, placed the wig on top of one of the sculptured busts and made himself comfortable for a long wait.

Tired out, he dozed from time to time but there was always that part of his mind that kept the antennae probing for signs of danger.

At mid-day he made sandwiches and poured orange juice and took them upstairs to the maid. He unlocked the door, removed her gag and helped her eat and drink. She wanted little of either; she was still very frightened but it was the best he could do.

He called on Carl who was now sitting up against the side of the bath and shot a look of pure hatred at Shaw. He strained to say something through the gag but Shaw did not help him except to pull the blanket up from where it had slipped. He offered no food or drink and closed and locked the door again.

Waiting became more difficult and he was now getting a nervous reaction with too much time to reflect, far too late, just how ill-prepared he was. He needed a tape-recorder and there was probably one in the house but somehow it did not seem to matter. He wanted the truth and was determined to get it. Given another opportunity he knew he would have done it all again and would have changed nothing. Terry would have done it this way, blundered in, played it by ear, and look what had happened to him. Yet, in the end, it was all about what had happened to Terry and the knowledge of how other

264

people had liked him and how little he had really known about him.

He expected Veida would return some time in the evening and as the hours dragged, each one longer than before, he became edgy and increasingly weary. He almost missed the crunch of tyres on the drive and was startled into moving fast and shakily. It was only mid-afternoon; had Veida returned so soon? He glimpsed the Jaguar through the lounge windows as it swung towards the garages, and he dived for the front door. He had waited a long time for this moment.

The sound of her footsteps was quite clear. She inserted the key in the lock, pushed open the door, and without turning pushed the door closed with her heel as she entered. Shaw said, "Don't twitch a muscle, Veida, hold your arms up where I can see them and go into the lounge."

She held her arms up, handbag dangling from one hand, and she said in a perfectly calm voice, "I wondered when you would pitch up. You poor man. Are you going to make me some tea?"

Once in the lounge she faced the windows and said, "This bag is damned heavy, Laurie. May I drop it?"

"On that table there. And don't try putting it down, just drop it."

She did as he bade and the bag slipped off the small table on to the floor. "I hope that's not a bad omen for you," she said. She went to pick it up but he stopped her and told her to sit down.

She tried to sit facing the door so that he might have his back to it but he made her shift position and when she was finally seated sat opposite her so that he could watch her and most of the room as well. He noticed her gaze drift to the wig on the bust but she gave nothing away.

"What's happened to Carl and Bette?" she asked as she crossed her legs and clasped her long-fingered hands.

"They're upstairs. Can't you hear them?" One of them was kicking at the bathroom door, probably because they had heard the car approach. He was watching her the whole time as if she could pull some sort of magic trick. She was so calm about it, no sign of surprise at all. Most women would have jumped out of their skin on finding a man with a gun behind their back. She was completely sure of herself and Shaw felt undermined. He had to cling desperately to what he believed.

Veida maintained the initiative as she asked, "Have you come to kill me? If you have you'll never do it."

"Really?"

"Your brother would have. He was wild. But you're different and you've been indoctrinated by years in the police. There's no way you will shoot me with that thing while I sit before you unarmed. You'll not leave here alive, Laurie. I don't have to ask you whether anybody saw you get in; otherwise, the place would be surrounded. Look at the state of you. Did you sleep rough in the grounds? You've got guts, though. But you're stupid. Nobody saw you come and nobody will see you leave."

"I just want the truth. Why the hell did you have to kill Terry?"

"I didn't kill him. He had met someone who knew something about me. It was one of those freak meetings that could lead a trail straight back to me. It was only a matter of time so I had to take him out of immediate circulation while I dealt with the rest of the problem. Prison was a good place. He went in happily thinking he was doing a job for me. He had done some nice work before. What happened after was not planned."

"You're a bloody liar. You sent him in to be murdered. And then you took care of Klatt."

Her gaze strayed to the wig again. "Is that what Judith Walker thinks?"

"It's what I think. What's behind it, Veida?"

She was silent for some time before she said, "You know I'm a very wealthy woman."

"That's evident."

"I mean really wealthy. Filthy rich." She gazed round the room. "I can justify all this by what my mother made. She is still a very astute business woman. But this represents only a big house and having money to spare. I'm talking

266

about owning two islands, a yacht. I don't even know my own wealth. If I chipped you in for, say five million, would you join me? There are few people I can trust these days. I do need help, things have become rather large and out of hand here and there. For years I've increasingly had to delegate. And I've made a lot of people rich on the way."

At first he thought she was trying to gain time and then realised she was absolutely serious. The fact that she had arranged the murder of his brother seemed not to touch her. He hid his outrage and replied, "I can't see myself joining you but I'll hear you out. What's it all about?"

"I hope you'll give it serious thought. You're the old-fashioned reliable type. I wouldn't have to look over my shoulder. At the moment I'm being creamed off too much. I have to expect it because the ramifications are huge." Veida smiled as she added, "And I can tell you because you are no threat either way. You discovered some of it in Greifswald. I run one of the biggest crime syndicates in the world, Laurie. Certainly the biggest in Europe." She waited for him to be impressed but he had begun to think along those lines ever since Judith Walker had given some background to the affair.

"Through your intelligence network?"

"A good deal of it. Why people think of agents as upright citizens I'll never understand. Some are the dregs of society but useful in so many ways. But my mother really started it all before the war. She was already into organised crime in the black markets of Europe; it was a matter of survival. Later I was able to use many of her contacts for intelligence purposes and built up my network from that. Villains are not just common thieves, as you well know. They are in every section of society whether fraudsters, inside traders, embezzlers or whatever. The two sides were complementary to each other, making blackmail an easy weapon to keep them in line, for they could be exposed for one thing or another. But they are paid so well I rarely had to apply pressure. I have complete records which you obviously have not found and which give me the power of control which others have in very limited form. It means, too, that I can shift emphasis from one issue to another from one country to another. You might not be surprised to grasp just how useful extortion can be in intelligence matters, apart from making money. Sex, the honey-pot, is an old friend of espionage and coins it at the same time. Drugs can hook not only for the need but as a useful carrot to obtain information. The Russians needed advice on the shifting of arms and now they fancy themselves in the protection racket. I carry more information, and my advice is sought for execution of these matters, than probably any other person. I am not involved in crime in Britain. I love my work at Century House."

"So you take your cut from everything that goes on in Europe?"

"That would be an exaggeration. I hold the strings that my mother built up before me. And I've done it without detriment to my adopted country. I have never entered the traitor game. I have always been loyal."

"Until recently."

"What do you mean?"

For the first time he had got through her barrier. "Once the Wall came down, and Eastern Europe broke up, a great many of your contacts went running scared. Some of the Stasi acted as doubles for you and were also making a lot out of the crimes you fingered. You were losing a lot of your agents and top villains too. And some were blazing a trail that could lead back to you. The civil war in Yugoslavia must have disrupted many of your contacts and control was slipping away from you in large chunks. And that created the risk of your exposure. There were some who found they did not need you or your contacts any more. I suppose it was one of those that Terry ran across. You provided an escape route for many of them, but you really wanted them where they were no longer a danger to you. Your safety net now had gaping holes in it. I suppose Klatt was one of them but couldn't keep away from something he enjoyed doing, stealing cars. Some of the men you are helping to escape are murderers and you know it. They are wanted by the German police whom you are not helping to find them, not because they supplied you with intelligence information but because they could finger you for crime. Your loyalty to your country has gone out of the window, Veida."

Shaw was so wrapped up in what he was saying that he did not see the gun appear. She must have had it tucked in her skirt or under her neat jacket but it did not matter. It was pointing straight at him.

"We could have made a deal, Laurie."

"My brother's life for five million quid and a life of crime for me? That's a deal? That's as twisted as the rest."

"Either hand over the gun, Laurie, or fire the bloody thing." She knew he could not fire unless she did and then it would be too late. But in any event, perhaps because he was so desperately tired and his concentration had lapsed, he was holding his gun loosely on his leg.

He said, "You won't get away with it, Veida."

"Oh yes I will. Nobody will know. It's a great pity. You've a great deal of integrity."

"Something you've never had."

He thought she was about to fire, and threw himself sideways, aiming the remote control at the nearest panic button. The whole house erupted as sirens on each side of the building burst out in chorus. He kept rolling as he shouted above the noise.

"They know I'm here now, Veida."

He had got behind the biggest settee knowing a shot could penetrate but that she could not place his exact position. He lay flat, heard her run out as others broke the door down and ran in. He lay flat on his back, arms out, staring at the ceiling, totally exhausted.

"I want a divorce," demanded a woman's voice he loved to hear and was somewhere above the long slender legs which straddled him.

"We're not bloody married, yet. You haven't damn well asked me."

He could barely see her through the waves of exhaustion but he summoned a smile as she knelt beside him.

269

KENNETH ROYCE
LIMBO

**The parcel bomb is the first warning.
Then the Ferrari blows up.
But the contract on his girlfriend is the last
straw . . .**

Not quite what Willie Jackson expects when he takes
on a discreet government investigation. People don't
usually try to kill you for asking questions about a bit
of stolen porcelain that has turned up in the wrong
private collection.

Forced underground with a price on his head, Jackson
still doesn't know who the enemy is . . .

HODDER AND STOUGHTON PAPERBACKS

ALSO BY KENNETH ROYCE

☐ 61735 7   Limbo   £5.99